Martha,
To a fine
friend and
neighbor, hope
something here
to your heart. Fondly,

from fragile fragments

Louise Rill

L O U I S E   R I L L

This is a work of fiction. The characters, incidents and dialogue portrayed in this novel are either a product of the author's imagination or used fictitiously.

Printed in the United States

ISBN: 978-1-7364577-0-2 (paperback)

ISBN: 978-1-7364577-1-9 (e-book)

Published by Louise Rill

Email: rilllouise17@gmail.com

Cover design by Damonza

In memory of my mother, M. J. S.

To my son, Douglas and my daughter, Liane
who bring so much sunshine to my life

ACKNOWLEDGMENTS

This book would not have been possible without the support of many people who read and advised me from the very beginning of my writing. A special thanks to Mary Jane Ryals who inspired me to begin the novel. Among the fellow writers who kept me buoyed with their constructive comments and enthusiasm, each deserves a big thank you -Bonnie Armstrong, who also reviewed my final draft, Carla Cramer, Jenny Crowley, Kate Kerr, James Nobel, Nancy O'Farrell, and Linda Wright. Thanks also to Kate Kerr, Pamela Krohn, Madelyn Skene and Linda Wright for their thoughtful comments in the beta review.

I am especially grateful to the talented women who kept inspiration flowing as we met together for years until we each progressed to a finished work-Patty Daniels, Judy Ray and our writing coach Heather Whitaker whose skillful guidance was invaluable throughout the writing and publishing process.

I am deeply indebted to Barbara Hamby whose talent enriched my prose and to A. Jae Lee whose editing expertise provided so many valuable improvements. To Janet Cowden, my editor, I have so much gratitude for her amazing devotion to accuracy of time and place and clarity of word.

Sincere thanks to Lt. Col. Lloyd Cory, retired, for his advice with military practice.

"As soon as one sees with one's own eyes the whole which one has hitherto known only in fragments and chaotically, a new life begins."

—Goethe, *Italian Journey*

CHAPTER 1

"Don't forget to cream your face." Marjorie's mother hovered in the bathroom doorway, inspecting Marjorie as she completed her nightly routine.

"Don't worry, I won't." Marjorie's stiff lips smiled, but a voice inside burned to shout, "Stop!" She was twenty-two, a college graduate, and a woman about to be married.

"Are you sure you're using enough?" Her mother peered over Marjorie's shoulder. "Your pores are a little large by your nose."

Marjorie felt her chest tighten like a coiled spring. "Yes, putting on a thick layer, just like I do every night."

At all costs, she would be agreeable to try to keep her mother in a pleasant mood. She had to so Les's visit this weekend would go smoothly.

Since their engagement five months ago, her fiancé had only been able to visit once, until now. Every time he had planned a weekend visit, her mother had found each date inconvenient. "That weekend doesn't suit," was her refrain. It was always something—your father's going hunting that weekend, the Critchfields are coming for cards that Saturday, we're going to take you to Florida that week. After months of delays, her mother had finally agreed to this weekend.

Until her mother turned and walked away, Marjorie hadn't realized she'd been holding her breath.

Marjorie leaned closer toward the bathroom mirror, staring. Instead of putting the Ponds cold cream onto herself, she dabbed a blob onto the reflection in the mirror. First the nose, then the mouth, then the cheeks. A clown? Her brown eyes shone bright. Her fiancé would arrive from New Jersey tomorrow.

She had met Les in summer school when each found the same quiet spot to study in the university's fireside room. He had been taking extra engineering classes to be certified as an electrical engineer, while she had been making up classes after a nervous breakdown had forced her to leave school in the middle of the semester the previous year. She was sure it was destiny that she found her prince that summer! She adored Les's kindness, his gentle confidence in the present and the future, and the puzzles he loved to challenge her with. She missed his handsome face, the curl of his dark-blond hair, and the warmth that enveloped her when he wrapped his long arms around her.

Quick footsteps interrupted her reverie. Marjorie grabbed a washcloth and hurriedly wiped the cream off the mirror.

"Still here?" Her mother appeared at the bathroom doorway, peering hard at Marjorie's reflection. What did her mother see there? A little girl in a pinafore? Certainly not a woman about to embark on married life. "Be sure to do your hundred strokes for your hair. It's important for keeping a good luster."

"Sure will." Marjorie fought for control as her teeth dug into her lower lip.

She turned to her mother. "Oh, Mother, I want to ask you about making an apple pie for dessert tomorrow. I'd like to make something special for Les, please?"

"Really? You've never made one before." Her eyebrows raised over her glare.

"We've got the apples. I'd really like to make a treat for him." Marjorie's lips held on to their smile.

"I already have the cookies made for dessert."

"Les loves apple pie. This would be something . . . just from me, a little surprise."

"That's a nice idea, but why don't I show you how to make a crust later on, then next time when he comes you can serve a lovely pie."

Marjorie hesitated, but pushed on. "I have a recipe that Lorraine gave me. She explained all the steps. I'm sure I could follow it."

"Marjorie, I've made my decision. We don't experiment on company by serving them something we haven't made before."

The air left the room.

"My mother always said, 'Never serve a guest what isn't tried and true.'"

Marjorie struggled to hold together the pieces of herself that threatened to fly in all directions. She shouldn't have to ask permission to make a pie.

"Now, Marjorie, don't get yourself upset over this. Marjorie, look at me. You don't want to get into one of your states again! Pie making is just too involved to try right before Les comes tomorrow. We have a lot to prepare."

Marjorie swallowed hard to keep the sour taste down and to steady her voice. "Next time he comes, then."

"Good night now," her mother said, waving her hand in dismissal. She turned and walked back to her bedroom, her long flannel nightgown flapping behind her.

Marjorie wouldn't let a darn pie get her down. She would keep her spirits up by thinking about Les coming tomorrow. In her room, she sat in her rocking chair, its rhythm soothing the prickle of her nerves. She closed her eyes and replayed the first moments of their engagement.

When Les had guided her from the graduation reception into the fireside room where they'd met about a year before, she felt like a bottle of champagne about to pop. He got down on one knee, took her hand, and asked, a boyish look in his brown eyes, "Will you marry me?"

"Oh yes!" she had burst out, giddy with delight. Her dream had come true.

Les opened the satin jeweler's box and gently slipped the diamond ring on her finger.

Marjorie's heart soared with joy. She leaped into Les's arms for a long kiss. Her life with Les would be filled with laughter and love. She squeezed him—he was really hers.

She remembered how they strolled back to the reception where they'd left their parents, arm in arm, their smiles wide and their eyes on each other. Her sorority sisters congratulated her with squeals and hugs, oohing and ahhing over her diamond ring. Her father shook Les's hand and wished them well. Les's parents hugged her, and his father gave Les solid pats on his back.

Marjorie's mother had smiled at the reception, holding back her words until they had returned home. No, she wouldn't think about what happened after that. Everything would be okay—Les was coming tomorrow. She imagined him in the mahogany twin bed in the room next to hers, his body long and solid under the sheets, his curly hair against the pillow.

After her parents were asleep the last time he visited, he had sneaked into her room. They caressed, careful to be silent. After lying together as long as they dared, Les tiptoed back to his bedroom and closed the door like a thief in the night. Her pulse ricocheted between excitement and resounding relief that her mother still slept.

Now Marjorie walked across the hall to the guest bedroom next to her room to close and open the door, checking for squeaks. She could hear her mother's warning echo, "These young girls who have relations before they are married get themselves pregnant, then the man takes a hike!" She remembered how her mother's eyes iced over. "You won't be one of those girls." Of course not. They used protection so she wouldn't be one of those girls.

As Marjorie climbed into her bed, she fretted over the pie she couldn't make for Les. She was practiced at stifling her ideas to maintain peace with her mother, but sometimes she repressed them so much they festered into a paralyzing sadness deep within her core. She took a long breath and prayed nothing would happen to delay their wedding. Only four more months. Four months until freedom. She fluffed her pillow and tossed from side to side.

The bedside clock seemed to tick louder and louder. She slipped out of bed and turned on the dresser lamp. Kneeling down, she reached under the bed and pulled out a box. She raised the lid and reached for her collection—potato peelers, paring knives, can openers, measuring spoons, potholders, and other little necessities of housekeeping she would need but were too small to be wedding gifts. She kept them in an old dress box, adding to the collection whenever she went to Woolworth's. Her father also enjoyed selecting small items for her at the grocery store when he helped her mother shop on Fridays.

She handled the items as if they were the golden keys to her independence. She could see herself peeling carrots and potatoes to make soup in her own kitchen. Calm washed over her as she placed each item back in its place and pushed the box far into the darkness under her bed. She crawled back between her sheets, flopping a pillow over the clock and another over her head. She visualized Les's car driving up to the house, him getting out and holding her close. Imagining his warm embrace, she fell asleep.

*

The next morning, Marjorie could barely eat her breakfast. She was drying the breakfast dishes, wondering if Les would arrive at four o'clock as planned, when her mother interrupted her thoughts.

"Marjorie, why don't you wash your hair now, and I'll come up in ten minutes to put the waves in for you?"

Marjorie placed the breakfast dishes back into the cupboard, then folded the tea towel and hung it carefully on the radiator to dry. The kitchen was her mother's royal domain, and she presided over it with the authority of a queen. Her mother did the planning, preparations, and cooking. Others might sometimes peel a potato, but mostly they just set or cleared the table and dried the dishes.

Marjorie strode upstairs to her mother's bathroom, quickly washed her hair, sat down at the vanity in her mother's dressing room, and gazed steadily into her own eyes reflected in the mirror. She would let nothing ruin this day. As Marjorie finished towel-drying her hair, her mother appeared and began to squeeze metal wave clips in rows down Marjorie's thick brown hair, moving down toward the ends as she went.

Marjorie hesitated. "I wanted to remind you that Les and I are going to Lorraine and Ned's tomorrow evening for dinner and cards."

"Yes, but remember, we need some time this weekend to finish Les's invitation list. The invitations take three weeks to be printed." Her mother walked over to the bathroom cupboard to get more clips, then shut the cabinet door with a whack. Marjorie inhaled sharply, startled at what seemed like a burst of anger.

Her mother plunked the cardboard lid full of wave clips on the vanity, adjusted her glasses, and continued to clip Marjorie's hair. "You know, Les's parents don't really fit in with our family, or with our friends. They're quite opposite—uneducated, unsophisticated, and most importantly, they are unable to speak English well."

Marjorie's stomach quivered. She watched her mother in the mirror. Her mother stopped, stood straight, and adjusted her glasses again.

"I never thought I'd have to face this situation. It's really quite an embarrassment." Her icy contempt froze the air between them.

"What? Mother, what are you getting at?" Marjorie knitted her brow, turning to look directly at her mother.

"I'm worried how his parents will behave at the wedding." Her mother dug a clip into Marjorie's scalp.

"Ouch!" Marjorie rubbed her head. "We just have to accept their uniqueness. After all, your parents came from a foreign country that had many differences."

"That's not the same. My parents spoke excellent English. I hate to say this, but I simply can't imagine introducing Les's parents to my women's circle, or to your cousin Audrey and her husband, or to your dad's colleagues." Her mother threw up her hands. "It's too much to ask."

Marjorie's jaw dropped as she watched her mother's face contort.

Her mother held her head high, her chin jutting forward. "It's a shame, dear, but it's much too humiliating. Their English is so poor. You have to think about how embarrassing it would be for them, too. It would really be a kindness for everyone if . . . well . . . if they didn't come. They wouldn't even understand what is happening."

"But Mother, that is so—"

"Why, at your college graduation, they looked like they'd just gotten off the boat! That awful long housedress she wore with the belt that didn't match, and a hat that looked like the cat had dragged it around, not to mention his father's pants were far too short, and they showed his white socks, no less."

Marjorie felt her face flush. She cringed at what might spew forth next.

Her mother drew her shoulders back. "I know you're set on marrying Les. But I just can't have his parents at the wedding," she said, shaking a wave clip in the air like a baton, peering at Marjorie over her glasses, her bottom lip curving downward.

Marjorie stopped breathing.

Her mother patted Marjorie's shoulder. "On the other hand, his sister is lovely, and as a bridesmaid, she would fit in, and give his family good representation."

Marjorie pressed her fist into her chest as if to force out her words. "I don't remember his mother's dress being like that. But regardless, they're his parents! They aren't educated, but they are shy, and they wouldn't say much." She dug her nails into her palms. "Besides, he's their only son!" Inviting his sister and not his parents would be a double insult.

Her mother stood firm as though planted on the carpet. "I'm sure you'll think of a way to tell Les. Kindly, of course."

Marjorie's mind reeled in disbelief. How could her mother ask such a thing? She couldn't bear another minute. She jumped up from the vanity and ran downstairs, her hair clips bobbing to the rhythm of her steps. How could she face Les with such a demand? Could this end their engagement? Wild thoughts poured over her spirit like scalding tea.

Her mother called down after her, "If they come, I can't be there!" and thumped her hand on the banister.

Marjorie ran out the back door, screen door slamming behind her. A flock of startled crows streaked upward from the yard. She drank in the fresh air like a drowning swimmer, almost tripping down the stone steps. Her knees nearly buckled, but she caught herself.

She wrapped her scarf around the hair clips to keep her head warm and paced along the driveway behind the house, numb to the coldness of the December morning. Her mother's intolerance of foreigners was a legacy she'd inherited from her own mother, who would say, "They're a wild bunch with no morals or manners." She knew her mother never made empty threats so she had to figure out something that would not ruin this weekend, or perhaps even her relationship with Les.

It was crazy. If his parents were at the wedding, her mother wouldn't be. If Marjorie said nothing to him and his parents came, her mother would have to be civil in front of all the guests. But then she'd be on edge during the months leading up to the wedding, fearing her mother might create an embarrassing situation for them.

Marjorie inhaled the icy air deep into her lungs. She needed time to think of the least damaging approach so Les would not hate her mother. Her hand pressed her chest as if there were a valve that could relieve the rising pressure. She would not allow those demons of depression to take hold again. Pacing along the driveway behind the house, she traced and retraced her footsteps in the snow. Her fingers ached from the cold.

Her mother's demand was not unlike her reaction after Les had proposed. Marjorie could still hear her mother's words. "You can't be serious about marrying him, Marjorie! We've raised you to be a lovely, well-brought-up girl. Your father is a doctor, a leader who is respected in this community. I have a reputation to uphold as well, being a doctor's wife. What would our friends think? Surely you understand, Marjorie."

She remembered her mother strutting stiffly across the living room carpet. "He's a pleasant fellow, but this is a lifetime commitment. You know I want what's best for you. We just can't have our only child seen marrying down to . . . to an *immigrant*. You can't keep that ring."

"Let's not make any hasty decisions, Sara," her father cautioned her mother, dropping the newspaper on his lap.

Marjorie swore to herself she would keep the ring. "I love Les and I want to marry him. I know his background doesn't match your wishes for me, but Mother, he is the one thing in my life I need to be happy."

Now she would fight, and not sink into that dark place. Marjorie continued to pace the driveway, rubbing her arms against the cold. Her world was spinning out of control. She closed her eyes and inhaled deeply. When she opened them, the white trunks of the birch trees were silhouetted against the heavy dark clouds that foretold snow, the inky skies reflecting the bleakness of her dilemma.

Suddenly she thought of Lonie, their former housekeeper, who had comforted her when she was young and used to wake with nightmares. Frightened, Marjorie would hurry to Lonie's room rather than to her mother's, stand by her bed, and whisper her name. Lonie would comfort her, pull Marjorie into her warm bed, stroke her back and kiss her cheeks, then Marjorie would fall asleep. Sometime during the night, Lonie would carry her back to her own bed, so when she awoke in the morning, it was as if an angel had transported her. She blinked, imagining Lonie hugging her right now, easing her anxiety.

Calmer, she realized that invitations didn't have to go out for more than a month. Her stress lessened when she decided she would put off any discussion with Les until his next visit. She couldn't risk losing him. She wrapped her arms across her chest and held the fragments of herself together.

CHAPTER 2

MOST OF THE afternoon, Marjorie tried to distract herself with a book she'd received as a graduation gift. After rereading one page several times, she said a silent prayer and ventured downstairs. She edged into the kitchen. Her mother stood beside the sink, slicing the tops off green peppers. On the stove, small clouds of steam arose.

Her mother turned when she saw Marjorie standing at the doorway, then she cleared her throat. "Let's have a nice meal tonight, and not let it be ruined by our talk earlier. I'm making stuffed peppers, which you say Les likes." Her knife chopped the top off the last pepper. "I hope he's not late," she said, her tone huffy.

Marjorie lifted her apron off the radiator. "What can I do to help with dinner?" Her peace offering was given.

"Why don't you set the table? Put the crystal water glasses on and use the linen napkins."

Marjorie nodded and began the routine of setting the table. *And the knife ran away with the spoon.* If only it were that easy. She checked her watch every few moments as she placed the crystal glasses and good china on the table. He should be here soon. Marjorie would pretend to him that nothing was wrong. She was an expert at wearing a smile when she was panicking inside.

"I'm going upstairs to change, unless there's something else I can do to help."

"No, go ahead. Why don't you wear that nice beige wool I got you last month?" Though her tone was quiet, Marjorie knew it was a command in disguise.

Marjorie nodded and headed upstairs. *Everything will work out.* She wouldn't think any more about her mother's hard line about Les's parents tonight. What about the blue dress? Should she wear this one she loved, or the beige dress her mother wanted her to wear? She hung the blue one back in the closet, then pulled the beige wool dress over her head and fluffed her hair.

She hurried down the stairs and into the living room to watch for Les. Staring out through the lead panes of the window past the rhododendron leaves curled from the cold, she watched the curve in the street, waiting for his car to turn into the driveway. No cars passed by.

These months apart had seemed eternal. The letters helped, but he did not write often. She read each one over and over until the paper was limp. Marjorie could not visit Les in New Jersey while he lived in his parents' small home since he was saving money toward furniture for their apartment. As an electrical engineer, he made thirty-five dollars a week, barely enough for a couple to live on.

"There's just no room for visitors with my sister still living there," he had explained during his last visit, brushing his hair back with his hand. She had suspected that he did not want her to see the simple house in the Polish neighborhood of Passaic where the family lived.

Long-distance calls were expensive, so they could not talk long or often. Sometimes, a week went by when they had no contact. Now he'd be driving in any minute.

A grey coupe roared down the street. Here he was! Her heart raced. The car slowed, moved closer, then it rounded the curve and kept going. It wasn't him. She had been so sure. Her watch said he was twenty-five minutes late. A grey coupe, like the other, cruised down the street and slowed. She held her breath. It turned into the driveway. She jumped up and ran out the door to greet him.

Les climbed out of the car, gathered her into the warmth of his arms, and kissed her. "How's my girl today? What, no coat?"

"I'm fine, now that you're here!" she said grinning. *My savior.* He wrapped his long arms around her and held her close. "I've missed you so much," Marjorie whispered, cherishing the heat that flowed from his body.

He leaned back and looked into her eyes. "Those beautiful brown eyes! You look so pretty. I'll be glad when you're with me all the time." She smiled, and the tension slipped from her shoulders. Les reached into the car and grabbed his brown leather suitcase, his thermos, and a box. "Candy for you!" Arm in arm, they ambled into the house.

Her mother met them at the doorway to the kitchen. "Glad you made it safely, Les. They said we might have snow. Homer will be home any moment. You can take your case up to the twin bedroom, as before, and relax in the living room while I finish dinner."

Marjorie was waiting at the foot of the stairs for Les to come down when she heard her father come home. He walked into the hall as Les was dashing downstairs.

"Glad you made it, Les, in this freezing weather. That was a long trip across these Pennsylvania mountains." The men shook hands like businessmen and exchanged polite smiles.

The three of them walked into the carefully arranged living room that had a large fireplace bordered by built-in bookcases at the end. French porcelains, which her mother collected, seemed to stare at her from their careful placement on the shelves. Antique English oak-style furniture complemented the Tudor style of the stone house. Tapestry drapes hung on wrought-iron rods over the French doors. Her mother had created a stage set, except for one chair that showed wear, her father's favorite wingback.

"How's the job going?" her father asked, easing into his worn chair.

"It's good. I'm doing more industrial engineering than electrical now," Les said, sitting close to Marjorie on the burgundy velvet sofa, covering her hand with his.

Her father nodded. He rarely said much. Marjorie watched Les cross and uncross his legs and smooth his hair. He moved forward on the sofa.

"How was the traffic on the turnpike?" her father asked in his usual calm tone, which reached across the room and soothed her nerves.

"The trip was good. Not much traffic, and the roads were clear. Only saw one accident, a blowout. Another car stopped to help them, which reminds me, I should check my tire pressure tomorrow. Do you know what the weather will be on Sunday when I have to drive back?"

"Not yet. We must look in the paper."

Les pointed to the mahogany radio console in the corner. "Isn't that a 1932 Philco?"

"It's a 1931 model, but it doesn't work," her father said sadly. "Quit just the other day. I listen to the little one upstairs, so I've been meaning to bring it down. Have to get this one repaired."

"It's a beauty," said Les, with a look of admiration.

"Maybe Les could take a look at it later. He might be able to fix it, if that's okay?" said Marjorie.

Her father beamed. "Be my guest, Les. I'd sure like to have it working again."

"I could give it a try," Les agreed. "I have my tube-testing kit in the car."

Marjorie noticed her mother standing in the doorway, her hands on her hips.

"Les's electrical engineering may come in handy at home! He's going to try to fix the radio. Isn't that wonderful?"

Her mother's lips maintained a straight line. "That would be quite a miracle," she said, her voice flat.

"It may take that," Les laughed.

Marjorie was relieved that Les overlooked her mother's tone. She whispered to him, "Let's take a little walk outside."

Les turned to Marjorie's mother. "I wonder if we have a few minutes for a short walk before dinner? I'd sure like to stretch these legs after all that sitting."

"Yes, but you'll only have fifteen minutes before dinner is ready," Marjorie's mother said. "I came to ask, Les, do you drink coffee with dinner? I know Homer does."

"That would be nice, thank you."

*

As they walked, Les's strength seemed to radiate to her. Marjorie's adoration for him fueled her warmth this icy-cold evening. She could almost shrug off her coat. They strolled along the sidewalk, chatting in front of the imposing, stone Tudor house. His arm cradled her shoulders. They stepped in rhythm, turning to stare into each other's eyes and blow puffs of breath at each other.

"I can't wait until I can cuddle you tonight. Is that still all right?" Les asked, hugging her.

"Yes, Dad and Mother still close their door at night."

"I'm not sure your mother likes me," Les said, looking down at his feet.

She squeezed his arm. "Why do you say that? Mother is a tough woman. She had strict British parents, so I'm afraid some of that upbringing shows." Marjorie looked at Les but his gaze was still down. "I visited my grandmother a few times before she died. She was very proper. We had to be careful of her pet goose in the front yard because it could rush at you and nip hard." Marjorie nudged Les to continue walking. "Mother didn't talk about Grandmother much, but I remember her saying Grandmother could be as mean as her goose! Anyway, I really do think Mother likes you," Marjorie said, her words crumbling in her mouth like dry cake.

Les wrinkled his brow. "I'll bring her a little gift on my next visit. It wasn't very thoughtful of me to not do that this time."

"Don't worry. Just be your kind self. Besides, I love you. That's what really counts."

He turned her to face him and said, his eyes dancing, "How special you are."

Marjorie's heart filled with affection that seemed to lift her to the treetops.

"We'd better head back. It's getting dark, and I don't want to disappoint the cook!" Les kicked a chunk of snow on the edge of the driveway. "Hey, let's go someplace warm for our honeymoon, somewhere far away, somewhere we've never been."

"Sounds great. Let's take time tomorrow to find a good place." Marjorie squeezed his arm.

Les gave her a kiss and opened the door for her.

Her mother looked up from closing the oven. "Dinner will be another few minutes or so. Go warm up in the living room."

Her father was buried in the newspaper, as he was every night before dinner. Les headed over to the radio and pulled it away from the wall to access the back. "Let's see if I can fix this pretty gal. I want to keep up with the news of events in Poland. I've been worried about my aunts and uncles these last months since Hitler's invasion. It's a miracle none of them were killed when the *Luftwaffe* bombed the roads and rails. They killed a huge number of Polish troops."

"Yes, it was awful," said her father, shaking his head sadly. "I heard they bombed villages, and the crowds blocked the roads so Poland's troops couldn't get to the front. I'm worried about this Hitler. I was a medic in the Great War . . . sure hate to think of another war happening," he grimaced.

"It must have been very tough for all the innocent people.

Europe's been a such a terrible battleground. My parents were lucky to leave just before the Great War. They still have family there I'm afraid." Les shook his head. "If you don't mind, I'll get my tube tester from the car, though I can often tell if the filaments aren't right just by looking."

One by one, Les began pulling the tubes, handling them delicately though his hands were large and his fingers thick. Marjorie cringed at what her mother might say about the radio tubes lying about but said nothing. She hoped he would be able to fix the darn radio so her mother would see how smart he was. Les's knowledge of electrical things amazed her. She had never seen her father even change a light bulb. While he was working on the radio, Marjorie told him about going to the Gordon's for dinner and playing cards the next evening.

"Good, that sounds like fun. I like Ned," Les said, holding several wires. "Maybe before that we can go for a ride on the incline. The Johnstown incline is supposed to be the steepest inclined plane in the US. It's got a seventy-one percent grade."

"It's really steep. Sure, let's go," she said, bobbing her head in agreement.

Marjorie's mother came to the living room doorway. "All ready for dinner!"

Marjorie jumped up to block her mother's view of the radio innards lying around. "I'm really famished, and you must be too, Les."

But her mother's eyes focused on the radio tubes scattered on the rug. A scowl formed on her mother's face, and she shook her head. "Come, or it will be cold." She turned and left the room with her officious stride.

Please say nothing. Let it go, Mother. Marjorie walked on tenterhooks, while Les stepped over his array of radio parts and followed her mother into the dining room. "It smells wonderful in here," he said, smiling.

The table made an elegant picture, set with fine, dark-rimmed china, an arrangement of evergreens and berries in the center, a lace tablecloth, and steaming serving platters. Marjorie felt a pang of pleasure when Les stood politely, waiting to sit until everyone else was seated. She hoped the evening would be as perfect as the table setting.

"Les, have you found any suitable apartments to rent when you are married?" her mother's eyes were glued on him.

Les swallowed his sip of coffee. "I haven't yet, but I'll do that soon." He tapped his fingers on the table.

"Les has a friend who lives in a nice garden apartment in Elizabeth, near Newark, and he plans to look there," Marjorie said.

"Several guys I work with live in Elizabeth. They like the parks, and the closeness to shopping and work."

Her mother formed a weak smile and put a bite of potatoes into her mouth.

Marjorie leaned back in her chair and took a deep breath.

"How is business at the factory?" Marjorie's father asked Les.

"We're doing pretty well. Sales are picking up in several states," Les said. "We're in the process of improving the conveyor belts at our plant so our assembly line can work faster. But the possibility of war might change the direction of our production."

"How do promotions work there?" asked her mother, leaning forward.

"You have to prove yourself to the managers. It may be awhile for me," Les said, looking down at his plate.

"You've only been there for a few months, so I'm sure when they see how good you are it will happen," said Marjorie with conviction. "Les was tops in his engineering class, remember?"

"Oh, yes. So nice. By the way, Marjorie, can you two go downtown to the hotel tomorrow and reserve the number of rooms you'll need for the wedding?" her mother asked.

Marjorie almost spilled her tea. Her mother had not mentioned this before. "Well, we were planning to go down the incline tomorrow, then to Lorraine and Ned's," Marjorie blurted. She bit her lip. Les did not have money for a deposit to reserve a block of rooms, she was sure of that. Somehow, she had to cover for him. Perhaps her perfect evening wasn't meant to be.

"Seems like there's plenty of time for reservations, Mother, since the wedding is almost four months away."

Les stiffened, lines deepening on his brow.

"But remember, the hockey teams will still be playing then, and the hotel fills up in advance," her mother said, punctuating her comment with her finger.

"Really, the number of rooms we should reserve would be a guess at this point since we don't know who all will be coming." Marjorie twisted the napkin on her lap. She and Les would have to talk later, figure out something that would not put him on the spot.

Her mother's jaw thrust forward. "I know that, but you can estimate. It's always better to be safe and reserve more than you would guess." Her mother pronounced each word slowly and with emphasis. "It's not something to take for granted."

Marjorie gathered her courage and persevered. "Les and I will discuss it and figure out what is best to do," she said, forcing a smile.

Her mother's eyes narrowed, and her mouth formed a thin slash. She cut her pepper to shreds.

Her father reached over and patted Marjorie's arm. "If we can help with the arrangements, let me know."

Her mother stared at her father and downed her coffee.

Marjorie's heart swelled at her father's offer, especially since he rarely disagreed with her mother. She was so grateful for this support. He must like Les. They'd find a solution to the reservation situation together.

When Les complimented her mother on the stuffed peppers, Marjorie warmed inside, and her mother sat up a little straighter. Her face softened.

"We wanted to have something you like," her mother said. "Do cookies sound all right for dessert?"

Les may have left the radio in pieces, but Marjorie felt almost whole.

*

After dinner, Marjorie suggested she and Les stay a few minutes in the dining room to discuss the hotel reservations that her mother had insisted were an immediate necessity.

"You know, Marge, your father means well, and I appreciate his offer to help with the reservations." Les studied her face. "But I think these reservations are my responsibility, my share of the wedding costs. After all, most of the people coming from out of town are my family and friends." Les looked down. "My folks aren't in a position to do much, but I want to do this with no help. You know, I've saved up $120 so far toward our apartment."

Marjorie grinned. "That's great you've saved so much," she said, patting his arm.

"The apartment I checked into costs thirty dollars a month, with thirty dollars in advance. So that leaves about sixty dollars that I thought we would put toward buying furniture. But I *could* use it toward reserving rooms for the wedding. The only thing is, I don't have that much with me, so we couldn't do it tomorrow."

"Dad would be happy to let you borrow it."

Les's fingers played with the lace tablecloth. "I just don't want to borrow that money, Marge. Maybe its false pride, I don't know." Les sighed and rubbed his forehead. They sat in silence.

"What if I get a check from my bank when I get home and send it to you? Then you could use the money to reserve the rooms for me. If we reserve ten rooms, that would cover all my family, the wedding party, out-of-town friends, and probably have a few left over," Les said.

"Sure, good thinking!" Marjorie hesitated. "On second thought, it would be nice if you sent the check to Dad. That way, he might be a part of the wedding planning. He could help by going down to the hotel and making the reservations for us. Mother doesn't include him in much."

"Okay, if that would make you happy, we'll do that. I want my gal happy!"

Flooded with relief, Marjorie hopped up and gave him a hug. She would tell her parents about their plan in the morning. Marjorie was delighted Les had saved so much from his pay. As a bonus, she had found a role for her father.

The evening was almost over, but what about Les's parents? That pot was simmering on a back burner in her mind.

CHAPTER 3

As she dressed the next morning, Marjorie floated in a wistful world remembering the night before when, wearing her blue silk nightie, she listened for Les's footsteps on the hall carpet for what seemed like hours. The door opened, and he closed it with the slightest click. He was standing beside her bed, just as she had imagined on so many nights that he would. He leaned over and kissed her, caressed her face. As he climbed in and over her, the bed groaned.

They lay still for a few moments, not daring to move. She was afraid her mother could hear the thundering of her heart. Silence. He kissed her hard and the swell of desire inflamed her. Her fingers pressed into his back. He kissed her again and again, pulled up her nightgown, then kissed her breasts gently, his tongue teasing her. Afterward, they lay together in the darkness, his warmth soothing her body and her soul. They whispered until they dared to no longer.

The next morning, as Marjorie pulled on her stockings, she knew the weekend was slipping by too quickly. She reminded herself they would be apart for only another month, until he visited in January, then less than three more months of separation until the wedding in April.

She was anxious to get downstairs to see Les. Pulling her

favorite blue dress over her head, she put lipstick on her smile, checked her teeth for pink smears, and glided downstairs. Marjorie peeked into the living room. Les was bent over wires, working on the radio. He looked up, smiled at her, and pursed a kiss. She returned the gift. Smells of bacon cooking shifted her focus. What mood would she find her mother in?

She called into the kitchen, "Mother, is there anything I can do?"

"You can put the juice and napkins on the table, then the coffee, while I finish the bacon and eggs."

Marjorie stepped lightly into the kitchen, relieved at her mother's conversational tone. "I'd be happy to," Marjorie said. She picked up the pitcher of juice from the linen tablecloth bordered with pictures of fruit. She did not allow herself the luxury of relaxing, although the road that portended deep potholes appeared smoother than she'd expected.

Les came into the breakfast room where her father stood waiting, and they exchanged good mornings. Sunlight poured in through the lead-paned windows where two ceramic roosters kept vigil on the windowsill. Her spirits rose with the promise of the day together. As she moved to her chair, Marjorie shared a discreet smile with Les.

"Have a seat, Les." Homer pulled his chair up to the table. "It looks like you have some sunshine for your outing today."

"I'm glad we've got good weather. I'm anxious to ride on Johnstown's famous incline." Les rubbed his hands together.

"You should have a good view from the top. From up there, you can see a strip of the Conemaugh River. It's hard to believe all the damage the flooding caused in thirty-six, almost four years ago." He tucked his napkin into the collar of his starched white shirt. "Many of my patients had to go up to the top floor of their houses to evacuate by boat. The incline carried many to safety," Homer said, pouring cream into his coffee.

Marjorie relaxed. Her father was sharing more than usual. She sent him an imaginary hug.

"It sounds like a radio in here with all your spouting, Homer," her mother said as she brought in a plate of bacon and scrambled eggs. "Let's eat." She passed the platter to Les.

Les served himself and toyed with his fork. "That same year, when I was a sophomore at Bucknell, the Susquehanna River in Lewisburg flooded most of the campus. My friend Phil and I got a rowboat and brought bread, canned goods, and meat to our housemother where we rented rooms." Les punctuated his comment with his fork, which slipped and skittered across the table to bang against her mother's coffee cup.

"Oh, no, I am so sorry. How clumsy," said Les, gaping at his fork as if he were willing it to return to him.

Marjorie winced, expecting reproach, but her mother said with a smile, "We don't allow surgery at the table, but cup clanging is alright." She handed Les back his fork.

Marjorie winked at Les's stunned look.

Near the end of the meal her mother leaned forward, holding her coffee cup in both hands, and looked at Les. "You have a busy day, but Les, save some time before you leave to give us your guest list for the wedding."

Marjorie's hand twitched, and bits of her scrambled egg slid off her plate onto the tablecloth. Since yesterday, she had pushed her mother's ultimatum about Les's parents deep down where only her darkest thoughts and secrets lay buried. She jabbed at the egg. Her emotions swirled and tugged. She forced a smile. "More coffee, Les?"

"No thanks," he said, raising his eyebrows at her in a look of concern before turning back to her mother. "I have the list, with all the addresses except one—a cousin of mine who's just moved. I can mail that one to you as soon as I get it."

"That will be fine. Also, we could get your measurements for your tuxedo today, or when you come back next month. Doing it in January will still give us plenty of time." Her mother stood and took the platter to the kitchen.

Les folded his napkin into a small square and turned to Marjorie. "Marge, I hate to disappoint you, but I won't be able to come in January, not until the end of February."

"Not until February?" Marjorie's eyes widened. Her chest began thumping.

"The company does their inventory in January and the first weeks of February. No one can take time off during this period," he said with a frown. "I don't know what I can do. We'll just have to talk on the phone more often." His eyes pleaded forgiveness. "I'm sorry I didn't tell you sooner. I didn't want to spoil our whole weekend."

"I understand," said Marjorie, scraping the bits of egg from the tablecloth. She couldn't be annoyed since she had kept the issue of his parents from him for the same reason. *Since he can't come next month, I have to figure out what to do about his parents' invitation today.* How could she broach the subject of his parents without embarrassing their family? Or without her mother turning into a monster? She just didn't know. But she would not risk ruining their time together today. She would talk with him tonight.

Les stood up and moved behind his breakfast-room chair. "While you're helping your mother with the dishes, I think I'll work on that radio for a while, if that's okay with your dad, then we can plan the rest of our day. The tubes are fine, so it must be a break in the wires somewhere. I'm going to try replacing some of them."

"Keep at it!" Homer encouraged Les. "You'll figure it out."

Marjorie hoped he could find the problem soon. She realized she was scrutinizing every move he made that could possibly cause her mother consternation. She had to stop being so vigilant. She followed them into the living room for a moment.

"Good luck finding the bad wire," Marjorie called to Les. She was proud of his tenacity, of his eagerness to help, and she was grateful that his visit was still amiable. She walked into the kitchen.

"Thanks for the nice dinner last night and breakfast this morning. I know Les enjoyed both," Marjorie said.

"Any guest must be treated well." Her mother stiffened her neck, plunking the silverware into the sink of sudsy water. A blanket of silence lay heavy between them as she washed the silverware.

Marjorie couldn't tell if her mother was somewhat pleased or annoyed. She was never a winner at this guessing game. If she questioned her mother, she risked a rebuff. If she was chatty and pretended all was well, her mother would likely see through it and be provoked to further annoyance. It was often better to say little. She dried the dishes.

"I'll need to get Les's tuxedo measurements after we're done here," her mother said, peering over her glasses at Marjorie. "It's inconvenient that he can't come until February, with so many decisions to make. Then, too, there are your honeymoon plans and all. We will pay for the honeymoon since his parents are on a limited income. Florida would be nice in April, don't you think?"

"That is wonderful, Mother." She hesitated. "But Les really wants to go somewhere neither of us have been."

"Well, beggars can't always be choosers, I'm afraid. We'll discuss it later," her tone dismissive.

Marjorie cringed. Her mother was still upset.

Walking into the living room, she saw her father sitting at his desk, head bent over the financial section of the newspaper—his usual Saturday morning activity. Les worked with the radio wires for an hour, testing one after another. A curl of his dark-blond hair fell across his forehead. He looked so boyishly handsome sitting cross-legged on the carpet. If he managed to fix that old radio, it might give her mother a reason to respect him.

Her mother marched into the room dangling a yellow tape measure from one hand and holding a pencil and pad in the other.

"Les, I'd better take the measurements for your tuxedo since you won't be here again until February. Would you stand up so I can measure you?" she said with upturned corners of her mouth that almost formed a smile. Wires lay around Les as he stood up. Her mother kicked at one that was near her foot as she whipped the tape across his shoulders, down his arms, and around his waist, jotting on her pad as she measured. She hesitated, then asked him to hold the tape at the top inseam of his pants while she measured the length.

Marjorie suppressed a grin as Les rolled his eyes to the ceiling.

"Your shoulders aren't as broad as I thought," her mother said. Her lips pulled into a tight smile she wore like a mask. "And I need your best man Phil's measurements too. I'll give you a list of what he'll need to do to measure. We're renting all the tuxedos here so they will be the same." She put her hands on her hips, the tape dangling from one hand. "You can't imagine the problems that arise unless everything is coordinated. I have one friend whose brother never could get the same pants as the others in the wedding party. He was mighty embarrassed."

"I'm glad that won't happen to us. I could send you my father's measurements too, if you like," said Les.

Her mother wrapped her measuring tape into a circle. "Certainly, but we may not need tuxedos . . . for the parents."

Marjorie flinched and looked down at her shoes.

Her mother swept out of the room, calling after her, "I'll be upstairs sewing."

Marjorie bit her lip, noticing Les clasp his hands.

"Let's sit down in the breakfast room a minute," she said, leading Les by his arm to the table. They sat next to each other, shoulders touching. She hoped he had ignored her mother's comment about the parents' tuxedos.

Les jumped right in, "The fathers wore tuxedos at my cousin's wedding. Isn't your dad wearing one? I don't know what your mother meant that the parents might not need tuxedos."

Marjorie, unprepared for such a direct question, scrambled for justification of her mother's statement. "Maybe I'd better read that wedding etiquette book more closely." She forced a chuckle. She would protect him now with a little lie and address the truth later, when this messy situation was resolved. If only she could figure out how to fix it. She burned inside at the dishonesty but said in as casual tone as she could manage, "Your cousin had a military wedding. Maybe the parents wore tuxedos because it was a more formal affair with swords and uniforms?" She bit her tongue until it hurt. Guilt seeped through her veins as she dug deeper into deception.

"I guess we'll find out later," Les said.

"Anyway, let's decide about the incline. Do you still want to go?"

"Definitely. Let's grab a little snack and go."

She knew Les was anxious to get out of the house and spend time alone with her.

*

They drove for a mile past rows of naked trees in their winter bones to get to the top of the incline. Waiting to board, they looked down from the top of the mountain at the sparkling miniature houses and shops below.

"It seems like a storybook, so peaceful and serene," Marjorie said. "Look how the river curves so calmly. It's hard to believe it grew into such a rage and caused all that devastation."

She relished the moment spent overlooking the city but nagging at her was the honeymoon dilemma. She didn't want to tarnish her time with Les, but while they were alone, she needed to tell him what her mother had said about Florida for their honeymoon.

Les pointed to the cables of the incline as the brown metal car with cloudy windows moved upward toward them. "Cables of this gauge could pull a house off its foundation, so it's safe, even if it *is* old," he said, nodding as if agreeing with himself.

Marjorie smiled. She loved his knowledge of things she knew nothing about.

They got into the empty metal car and sat close together, facing downhill as the agent closed the door with a loud clank. Les kissed Marjorie on the cheek. She wrapped her arms around his shoulders feeling his strength beneath his coat.

As they descended, the city slowly rose to greet them. She wondered if this was like flying, the tiny houses growing larger as they moved down the mountain. Near the bottom, she could see porches of old homes leaning off balance, relying on precariously tilted posts to keep them from collapsing. Torn fences, houses in need of paint, and untended yards came into view. They stood a few minutes at the bottom before catching the next car going up. As they rode back up, the shabbiness seemed to disappear, as if the scene mended itself like an enchanted village.

Later, walking to the car, Les said, "That was great. Quite an engineering feat. It was both fantasy and reality in one-half hour."

Like my hopes and dreams for a sweet life with Les, and Mother's demands that could suddenly pitch me off balance like those ruined porches ready to tumble. Then Marjorie pinched her hand and dismissed these negative thoughts. She wanted their time together to be foremost in her memory. "Wasn't riding the incline fun? We were lucky to have such good weather for the view, especially since the clouds are moving in now."

"It's so good to be alone with you." Les stopped and swung her hand.

She sensed his body tense.

"I shouldn't say this, but, you know, Marge, I thought your mother was a bit hard on me at dinner last night." He looked down at the street and brushed his shoe on the pavement. "I don't think she approves of me."

Marjorie's mood tumbled down the incline. She grabbed his arm. "Oh, hon, that's just how she is. She's often all business, wanting everything planned and organized so that she's in control and nothing unforeseen will ruin things. Please don't make anything of it."

"I want her to like me." His eyes reflected hope. "Maybe it'll just take time."

"Gosh, Les." She shook her head. "You know she's not big on giving compliments. Like I said before, I really think it has to do with growing up in a straitlaced family from England."

They neared the car and stood by it. Les's brow wrinkled as he listened.

"So, hon, don't make anything of her questioning." She put her hand on his arm. After all, she made cookies for you, and wanted to please you with the stuffed peppers."

"Okay. I guess I just have to be patient."

She heard a tinge of doubt in his voice. "Please don't think any more of this." She gave him a hug. "I love you, that's what counts most!"

Les unlocked the car and opened her door.

Marjorie scooted into her seat. Les closed her door, walked around and slid into the driver's seat, folding his long legs under the wheel.

Marjorie took a deep breath. "Before we go back, I want to talk with you about something Mother mentioned this morning. Sorry, but we've got so little time alone."

He turned to her. "Okay, shoot."

"She said that they want to pay for a trip to Florida for our honeymoon." Marjorie watched his face change from a slight grin to pursing his lips.

"That's very nice of them to pay for the trip, but you've been to Florida several times. Heck, they just took you to Miami a few months ago. It's not like we would be discovering a new place together."

"I know. I want to go somewhere new too." She patted his arm.

"Couldn't we go somewhere else? Does it have to be Florida?" he said.

"I did tell her we wanted to explore somewhere we haven't visited."

"What did she say?"

Marjorie looked down and hesitated, torn between distorting the truth again and admitting her mother was in control of their honeymoon. She struggled to say the right thing. If Les knew her mother's hard nature, he might change his mind about marrying her. She measured her words. "Something about in April, the South is the only place where the weather is warm and nice," she stumbled. Her sin of omission plunged her back into a gully of guilt.

"It seems like we're always bending to meet your mother's wishes. She wants you to have the best, I know that," Les said, pressing both hands against the steering wheel. "I just wish I'd been able to save more so we weren't depending on anyone. I've been living at home so I could save everything I possibly can."

"You've done wonderfully, Les, my goodness." Marjorie leaned her head against his shoulder. "You're working as an engineer for a strong company. I'm really proud of you, especially because these times are hard for many people. What with the war in Europe, jobs are changing, and who knows what could happen here soon."

"But your folks are paying for so much, like the wedding, furniture, other things for our apartment, and now the honeymoon too. I'm afraid my folks can't help us out." Les's frustration was seeping out again.

"Don't worry about that. Dad and Mother are lucky they are able to help. They really want to do this for us," Marjorie said confidently.

Les took her hand. "That's good, Marge, but I want us to decide where we go for our honeymoon. Maybe I could save up for a while longer and we could take our honeymoon later."

Marjorie's spirit sank. She wanted their honeymoon to be the way she thought it should be—right after the wedding, not later. Her dreams for her wedding day were drifting up into the clouds overhead. She gripped Les's arm as if she could squeeze a solution out of it. Someplace warm, drivable, but not Florida. She needed an answer so they could get past this pitfall and get on with their weekend. They sat in silence.

"Maybe we could go somewhere else in Florida? Somewhere I haven't been. I've only been to Miami Beach." *Why didn't I think of this sooner?* She watched the lines in Les's brow fade.

"Well, maybe we could find another city that would be good to explore. And guaranteed to be warm in April. I think I've heard some good things about Tampa."

The strain eased from Marjorie's neck. She breathed a sigh. This solution would please everyone. "You're a genius." Marjorie grabbed him and kissed him.

"We'll work on it!" he said with a smile as he turned the key in the ignition.

*

As they drove to Lorraine and Ned's that evening, a rosier perspective began building. Marjorie felt like a bird about to flee its cage, soon to have her own apartment and a wonderful husband, far from Johnstown. She was eager to enjoy this night out with Les, Lorraine, and Ned, making memories she could relive after Les left in the morning.

She mused about how lucky she was to have Lorraine as a friend. She and Lorraine were both only children who had played together like sisters throughout childhood. Lorraine had helped her select her wedding dress from an array of fussy choices. And later, when her mother preferred a shorter veil than what Marjorie had chosen, Lorraine, always the diplomat, agreed they were both beautiful.

Ned greeted them at the door. "Come in, it's so good to see you both. Lorraine is fighting with the roast, but she'll be here in a minute."

They chatted and teased about married life during a dinner of pork roast with baked apples and mashed potatoes—a specialty of Lorraine's.

"Great dinner, and lemon meringue pie too, Lorraine," Les said. "Now, Ned and I are going to show you what we're made of." They played four games of canasta, the men against the women.

At first Marjorie was absorbed in the game, and it was a good distraction. But as the evening progressed, she missed some obvious plays.

"Hey Marge, you could have added those sevens to my meld, and now they count against you," Les said, disappointment in his voice.

She had overlooked another play. Her thoughts of what to say to Les about his parents invaded like a persistent pest. She rehearsed approaches that would not damage any relationships. Nothing seemed right.

When Les suggested it was time to go, Lorraine said, "I meant to tell you, Marjorie, the bridesmaids' dresses are really lovely in the picture you sent, and I think the hats make the whole outfit very elegant."

"My sister likes them too," Les added. "I heard Emilie oohing and ahhing at the magazine picture you sent."

Marjorie grinned, "I'm so glad you like them."

"Has your mother decided on a dress yet?" Lorraine asked Les. Marjorie shrank in her chair, focusing on the white doily under the table lamp, tracing the pattern with her eyes.

"Oh, she hasn't gone shopping yet. She likes to wait for sales." Les glanced down at his feet. "Plus, she's a little nervous about coming to the wedding since her English is so limited. She doesn't go out much. Emilie will help her, though. Thanks for a great evening. Next time we play canasta, we men might even win again!"

"Before you two run off, Marjorie, I'd like to show you what I did with the old bookcase your mother gave me," Ned said.

Marjorie took a step toward Ned.

"And I'll ask Les's opinion of the leak on the porch roof," said Lorraine. "Follow me, Les, I need your expertise."

Ned ushered Marjorie into the den. "Someday we hope this room will be a nursery. Please, sit for a moment." He gestured to a wooden chair.

This is odd, Ned wanting me to sit, What's up here?

Ned sat down nearby, then after a moment he stood back up. "You know, Marjorie, I debated whether to say anything to you, but I wanted to talk with you alone for a minute."

Marjorie swallowed hard. *Where was this going? Was this something about Les?*

"I told myself it was none of my business, that I shouldn't interfere." Ned wrung his hands. "It's difficult for me. I thought about it a bunch. Lorraine doesn't know I'm telling you this. She thinks I should stay out of your business."

Marjorie's curiosity became anxiety.

He threw up his hands. "I decided I should talk to you anyway."

"Ned, what is this about? Is it about Les?" Marjorie's eyes narrowed.

"First, I want you to know I appreciate what your mother has done to help me, giving me that job taking care of your dad's office before I got work at the mill. That was really a big help for me."

"Mother wanted to do that. After all, Lorraine's mother is a good friend of hers."

"Anyway, well . . . uh . . . Lorraine told me how you went through a bad time after your engagement. Several times she invited you over, but you wouldn't come. This bothered both of us. At first, Lorraine thought you were mad at her." Ned began to pace, his hands pushing in and out of his pockets. "Then, on the phone, your voice sounded so strange. It reminded us of when you were sick in college. We didn't know how to help."

Marjorie flushed with embarrassment that Lorraine had discussed her depression with Ned. It was not a time in her life that she wanted shared. Her mind slipped back to those dark weeks when her mother had refused to accept her engagement to Les and wanted her to return the ring. She remembered lying in bed for many days in her pajamas, having lost her ability to enjoy simple things that used to give her pleasure. Even the decision of what to wear demanded enormous deliberation and energy. After weeks of little hope, she could hear strong voices, her father intervening and insisting to her mother that they must support her engagement to Les. The dreary fog that had kept her prisoner lifted a little each day after that.

"That was a difficult time, but I'm better now," Marjorie stammered. She noticed Ned fidgeting. "Thanks, Ned, for thinking of me."

"Lorraine and I both wish the best for you and Les. He's a fine fellow. But between you and me, well, I think you might need to take a stand with your mother if you want to be happy. She's a strong-willed woman, and that might make things hard for you . . . that is, unless you set your limits." He clicked his tongue. "Just had to say this." Ned patted her shoulder. "Uh . . . please don't tell Lorraine I said anything."

Marjorie sat stunned that Ned would share this very private advice. "Ned, thanks. It'll be our secret. I appreciate your honesty. It has been hard to do everything Mother wants. Maybe it's impossible to please her. Thank you for your advice." Marjorie hugged him. "I will try to keep your words as my support. Your concern means very much to me." Marjorie was surprised that even Ned had seen this aspect of her mother's personality. Imagine what he would think if he knew about her mother's refusal to have Les's parents at the wedding.

"Now have a look at this bookcase. I've stained and shellacked it." Ned beamed.

"It looks new. You're a clever man, Ned," Marjorie said, smiling at him.

They moved back into the living room, where Les and Lorraine were talking and laughing. They exchanged hugs all around and said their good nights.

There was no time left. She had to make a decision about her mother's ultimatum. Marjorie's heart pulsed faster as they walked down the steps to the street. She fumbled with her gloves, angry that her mother had put her in this impossible position. She had to talk with Les while they had time alone. Her thoughts whirled and dodged, a kite buffeted by blustery winds. As she slid into her seat, she struggled to find words that would do no harm. She glanced over at Les. The storm in her mind suddenly subsided, and she knew what she would do.

The car choked, whined, then rumbled to a start. Marjorie said, "Could we sit here a few minutes? There's something I'd like to talk to you about."

"Sure, if you don't mind the cold. The heater is slow." He turned a dial and snickered. "My car seems to be the cozy place for our conversations!" Les turned to her, his brow furrowed. "What's up?"

Marjorie swallowed. "It's about your parents." She put her hand on his arm, drawing in his strength. "I want you to know that I hope they will come to the wedding. Your sister and I can help make them comfortable." Marjorie was giddy with relief. There would be a hefty price to pay, but she was sure she'd made the right decision.

"Thanks, I know they want to. It's just that they are so self-conscious about their English. I wish we could just elope. Everything would be simpler," Les said, sighing.

"I know what you mean. We could save a lot of anxiety if we

just ran off and got married," Marjorie said. "Actually, Dad and Mother did that. They were married by a justice of the peace."

"No, we'll do it the right way so there are no regrets." He took her hand.

Marjorie hesitated, "You're right, a wedding is the best way." Marjorie hoped this would be true. She pressed her lips together. How would she face her mother with this decision? She had to prepare for her anger, her rebuff. Her head began to throb. She consoled herself with the thought that during Les's visit there had been no ugly incidents between Les and her mother. At least that much had gone well. She was grateful.

*

The next morning the weathermen were predicting snow, and she knew Les wanted to get an early start. It took seven hours to drive from Johnstown to Passaic, New Jersey.

"I hate to run off before fixing the radio," Les said as they all stood in the hallway, "but I don't have new snow tires yet. The old ones don't get much traction, so I should get started. I'll be sending the check for the hotel reservations to you, Dr. Hill. Thank you for helping to make them. I hope you have a wonderful holiday."

"Come back when you can." Her father shook Les's hand. "That old radio will be waiting for you! I have a house call to make now, a stomach ulcer I think, so I'll be right behind you in the driveway."

"Have a safe trip," added Marjorie's mother. "Here are instructions for Phil so he can measure for his tuxedo, your thermos, and a sandwich and cookies for the road."

"Thank you for your fine hospitality. I appreciate the hot coffee and sandwich."

Marjorie threw on her coat and walked outside with him. "I'll be sending your Christmas present next week," he said to her with a smile as they reached his car. "This is the last Christmas we'll be apart." They hugged and kissed, then hugged again.

"I love you, sweetheart. And don't let your mother get you down. You must stay strong—I see what goes on." Les held her close, reassuring her of his support.

He looked deep into her eyes. What did he see there? A weak woman? Or one trying to be strong?

"I'll work hard on that, honey." She gave him a big smile and a last kiss.

He got in the car. She waved at him, watching the car through her tears until it disappeared around the turn.

As Marjorie walked slowly back into the living room, her mother sat in her chair cutting a thread with her teeth. She was sewing a button on her husband's shirt.

"You know, he left that radio still broken!" her mother said to Marjorie over her shoulder. Marjorie braced herself against her father's wing chair for support. She wished there were a way she could avoid this confrontation. She sat down opposite her mother.

"He didn't have time to get all the wires checked. He said he was sorry, and he would finish next time," Marjorie said.

"So, did you tell him about his parents?" Her mother's lips formed a tight line.

Marjorie took a long breath, knowing she had to face this now. "Yes."

"What did you say?" her mother asked, staring at her with a piercing look like a bird of prey.

Marjorie was walking a tightrope over an abyss. She cleared her throat. "I told him we were hoping his parents will come."

"Ouch!" her mother yelled, flinging her hand up after sticking her finger with the needle as she shoved the shirt down on her lap. "What? I told you I would not be there if they came!" she sputtered, her eyes blazing. "I cannot believe you defied me!"

Marjorie didn't know where her strength came from, some untapped inner core, maybe, but she gathered every fragment and pressed ahead. "Mother, *I* can't be there if *they aren't* invited."

CHAPTER 4

MARJORIE TOSSED IN her bed that night, her sheets as twisted as her thoughts. The clock read 1:35 a.m., 3:20, 4:15. Her mind spiraled. Would her mother change her mind? What should she tell Les? What if he decided he'd had enough of this family?

A grey fog filtered through the curtains. Daylight already. It had been only one day since Les left. Marjorie forced herself out of bed and ran water to soak in a hot bath. She lay back in the tub, staring at her tummy rising and sinking below the surface as she breathed, the warmth soothing her. She soaked until her turmoil subsided.

She would never agree to not inviting Les's parents. "Everything will be okay," she repeated aloud as she stepped out of the tub and rubbed her skin with a rough towel. *If only my worries would swirl down the drain with the dirty water.* She pulled on her nylon slip, and over it a navy wool dress. Glancing down the hall, she saw her parents' bed was made. She smelled toast as she scuffled down the stairs. Somehow, she had to convince her mother to change her mind.

When Marjorie entered the kitchen, her mother was bent over the kitchen sink rinsing dishes. She did not look up.

"Has Dad gone already?" Marjorie asked. Her mother nodded

her head yes, but she did not turn around. Water ran, but no words dribbled forth.

Marjorie supported herself against the doorframe, a tight smile welded into place. "You're upset about what I said yesterday. About Les's parents," she stammered in the most neutral tone she could muster. No response. Silence had always been her mother's way of controlling a situation when she believed she had been crossed.

Marjorie's neck stiffened—she could feel a headache coming on. She stared at her mother. She saw flesh and blood and stone.

Marjorie inhaled deeply, her nostrils flaring. "Mother, I'm sorry I offended you. I've always tried very hard to do as you wished. I've always put aside my own wants and ideas since I believed you knew what was best for me." Marjorie cleared her throat. "I hate to contradict you." She hesitated, pooling the droplets from her reservoir of strength. Her mother said nothing. "Now, I have to do what I believe is the right thing, what my heart and head tell me is best." Her voice caught. She waited.

Her mother dried her hands on her apron, pulled it off her waist, and laid it on the radiator to dry. She did not look at Marjorie and headed toward the back stairs. Marjorie followed her.

"I can't hurt Les by not inviting his parents. It would be a wound that wouldn't heal. I just can't agree to anything else. They are shy about their English, and I'm sure will say very little."

Her mother snapped her head around, her eyes on fire. "That's just it, their English!" she spat. "I won't be made a fool of by people whispering that middle-aged adults can't speak English!" She whipped back around, then stomped up the wooden stairs, her shoes like a hammer hitting a board.

Marjorie retreated to the breakfast room. She dunked cold toast in her coffee and stared at the crumbs that floated in her cup. Her mother's silent episodes usually ended when she received an apology, full of penitence and regret. Humility was essential. Apologies were validation that her mother was right. This time,

Marjorie's apology wasn't good enough. She had dared to defy her mother, a crime requiring due punishment for a rebel.

Marjorie squinted at the rooster on the windowsill, remembering Les eating in this room with her only a day ago. If only he could tell her what to do. The room dimmed as thick snow clouds darkened the morning. Moisture condensed into droplets on the lead windowpanes.

Marjorie went up to her room. If the impasse continued, there couldn't be a family wedding. If she confided in Les, she'd have to tell him the truth about her mother's unwillingness to have his parents come. That could ruin any hope of a positive relationship between Les and her parents. Perhaps that was questionable anyway.

After settling in the rocking chair in her room, she began a letter to Les explaining her need to talk to him about a problem she was struggling with. She explained she did not have the privacy she needed on the family phone for this discussion, but perhaps he could call her at Lorraine's. They could arrange a time that was good for all.

She reread the letter and wadded it into a ball. Surely he would find this letter vague and the arrangements silly. She began another, finally crumpling it, too, and tossing it into the wastebasket. He was a practical man. She had to be more patient.

Marjorie remembered that her mother hadn't wanted her father's parents, who were farmers, to embarrass her family that had proper manners. She opted to forgo a formal wedding, wore a suit, and was married without family present by a justice of the peace. Perhaps a wedding like her mother's was becoming a more realistic option for her.

At dinner, her mother clanked the plates and banged the salt and pepper on the table, her lips set in a thin line. She avoided all eye contact.

"Mrs. Thorn had a tumor the size of a grapefruit," her

father offered. Usually details from the hospital would interest her mother. Today, his attempt to engage her was rebuffed. Her mother glanced over her eyeglasses, stabbed her fork into the pork chop, and furiously sliced her meat. She broke her roll with a savage thrust. With each jab of her fork, she rhythmically clenched her jaw, maintaining her veneer of silence.

In the living room after dinner, Marjorie pulled the desk chair close to her father's and whispered to him, "What can we do, Dad? I'm afraid Mother's anger will go on for a long while. I apologized and explained to her why it was so important to me that Les's parents be invited." Marjorie shrugged and shook her head. "But she's so upset about their English, fretting about what people will think about my marrying into an uneducated immigrant family."

Her father studied her, his pale-blue eyes reflecting concern.

Marjorie couldn't speak for a moment. "Maybe it's even more than that. Maybe she hasn't gotten over the fact that I'm not marrying Bob. Self-centered, boring Bob." Marjorie hung her head, surprised at her own acrimony. "After all, turning Bob down keeps me out of the social circle she wanted me to be part of." Marjorie paused. "Could you please talk to her?"

Her father sat forward in his chair, moving closer to her. "I know you want Les's parents to receive an invitation. And, of course, they should." He straightened his glasses on his nose. "I'll try to talk to her again tonight. But, Marjorie, you know it is best to be a little more patient, to allow her upset to ease off, for her to come around on her own." He seemed to focus on something far off and stroked his mustache. His mouth opened as he started to say something, but he hesitated, then pressed his lips together. He looked over at her and patted her hand. "She wants what is first class for you. She loves you and needs to protect you, but she doesn't always know the best or kindest way. Sometimes she's just bluster and spittle."

"It's more like flames and dynamite."

"She will come around soon, Marjorie, you'll see. Please don't worry." He picked up his newspaper and began reading, her cue that their talk was over.

So, he had talked with her mother already. Soon? She'll come around soon? Why couldn't her mother see her side, show her some consideration?

After a few minutes of staring at the same page in the Saturday Evening Post, she put it on the table. "Good night, Dad, I'm going up early."

Her father folded his paper. "Give her a few more days, Marjorie. You'll see, it will work out." He reached over and patted her leg with the paper.

She got up, forced a smile, and walked out of the living room, through the hall and into the kitchen. She knew her mother was upstairs ironing in the back room above the garage, so she called up the back stairs, "'Night, Mother."

There was only silence.

*

The tension emanating from her mute mother hung like a dense, grey cloud for weeks. Her mother was as icy as the bitter weather outside.

Late one morning, Marjorie noticed a brown box tied with string on the hall table. The mailman must have brought it. The return address said Arlans, Printing and Engraving. The invitations had come! Her initial excitement immediately dampened. Should she open it and send one to his parents? Or should she and Les just elope? She was stretched one direction, then yanked to the other, caught in a tug-of-war. Her spurt of defiance that Sunday had left her in a quagmire.

She filled her lungs with a deep breath and slowly climbed the stairs. She decided to approach her mother once more. The rhythmic hum of the sewing machine reached her in the stairwell.

Her mother worked the foot treadle like someone speeding on a bicycle. Her father had wanted to get her an electric sewing machine, but she preferred the manual one to control every stitch. When Marjorie entered the sewing room, her mother glanced at her sideways over her glasses and continued her pedaling.

Marjorie leaned against the frame of the French door that separated her parents' bedroom from the sewing area and gathered her thoughts. "Mother, I have to talk to you." She clenched her fist. "I think the only thing I can do is to call Les tonight and tell him that you're afraid if his parents come, it might be embarrassing for everyone since their English is so limited." Her mother stopped pumping the treadle. She raised her head and looked at the wall ahead without turning.

"Do what you want, it's your wedding."

Marjorie's heart pounded. She stammered. "Of course I don't want to call and say that, hurt Les's feelings, but we have to come to some sort of an agreement. Can't we please work something out that will be suitable to everyone? They're going to be my in-laws."

Her mother's back stiffened. "You know what I said. I'm not changing my mind." She pronounced her words slowly, emphatically, as if speaking to someone hard of hearing. She started pumping the pedal again, the rapidly piercing needle stabbing the plaid fabric. A lump formed in Marjorie's throat. She turned and shuffled downstairs, running her hand on the oak banister, feeling each joint in the wood.

Marjorie felt dizzy, her head beginning to ache. Her mother's rigidity covered her like a thick wool blanket, smothering and rough. Her mother wasn't budging. What if she didn't come to the wedding? There would be decades of silent treatment. *I have to stay strong.*

Marjorie needed some fresh air to clear her head, even though it was freezing and about to snow. She wrapped herself in a sweater and scarf, donned her wool coat, and sat on the back stairs to pull on her boots. As she stepped off the porch her foot hit an icy spot on the sidewalk and she nearly fell, pressing herself against the stone wall of the garage to regain her balance. She pulled on the gloves she kept in her pockets and tightened her scarf up to her ears. If only she could dodge the present, leap up, and jump into the future. But the future she needed wasn't in place yet. For this moment, she was suspended in a cold grey world.

After clearing her head a bit, she noticed how the fresh snow blanketed the walks, the driveway, shrubs, and trees. Magically transformed, the scene appeared so peaceful. She would find harmony.

She retrieved the snow shovel from the tools in the garage and began digging in the mounds of snow. With each shovelful, she created a path that became clearer as she moved toward the driveway. She was accomplishing something worthwhile. Digging in with fury, she blew out clouds of air like steam puffing from a kettle. When she had finished, she looked at her handiwork and felt a sense of tranquility. She remembered Les in the driveway as he left, saying, "Don't let your mother get you down." But he had no idea how hard this was. She climbed up the porch steps and opened the door, glancing back at the clean walk. The warm air was a balm to her face, tight from the cold. Her headache was a little better.

She hung her coat on the banister in the back hall where it could dry, pulled off her boots, and placed them on the rubber mat by the back stairs. With a calmer mind, she decided to ask her mother about opening the invitations. If she could make progress writing a few invitations, a resolution might miraculously evolve.

She found her mother in the dining room putting the crystal glasses in the china cabinet.

"Do you mind if I open the box of invitations?" Marjorie said with hesitation.

Her mother gave an I-don't-care shrug and climbed up the stairs.

Marjorie stood for a moment ruminating over her mother's response. She got her mother's favorite paring knife from the kitchen drawer and placed the package on the kitchen table, cut the string on the box, and opened it. The invitations stood like soldiers, ordered in perfect formation. She picked up an invitation with its gold embossing on a heavy, cream-colored panel and ran her finger over the raised engraving—*Dr. and Mrs. Homer L. Hill request the honor of your presence* . . . but not her future in-laws.

Perhaps she would address a few friends' invitations first. She found the invitation list in the kitchen cabinet. As she stared at the names, they melted into a blurred sea of black and white. She blinked hard in order to focus better. Her head felt like spikes were being driven into her eye sockets. Her eyes slid over to the paring knife. She picked it up and tested the point on her finger. Her head was pounding. She flicked the knife on the little blue vein at the center of her wrist. Then she pressed a little harder. Suddenly, blood began to flow down her hand. She stared at what she'd done, then shoved the invitations away so they would not get soiled. She cupped her other hand under her wrist to keep the blood from dripping onto the carpet and ran into the kitchen to wrap a tea towel around her arm.

Just then, the back door opened and her father walked in. He draped his coat over hers on the banister of the back stairs and plopped his hat on top of the newel post.

"What happened?" he said, walking over to her, frowning. He bent over the sink to see better.

"Oh, I . . . I was opening the box of invitations and the knife . . . slipped and caught me on my wrist," Marjorie stammered.

He took the towel off and lifted her wrist. "Well, that knife cut a little slice. Let's get some pressure on it to stop the bleeding. Sit down here," he said, pointing to the kitchen chair. "Press with this towel while I get my bag." He rushed out the door without his coat and returned from the car with his black medical bag. "Who shoveled the walk?"

"I did," she said, her mind numb.

"Well, good job, thanks. It's getting icy. Now, I'm going to wrap this up." He put a drop of iodine on the cut and quickly pressed a pad of gauze on it. It felt good to have him leaning against her. A solid support. After a few minutes of putting pressure on her wrist, he gently wrapped it with gauze.

"There," he said, patting her shoulder, "keep your hand above your heart for a few minutes. Where is your mother?"

"Upstairs sewing. Dad, I tried again. She still won't change her mind."

"We'll see," he said, trudging upstairs.

Once it was clear the bleeding had stopped, Marjorie followed him up. She put a cold washcloth on her face and lay down on her bed, leaning her forearm up against the headboard so her wrist was above her heart as her father suggested. Did he believe her about the knife? He seemed to. How could she have done such a crazy thing? One moment she had the thought to poke herself, then it was done! She was shocked to see the blood. It was as if someone else had pushed the knife into her wrist.

She'd been so furious with her mother, who didn't seem to care a whit about her feelings. Everything had always been her mother's way. But she never should have reacted like that. She rubbed her aching head with her free hand.

Lying there, she made out her father's voice from her parents' bedroom. He wasn't speaking loudly, but both their bedroom doors were open. Her ears perked up at his stern words. "Hon, this is enough. We are going to invite Les's parents. This is Marjorie's wedding, such a special event in her life, and I won't let her be miserable." Silence. "I'm going to tell her I decided to invite them,

and you'll go along. Now, let's have some normalcy around here."
Their door closed with a click.

Marjorie was stunned. She had rarely heard her father speak like this to her mother. The few times he did, she knew he meant what he said. She remembered him intervening before, when her mother refused to acknowledge her engagement, giving her a new lease on the life she wished to have with Les.

Marjorie lay on her bed with a wide smile underneath the washcloth and a loving feeling for her father.

CHAPTER 5

MARJORIE'S MOTHER CONTINUED the wedding planning soon after her father demanded that Les's parents be included. At first Sara affected nonchalance, contradicted by chord-tight tension, but after a few weeks she became absorbed in the arrangements. She maintained firm control over the details, such as the bridesmaids' flowers, the order of the receiving line, and seating arrangements at the reception. The wedding became a performance she was orchestrating. Marjorie was still able to choose her own bouquet, and the music at the church and the reception—things her mother did not care about. She hadn't seen Les for over a month, but here they were, at the church on their wedding day.

"You look like an angel," Marjorie's father whispered as they waited in the vestibule. Her eyes widened. A pearl for her pocket. She shrugged her wings and stood straighter. "Thank you, Dad." She smiled at him and stroked her satin sleeve where he had touched her arm. She prayed her dream day would bring peace and harmony.

Her father smoothed his mustache with his thumb and fore-finger, then fidgeted with his bow tie. He pulled out his pocket watch, stared at it a moment, then slipped it back into his pocket as he pursed his lips. He was always so prompt. This delay must annoy him, but he said nothing. She thought of the nurses at the hospital who would wheel the patients into the operating room in advance, but only for him. It was now ten minutes past the scheduled time for the wedding to start.

Her bridesmaids poked at their bouquets, straightened each other's hats, practiced the paced stepping, and fussed with stray curls. Lorraine, her dearest friend and maid of honor, always calm and stoic, fixed the folds of her train for the third time.

"Stop hopping around, Marjorie, or your caboose will be crooked! Les is probably fixing his carburetor and forgot the time," Lorraine chuckled and winked.

Marjorie had to do something—at least she could see if Les's car was parked out front. She edged to the door to peek outside, cracked it open, and scanned the cars looking for his grey sedan. It wasn't there. Lorraine rushed over and pulled her away.

"You can't see anything from here, Marjorie. They'll be here any minute."

Marjorie smiled at her, but a lump swelled in her throat. *Where were they?* The organist played Bach's Prelude in C Major over and over, then finally changed to an excerpt from Handel's *Water Music*. Dampness crept under her arms. Hopefully the satin wouldn't show a dark ring. She shifted her weight from one foot to the other to ease the discomfort of her shoes.

She would think of the future. Goodbye, 330 Gardner Street—hello, 226 Salem Avenue. She would live in their apartment in Elizabeth, New Jersey, a stone's throw from New York City and its Broadway lights. Country mouse in the city.

Lord knows she had struggled to keep a semblance of composure to reach this moment. She'd bitten her nails, agreed to plans she didn't want, and smiled when she felt like screaming. Now that was behind her. A new life of love, truth, and freedom was waiting. *If only the groom would get here.*

In spite of Lorraine's scowl, Marjorie stepped forward and peeked through a crack in the door to the sanctuary. A sea of hats and heads, but up at the chancel no men stood tall in grey tuxedos. She froze. What if Les had changed his mind? He hadn't sounded himself on the phone last night.

"We've had some complications with my parents," he had said hastily, without further explanation. What could have been wrong last night? His parents seemed to want to do things right, to make Les proud of them. Marjorie agonized silently. *Please, please let everything be all right. I can't lose my chance.*

The prelude was over, and the organist began playing "Here Comes the Bride." Marjorie let out a loud sigh as the first notes began. She knew all was well. She quickly fanned her armpits with a church bulletin and whisked her bouquet from Lorraine.

The bridesmaids stepped forward, dwarfed by huge bouquets of cascading yellow roses and purple orchids. Then her moment came. Her father firmly grasped her elbow as Marjorie took her first steps down the aisle. Her eyes locked on Les's, her veil billowing about her like a flock of butterflies, and she floated. Elated, Marjorie's wide smile seemed to stretch to the stained-glass windows. The church was nearly full. Women's hats, resplendent with a rainbow of flowers and feathers, dotted the pews.

She searched for Les's parents. There they were. Both Casper and Catherine were sitting stiffly in front. Casper sat very erect, as if his tuxedo would fly apart if he slouched. Catherine wore a blue silk dress. She patted her hat to adjust it. A sweet swell rose in Marjorie's chest for them. They showed love and courage by coming.

Some of the guests who turned toward her were patients of her father's. She remembered a few of them had paid him with berries, eggs, or vegetables. She glimpsed her father's colleagues, friends of his and her mother's, college friends of Les's and hers, a cousin, and some of her uncles had come to witness their joining into matrimony. And near the front was Robert, her first college boyfriend whom her mother adored. *What is he doing here?* Her mother must have invited him. Trying to repress her anger, she quickly shifted her focus back to Les and his boyish grin.

When she and her father reached the chancel, he stood on his tiptoes to raise Marjorie's veil over her head. She bent down a bit to help him. Wearing her satin pumps, she stood five nine to his five eight. But at this moment, he was a giant in her mind. She was ever grateful for each time he had buffered her mother's harsh opinions.

"Who presents this woman to be married to this man?" the minister asked.

"I do," her father said firmly, taking Marjorie's hand and gently placing it in Les's. Her hand warmed at his touch. Les stood beside her, so tall and stylish in his grey tails. His eyes met hers, and her heart melted into his. A coil of strength sprang alive in her. She would soon be her own woman.

She glanced to the side. The groomsmen were handsome in striped grey tails, the most appropriate attire for her mother's taste. All was well.

The minister adjusted his glasses. Marjorie savored every word of the traditional ceremony, knowing that each phrase brought her closer to dashing out of the church with Les. They each said their vows, then the minister asked for the ring. The best man, Phil, eyes bulging and fingers furiously probing each pocket, was without success until Les pointed to his friend's inside jacket pocket. The ring was recovered, the ceremony saved! A murmur escaped the lips of many guests.

Marjorie heard the words she had longed for, "I pronounce you husband and wife. You may kiss the bride." She and Les sealed their vows with a long kiss, then Les stepped on Marjorie's train as they turned to leave to the exhilarating recessional music. She jolted to a stop. Crimson rose up Les's neck. Then they laughed as Lorraine adjusted the train, and they glided down the aisle arm in arm to Mendelssohn's *Wedding March*. Once outside, they rushed to the waiting limousine.

*

In the back seat of the limousine, Les put his arm around Marjorie. "This ride would be two weeks salary, Mrs. Stoltz."

"Don't fuss, Mr. Stoltz. This was Mother's idea." Marjorie snuggled against him.

"She has lots of ideas, doesn't she?"

"Too many, I'm afraid," Marjorie whispered grimly.

"You look beautiful, Mrs. Stoltz," he said, and kissed her.

"I love you, Mr. Stoltz."

Marjorie wanted to know why Les sounded so remote on the phone last night, but she was reluctant to bring up an issue that might be uncomfortable. She risked her question anyway. "So what was wrong last night? On the phone you sounded like there was a real problem with your folks," Marjorie said. "I was afraid they wouldn't come."

"Oh. Nothing, really. Emilie and I were practicing the receiving line with Dad and Mom. Mom got a little confused and upset. She wanted to grasp with both hands. It doesn't matter. I just didn't want them to embarrass your mother."

"How thoughtful. I've been concerned about them feeling uncomfortable. You know I'm going to do all I can to make sure they're at ease, and that Mother doesn't ruin anything for your family."

"Hey, it's your wedding. You can't be on patrol. Everything will be fine."

"Yes, it will." Marjorie smoothed his jacket and asked, "And why were you all so late?"

Les squirmed awkwardly. "Do you have to know?"

"Yes, please."

He grimaced, then lowered his head and shook it. "I'm really sorry. I noticed your mother had a look to kill when the men and I walked in late."

"It wasn't part of her master plan, I'm afraid. Honey, please ignore that. So . . . ?"

"I couldn't find my socks. I was finally able to borrow some from the minister! I had tucked them into my dress shoes to bring over, but when we started changing, they weren't there. Don't laugh, or cry!"

"A sock thief! I'll be on the lookout," Marjorie said with a chuckle, relieved it was nothing more serious.

*

The limousine stopped in front of the large stone staircase of the Susquehanna Country Club. Marjorie had told Les that her parents did not belong to the country club because her mother forbade her husband to join. Several married men had gotten involved with other women at club parties, and their marriages soon dissolved. Her mother would have no part of that situation. Mr. Hoyt, the country club manager, had still been happy to offer the club's ballroom for Marjorie's reception, as her father was both Mr. Hoyt's doctor and his hunting buddy.

The rest of the wedding party drove up in their own cars soon after Les and Marjorie arrived.

Catherine hurried over to them. Her hat fell back when she raised her hands to hug Marjorie, then she gave Marjorie a kiss on the cheek, saying, "So pretty. Welcome to family." And to Marjorie's mother, she said with a smile, "Very nice, very nice— everything." Casper kept nodding, almost like a bobbing pigeon trying to remain very erect.

Her mother and father each hugged Marjorie and pecked her cheek. Her mother held her hand a moment and said, "I hope you will be happy, dear."

"I am, Mother. Thank you for a lovely wedding."

Once inside the country club ballroom, Marjorie's mother ushered Les's parents and the wedding party into their correct places in the receiving line.

Marjorie was delighted at the festive picture the room presented. Round tables covered with ivory linen cloths, flower centerpieces, and formal dinner table settings curved around the head table. The walls were covered in a tasteful flocked wallpaper of blue and gold, softly glowing under the glimmering light of a giant chandelier.

Catherine and Casper were placed between Les and Emilie in the receiving line in case communication needed clarification. Warm greetings poured forth. Marjorie was sure the whole club could hear the beating of her heart over the quartet. As congratulations were shared, her mother stepped out of the receiving line.

"Les, this is Robert, a friend of Marjorie's. You all attended Bucknell together and may enjoy chatting a bit."

"It would be a pleasure," Robert said to Les. "I'm representing my parents, who are vacationing in Europe, and of course I wanted to meet the lucky man who won Marjorie."

"I hope we can talk later," Les said with polite enthusiasm.

Marjorie was annoyed that her mother had singled Robert out to Les. Les knew he was an old boyfriend from a wealthy family.

Then, Marjorie overheard her mother say to Ethel, her mother's friend, and the next guest in line, "Robert is a peach—the man I always thought would be my son-in-law. You know, he's an estate attorney now. But you can't choose for them."

Furious, Marjorie spun to look at Les to see if he had heard. She bit the inside of her cheek. He was busy speaking to his mother and didn't react. *Thank goodness.* She closed her eyes for a moment and told herself it wouldn't be long until she could escape. She noticed that Catherine grasped each guest with both her hands in a sweet, friendly gesture. Marjorie smiled.

After dinner and one glass of champagne with the toasts, they danced a successful waltz. Les did not step on her toes, and guided her nicely, almost to the beat.

"I spent hours practicing," he whispered to Marjorie.

"It's wonderful," Marjorie said, resting her forehead on his shoulder for a moment. As they walked off the dance floor, her mother motioned Marjorie over to where she stood by the cake. "Marjorie, I'd like to introduce you to Helen Hoyt, a dear lady who has helped the evening run so smoothly."

"Mrs. Hoyt, thank you for all you've done to make our reception so lovely."

"Oh, it's just a little overseeing at dinner. My best wishes for you and your husband," she said, offering her hand with a broad smile.

"Thank you very much." Marjorie shook her hand, noticing the diamonds on her necklace.

"Your father and my Bill have had many enjoyable hunting trips together. Now, it's a treat to finally meet you, Marjorie." She clasped Marjorie's hand. "I chatted with your husband's parents a little while ago. They seem very happy about your marriage." She paused, "I had a little trouble understanding if they live near your new apartment."

Marjorie was about to tell Mrs. Hoyt how close they would live when Marjorie's mother interrupted. "Their English is quite poor. I can't understand how adults their age, after being in a country for over twenty years, haven't yet mastered our language."

A flush moved up Marjorie's face. She clenched her free hand. "Really, it's quite difficult to learn a new language as an adult, especially if your friends and neighbors speak your native tongue."

Despite the daggers her mother was hurling, she pushed ahead. "One tends to rely on what is familiar. It takes a lot of effort to become fluent."

Mrs. Hoyt glanced away, revealing a look of embarrassment.

"Yes, I've been studying French for years and still can't manage it," she offered.

Marjorie's mother seemed to shrink a few inches. She glared at Marjorie. Then, after a moment, her mother forced a smile, "I think it's time to cut the cake."

Marjorie saw Les looking at her from across the room. He gave her a puzzled look, but she just smiled. She had delivered her warning shot against belittling her in-laws.

*

Everyone feasted on the four-tiered cake, which towered like a museum sculpture. Marjorie's mother beamed at the numerous compliments of its moist lightness. The baker would have been proud. Les's parents ate their cake with spoons, after which Emilie ushered them, smiling, to Marjorie's parents.

"So nice, everything, thank you. Please come to house for visit," Catherine offered to Marjorie's parents, grasping both their hands. Marjorie glanced at her mother. Her mother's expression was the smile that said it was not too soon for their departure.

"Can we leave now too?" Les whispered.

"As soon as I thank a few people. I'll be right back."

Walking over to Lorraine, Marjorie heard her mother say to her friend Ethel, "If you don't count the fifteen minute delay, Phil's fumbling in his pockets for the wedding ring—which left us gasping for what might happen next—Les stepping on Marjorie's train, nearly tearing it off her, and the candle that wouldn't light, the ceremony went all right."

Marjorie stood a little straighter, grateful for the bits of tranquility that had held through the day. And it was lovely, and it was over.

*

As they ran out of the country club, Marjorie and Les were sprinkled with clouds of rice. Guests said goodbye with applause, as though the bride and groom had performed some admirable feat. From Marjorie's perspective, an exceptional feat would be more accurate.

They drove off with cans clanging and streamers flying behind the Buick coupe to leave for their honeymoon in Florida.

"We're off!" Marjorie said with a big smile, snuggling up to Les. The drone of the car engine soothed her soul.

"Miami Beach or bust," said Les, tapping the steering wheel.

Suddenly, memories filled her mind of Les's disappointment that their plans for honeymooning in Tampa didn't work out. Because of the roads, it would have taken an additional two days to go to Tampa and back. Les did not have the extra vacation time. She replayed their conversation.

"Miami Beach is a big place. We'll discover many places I haven't been," Marjorie had offered.

"Well, I guess not much can be done," Les had said in a low tone. She knew it wasn't fair to him. She promised herself this would be the last time she placated her mother!

"Then, after our honeymoon," he said, "we will go home to our apartment in New Jersey, where the furniture, lamps, and rugs were picked out with your mother's guidance, and paid for by your dad. It's not that I'm ungrateful, Marge, I just think we need to watch out for our independence."

"And so we will! I promise." She'd patted his arm. "We'll be together, isn't that what really matters?"

"Sure, sure it is," Les rubbed her knee.

She put her head on Les's shoulder as he drove. "I am so happy, honey. Just the two of us."

CHAPTER 6

AFTER THE HONEYMOON, the movers brought everything from Johnstown, where the furniture, lamps, and rug had been purchased. She and Les had so much fun arranging everything. Marjorie loved her new home, a second-story, one-bedroom apartment with a view of the grassy courtyard. Most of all, she adored being with Les, greeting him every night with a long embrace when he came home from work. She enjoyed listening to him talk about his day at the factory, how he was planning to make the plant more efficient by improving processes, putting job reminder signs up in critical places, and redesigning the assembly line to make it safer for the workers.

Marjorie unpacked the boxes and wedding gifts. She organized her own kitchen, placing the cookware, glassware, and utensils where she wanted them. In the meantime, Les set up the phonograph and calculated the best placement for the fans to allow the greatest flow of cool air through the apartment in the evenings. Even with all the windows open, in mid-summer the apartment got quite warm by afternoon.

She and Les developed a routine of relaxing after dinner, cuddling on the sofa, listening to news on the radio, then putting on records they'd received as wedding presents. Selecting classical Beethoven, Mozart, or Wagner, or more lively popular tunes such as "When the Saints Go Marching In" or "Beer Barrel Polka" was entertaining. Once, when Les raised the volume as he pretended to conduct, the downstairs neighbor thumped on their ceiling.

While Les was working, Marjorie hung curtains in the living room, shopped for groceries, and did the washing and ironing. She made sure Les had an ironed shirt each morning. She had read in *Good Housekeeping* that providing her husband with affection, a clean home, a good meal, and lively conversation were essential for a successful marriage. She was determined to follow this advice. However, she knew she was still at the low end of the cooking curve. She felt overwhelmed when her cookbook did not contain what Les was used to eating—*kielbasa*, *pierogi*, and stuffed peppers.

She once thought of calling her mother for advice but resisted the temptation. No, she had to do this on her own. Instead, she relied on her new friend and neighbor, Betty. They had met in the courtyard of the apartment building while hanging clothes out to dry, their matching wicker clothesbaskets in tow. One day when they were bringing clothes in, Marjorie discovered a pair of lacy black underpants in her basket. She held them up to Betty. Betty laughed, throwing her head back. Indeed, they were hers, mistakenly put in Marjorie's basket. Marjorie blushed as Betty pretended they were hot before dropping them in her own basket.

The two women became fast friends over the lost lingerie. Betty claimed she should leave a trinket in everyone's laundry basket, just for a reaction. Five years older, Betty was like a sister, offering advice without telling her what to do.

*

Marjorie had walked to the grocery store, and now, walking home from shopping, she realized she had bought more than she could easily carry. She was excited to make a Polish dinner for Les and didn't realize she was buying more than she could handle. Four blocks to go. Each arm squeezed a bag of groceries.

Her dark, wavy hair dripped perspiration on her neck and brow while rivulets rolled down her cheeks in the late August heat. She adjusted her load and wiped her face on the side of the paper bag. Finally, the sign for her apartment house, Salem Gardens, rose ahead. She began trudging up the stairs to their second-floor apartment. She was going to make stuffed peppers for Les if it killed her.

"Hey there, Marge, do you want a hand?" Betty called down from the apartment landing, her poodle-like curls poking out of her apartment door.

"Thanks," she huffed as Betty met her halfway and grasped a bag.

Betty teased, "What have you got in here, bowling balls?"

"Grapefruit. They were on sale. Les likes me to buy things on sale," she said, looking down, her cheeks feeling even hotter. "So I bought four."

"Why don't you shop on Saturday when Les is home?" Betty took the second bag while Marjorie fumbled for her keys. "Then you'd have a car and wouldn't have to walk six blocks with a load." Betty's brow wrinkled, waiting for Marjorie to unlock the door.

"I needed ingredients for tonight's dinner because I wanted to make stuffed peppers for Les. He's suffered through so many of my botched dinners. Besides, I was out of meat and vegetables. My freezer is so tiny it won't hold much." She didn't want to tell Betty they were trying to save gas money.

In the kitchen, Marjorie turned on the rotary fan and ran cold water over a towel, dabbing her face. Betty pulled the grapefruit out of the bag she was carrying and put them on the counter while Marjorie pulled the groceries out of her bag one by one. She placed one butcher-wrapped pack of meat in the refrigerator and the other on the counter. She handled each item as though it were a cherished valuable. "Betty, can I get you some iced tea? I made some before I left."

"No thanks, I have to get dinner going in a minute myself." Betty leaned against the red Formica counter.

"Les really loves stuffed peppers, but stuffed with meat and rice, not bread, the way my mother served them. He ate hers with bread stuffing before we were married, but he never said a word until our honeymoon." Marjorie lifted the wrapped package from the counter. "Do you think I should cook the meat before I stuff the peppers?"

"I wouldn't. Cook your rice, then add a little tomato soup to the raw beef, onions, and rice," Betty offered. "Then mound it on half a pepper."

"Oh, okay, thanks. How much rice should I cook?" asked Marjorie.

"One-half cup raw rice should make plenty to mix in about a pound of ground beef."

"Betty, I don't know how I'd manage without you. You are such a dear. My special chef! My real-life Betty Crocker!" Marjorie laughed. Then she heard herself saying, "Would you and Cal like to come for dinner on Saturday? I'll try a pot roast, if you're willing to be guinea pigs." She gulped. Her offer had spilled past her lips, a gesture of gratitude. Then fear crept into her stomach. She had never made dinner for guests. What if Les wouldn't want to do this?

"Sure, sounds great. I'll check with his majesty and let you know tomorrow. Oh, and I can bring the dessert," said Betty.

"I'll make sure Les doesn't have other plans. It would be fun." They shared a hug.

"You're precious, gal, and I'm happy to help anytime. You didn't get much practice cooking at home, I can tell. I'd better get on over to the palace. Cal's shift is over at five, and I have some prep to do."

Marjorie was relieved to have Betty willing to help her learn to cook. Her failures outweighed her successes, but she had made one tasty roast chicken and a perfect angel food cake. Tonight, she was determined to make Les a home-cooked, Polish dinner.

*

It was almost five o'clock. Marjorie cooked the rice and steamed the peppers a bit to soften them. Then she followed Betty's suggestion and mixed in a little tomato soup. She guessed at the oven temperature and put the peppers in for forty-five minutes. Darn Betty Crocker for not having a recipe.

She heard Les at the door and went to meet him. "Something smells so good," Les said as he threw his felt hat down on the living room chair. She had not yet been able to convince him to put his hat on the clothes tree in the hall. She gave him a kiss.

"The manager called a meeting at lunch time," he said, "and I had to check on the assembly line right after, so I missed lunch."

They entered the kitchen arm in arm. Les peeked into the oven. "Hey, they're getting kinda brown on top," he warned.

"Oh, gosh, I only had them in for forty minutes." Marjorie dashed over to the oven with a potholder and pulled the browned peppers out. "I'll put the rest of the soup on now."

"You're supposed to cook the soup over the top from the beginning," he said.

She sighed, deflated. Would she ever get a meal right? She'd tried so hard.

"Hey, it'll be okay," Les said, putting an arm around her. "Let's eat. I'm starving."

Les downed his peppers and had second helpings. He chatted about his work—the demanding plant superintendent, increased production quotas, and budget problems. Then their own budget surfaced.

"I got some grapefruit on sale today," Marjorie said, hoping he'd be pleased. Les didn't say anything or look up.

"Thirty-five dollars a week just doesn't go far," he frowned. "I'm worried about making ends meet. We have to cut down, Marge. I take care of the car repairs and do my own oil changes, but . . . . Maybe we could cut down on gas, not drive so much on the weekends. It's only nineteen cents a gallon, but it still adds up." He looked at the receipt Marjorie had left on the counter. "These groceries were nine dollars. Maybe you could keep to a list and cook more stews or something?"

Stunned, Marjorie weighed what to say next. She knew she needed to be more careful finding bargains at the grocery store, but it wasn't easy. "I can do better at taking advantage of sales, I'm sure." She bit her lip. "I'm still learning how to keep to a budget."

"I know you're not used to it."

"Also, Les, to save gas, we can find some fun things to do at home. Maybe getting together with friends?" Marjorie hesitated, clasping her hands together, fearing that their budget talk might sour Les on the idea of dinner with Cal and Betty. She probably should have talked with him first, before inviting them. "I wonder, what do you think of Betty and Cal coming for dinner on Saturday? Could we afford that?"

"Golly, I'm not sure." His brow furrowed. Les paused. "Do you feel okay about cooking for company? I don't want you to be too worried."

Marjorie felt her cheeks burn, but she pressed on. "Well, I have a recipe for pot roast that seems pretty easy. Besides, I can always ask Betty. I was more worried about the budget."

"I guess we can handle it this time. Besides, as a cop, Cal has interesting stories about the precinct, and Betty's fun." Les smiled at her. "Sure, let's do it."

"Good, I'll tell them. I already bought the roast."

"Y'know, Marge, the peppers tonight looked different, but they tasted just like Mom's!"

Marjorie beamed. The dish wasn't perfect, but she'd done it. He liked her Polish peppers.

*

Saturday morning, Marjorie began preparing for her guests. She delighted in using the tank-style vacuum cleaner that Les chose to buy, instead of getting the Hoover upright that her mother recommended.

"This motor is so strong, it can suck up a sock in a second," Les had assured Marjorie.

In her mind she saw herself vacuuming all the socks he left lying around the bedroom floor. Her mother didn't like the tank style because it required bending and pushing. She was so annoyed they hadn't taken her advice that she said she'd bring her own vacuum when she visited. Marjorie smiled as she pushed the vacuum across the living room rug.

After she cleaned the bathroom, she picked up the odds and ends, dusted the living room furniture, and ironed the lace table-cloth. She slavishly followed the recipe for chuck roast in her *Betty Crocker Cookbook*. This time, her dinner would work out. She borrowed some thyme from Betty and put the roast in the oven, adding carrots and potatoes later so it would all be done at 6:00. She hoped all would go well for her first real dinner guests.

Les worked on his electrical equipment much of the after-noon. He was building a battery charger for the car. Though Marjorie never understood his love of motors and electricity, she was charmed by his devotion to his tinkering. He told her he was also working on a little surprise for Betty and Cal.

That evening when the doorbell rang, Les answered.

"Hi there, Mr. Engineer." Betty's purple dress rustled as she entered. "Got any electrical surprises for us tonight?" she asked Les as she handed a chocolate cake to Marjorie, who whispered "lovely," and disappeared into the kitchen returning a moment later.

"I sure do. Come sit down and I'll show you in a minute. How ya doing, Cal? Catch any thieves or murderers today?"

Cal, a little taller than Les, blond, and broader in the shoulders, gave him a solid handshake. "Just wife-beaters and drunks today, but there's always hope for tomorrow." Cal dwarfed the green occasional chair as he sat with his legs straight out in front of him. He surveyed their traditionally furnished living room like a detective inspecting a crime scene for evidence.

Betty looked around the room. "Your apartment always looks so nice—matching end tables and coffee table, and that rose-and-gold striped sofa with the rose rug look beautiful together."

"Thanks, it's Duncan Phyfe style. Mother helped me pick it out."

"And pay for it," added Les. "Not on my salary."

"Oh, excuse me, I have to check on the roast. Les will pour you something to drink," Marjorie said, scurrying into the kitchen. From their kitchen, she heard Les continue.

"Not that I am complaining or anything, but with the war in Europe, we're lucky to have civilian jobs here. Those Germans are darn scary, shelling Dover with their long-range artillery, and bombing Wales and Northern Ireland too."

"The Nazis are a huge problem," said Cal. "In September, we'll have to register for the draft. I'm hoping my job in the force will keep me here."

"You'll be fine, Cal but I'm not sure about my situation," Les said, doubt in his voice.

"We'll be ready to eat in five minutes," Marjorie called from the kitchen doorway.

"Now, if I may have your attention, I have a little something to show you before dinner," Les said. "I was working on it this afternoon. I'm going to stand by the bedroom where you can see me. Marge, come here a minute," he called, leaning toward the kitchen.

"But dinner's almost ready," Marjorie said. "Could you do this later?"

"I'll just take a minute." Les walked into the bedroom. After a few minutes he took several steps into the hall from the bedroom and adjusted the rug.

He waved his arms pretending to clap. Nothing happened.

"Okay, now listen carefully." He clapped his hands. All was quiet.

"I'm worried about that roast," Marjorie said under her breath, but no one seemed to hear.

"Good job making silence, Les. I wish you would come down to the precinct and do more of that!" Cal laughed.

Les brought his hands together again with a single clap, pressing them firmly together, and suddenly the radio was blaring.

"You are Mister Magic, Les! How did you do that? And where's the rabbit hiding?" Betty laughed.

"I'm holding onto my wallet," said Cal.

"Les is amazing! I think we better come to the table now, though, before we have charcoal and mush for dinner," Marjorie said.

After they were seated around the table, dinner conversation centered on how Les had turned on the radio. He explained that he had wires from his wrists under his shirt, down his pant leg, and under the rug to the radio. Electrical entertainment.

Marjorie watched her guests. The roast was dry and a little overcooked. She kept passing the gravy, which she thought turned out tasty. Not a total disaster. She wondered if Les thought the cost of the roast was not worth this result. Next time she would take food out of the oven when it was done, no matter what else was happening. But she'd never tell Les that his experiment interfered with her dinner success.

The dinner conversation turned back to the German aggression in Europe. They talked about the Germans' horrific bombing of Great Britain, and of their occupation of France. Finally, they discussed their own financial challenges. Budgets were tight.

Marjorie served Betty's cake, which inspired well-deserved compliments.

"I'm going to look for a part-time job," Betty announced. "I can do accounting somewhere."

Betty is so adventurous and confident, while I can barely cook a dinner.

"That was a great dinner," said Betty, touching her fingertips to her lips and blowing the kiss to Marjorie. "We enjoyed this evening with you two so much."

"I'll have to learn new card tricks to keep up with Les," said Cal.

"You can just entertain us with your stories of burglary and mayhem," Les said. He stood and gestured for Cal to move into the living room.

"Let me help you with the dishes while the guys talk shop," Betty offered.

"Oh thanks. I'll wash, if you don't mind drying." Marjorie was anxious to talk to Betty about how she was going to find a part-time job. If she could also work a few hours a day, it could help their finances and ease the strain on Les.

"I'm going to check with the personnel office at Bamberger's and Kresge's. If they don't work out, I'll keep looking until I find something in accounting," said Betty.

"You're so confident, Betty. I don't know what I could do." Marjorie stopped washing dishes for a moment and turned to look at Betty.

"You've got a college degree for Pete's sake, Marge. You could certainly find something. You just have to get out there and try. Maybe a salesperson in a nice department store to start," Betty said, drying the last of the glasses.

"You've given me a great idea. I'll talk to Les about it. A

little extra money would mean a whole lot." Her eyes grew wide with excitement.

After Betty and Cal left, Marjorie was anxious to talk to Les about the possibility of finding a job. She thought he might be pleased. Money was important to him, maybe more important than the pride he would lose by having a working wife.

She waited until he seemed relaxed. "What would you think about me looking for a part-time job?"

Les, who was sitting on the bed bending over to take off his shoes, suddenly sat bolt upright, his eyes wide open, staring at Marjorie. "Well . . . sure. I guess that would be good. Get you out of the apartment and give us a cushion for expenses." A wide grin spread across his face.

"I don't know who would want me, but I could go to the personnel offices of a few stores and see what's available. That's what Betty plans to do."

"You would do a fine job at sales. How about Bamberger's on Market Street? It's on the bus line. You could get the bus a block from here."

She was excited. Les thought a job was a good idea. Now, if she could somehow make it happen. She hadn't mastered housework completely yet, but she wanted more than that. She wanted to be a support to Les, to contribute.

On Monday, Marjorie convinced herself to go to Bamberger's to try for her first job. She bathed, selected a beige summer suit, heels, and a pair of stockings. When she got off the bus, she saw an imposing store the length of a city block. Once inside, she walked down a wide aisle between glass counters. She wandered past one counter after another before asking a clerk in the fragrance department how to find the personnel office. The clerk directed her to the third floor. Marjorie took the elevator up, then navigated a long hallway. On the left, she found a door with *Personnel* lettered on the glass. She decided to find the ladies' room first.

She combed her hair, freshened her lipstick, making sure no pink blotched her teeth, and checked that the seams on her stockings were straight. At her ankle was the beginning of a run. *Darn, these stockings are new, too. Another expense.* The annoying run was slightly distracting, but she put her mind firmly back on what she was about to do. Once outside the ladies' room, she paced back and forth. Why was she so nervous?

She took a long breath, opened the door slowly, smiled at the grey-haired woman behind a desk, and asked if there were any vacancies in sales.

"Yes, we have a few."

"My name is Marjorie Stoltz. May I have an application?" Marjorie affected a tone of cool confidence.

Marjorie took the papers she was given, carefully completing each line with her name, age, marriage status, and her education, answering each question in her neatest handwriting. She handed the papers back to the woman with a smile. There, she had done it.

"Oh, you've got a college degree. I'm afraid we only have openings in women's clothing." The woman frowned.

"I'm really looking for a half-time sales position in women's wear, if possible. I love working with people to help them find just the right thing." Marjorie flashed her biggest smile. She would do all she could to get this job.

"Well, could you stay for an interview with our sales director at 11:00? "

"Yes, of course," Marjorie grinned. "Thank you." She would make the most of this chance.

*

That evening, Marjorie jumped to open the door when she heard Les's key in the lock. "Guess what? Guess what?" she almost exploded with excitement.

"You made a pie?" he guessed.

"I've got a job!" she said, throwing her arms around him. "At Bamberger's."

Les put his briefcase down, threw his hat on the chair, and twirled her around.

"Can you believe it? They wanted me! I'll be working in hats, gloves, and scarves to start. Wednesday through Saturday, nine o'clock until one. I start this Wednesday."

"That's my gal. Really good, Marge." He held her shoulders. "You should be proud of yourself! Okay, we have to celebrate. How about some of that champagne we got for a wedding present?"

"Sure! I'll get it!"

Les followed her into the dining alcove. "I knew you could do it, but I'm surprised it happened the first day you tried! How much will you get an hour?"

"Two dollars a day for part-time," she cocked her head, grinning at him as she bounced to the kitchen.

"That's great, honey. That will be a real help to our budget."

She dusted off the champagne bottle and placed it in the refrigerator to cool. Glancing out the window, the golden maple trees appeared brighter. The last of the sun poured through the venetian blinds, throwing shafts of sunlight where she stood. Her spaghetti sauce bubbled gently under the lid.

But then she thought of her mother. Her mother would disapprove, so maybe she just shouldn't tell her. After all, it was none of her business. This was her very own job. Hers.

Later, when Les toasted to her success at getting her new job, she added, "And, to our secret. This job. I don't want Mother to know. She wouldn't like me working. Promise me that if she calls, and you get the phone, you won't say anything?"

Les scowled. "Well, I'll go along with it, though I would rather tell her what she could do if she didn't like it!" Les held up his empty glass and reached to pour more champagne for them.

*

On Marjorie's first day of work, Mrs. Dowling, the supervisor, showed Marjorie the stock where extra hats were kept, pointed out which hats were one-of-a-kind, and demonstrated how to use the cash register. Hats were the primary sales item for this department. Mrs. Dowling then explained how to interact with the customer. "Always compliment the customer on her choice no matter how silly the hat might look on her." Marjorie listened carefully but had her own thoughts about how she might vary this policy.

"If she decides on a hat, select a scarf that would accent it. I know you'll be good at colors by the lovely way you dress."

Each evening, Marjorie planned for the next day with a new sense of purpose. She ironed blouses, polished shoes, and fixed her nails. At work, she enjoyed interacting with customers, helping them find a hat that complimented their coloring and hair. She would hold the mirror so they could see the back of the hat and suggest another they might also like. After two weeks, Mrs. Dowling came by.

"You are doing a fine job Marjorie. I've observed how helpful and friendly you are, always attractive, poised, and nicely dressed. A good example of a Bamberger's employee."

Marjorie glowed. "I'm sure my success is due to your excellent instruction."

*

After three weeks on the job, Mrs. Dowling told Marjorie that she had sold more hats in three weeks than anyone had before. If her performance continued, Mrs. Dowling would consider her as a trainer for women's wear in other departments. Stunned, Marjorie walked out of the store that afternoon with her heart full. Everyone she passed on the street wore a smile, and the sky was a brighter blue.

The phone was ringing as she entered the apartment, two

short rings for their party line. She reached the phone before it stopped. She heard her mother's voice.

"I've been talking to Hanna every morning this week instead of you, Marjorie. Hanna picks up the phone if you don't answer your rings. That party line is a nuisance. I wish you'd get rid of it," her mother cleared her throat. "Where have you been every morning?" her tone softened.

Marjorie was caught off guard. "I've been at Bamberger's."

"Shopping? Every morning?" asked her mother.

"I've been helping people find hats and scarves," she said, her mind searching for how to be truthful yet assuage her mother.

"Are these indigents or cripples?" she asked, sounding confused.

"No, Mother." She should have prepared some answers. No way around this now. "I have a little part-time job, just a few mornings. I really enjoy it. And I have all afternoon to do the housework."

"A job?" her mother screeched into the phone like an angry parrot.

"Yes. It's fun, and it's important to me. I feel good going into the store and helping women find the right hats." She collapsed onto a nearby chair. A draining feeling poured down her stomach.

"You know you have a weak constitution, Marjorie, and a job will be too much for you. I don't want you to get down again, what with the stress of a job and keeping up a home." Her tone hardened.

"Mother, I am really enjoying this little job," she murmured. "It isn't stressful. In fact, I feel better than I ever have."

"Marjorie, you need to quit before it becomes too much," she said with authority.

First the ceiling moved down, then the walls closed in as her airspace tightened. She was suffocating.

"You know what happened before when you became depressed. I'm only looking out for what's best for you, dear."

Marjorie's spirit hemorrhaged. She was silent, sinking into darkness. She had to get away. "Oh, there's someone at the door, sorry, Mother."

"Get the door. I'll call you back later," she said mechanically.

Marjorie hung up the phone and stared at the rose rug, which was turning grey before her eyes.

CHAPTER 7

MARJORIE TEETERED ON a slippery slope between darkness and light. She thought back to years ago when she was nine and wanted to go to a party at her friend Helen's house, but her mother said no. Marjorie had insisted she should be able to go. All her friends were going.

"I told you, they are not a reputable family," her mother said, banging a wooden spoon against the kitchen sink.

"But Helen is really nice. We have fun together, and she gives me cookies. Why can't I go?" Marjorie pleaded.

Her mother's answer was to thrust her outside without her coat. "Stay here a few minutes until you cool off and can speak respectfully." After a while Marjorie tried the door, but it wouldn't open. She knocked, but her mother didn't answer. She kept rubbing her arms and hugging herself to keep warm in the chill of Pennsylvania's November. Shivering, she went into the garage and found a musty old army blanket.

Her father found her huddled outside under the yew bushes near the back door when he got home from his office. Later, she heard muffled voices, then her father's stern voice in her parents' bedroom upstairs. This was a tone she hadn't heard him use before. Her mother said, "My goodness, she just didn't push the door hard enough. You know how it sticks." Her mother did not speak to her for days. It was as cold inside the house as it was outside, which was far worse than the time she spent outdoors shivering.

*

Marjorie's thoughts turned back to what she might say when her mother called again. She was determined to do whatever it took to keep her job. Her supervisor's acknowledgment of her success at work gave Marjorie a sense of fulfillment she'd rarely experienced.

Tiny crumbs and lint dotted the carpet before her. The scattered residue seemed as messy as her dilemma. Marjorie stood up. It was time to exercise her instrument of rebellion. She pulled the tank vacuum from the closet and swept the rug with a vengeance, pushing and pulling the wand, banging it down as if she were killing bugs, then sucking it all into oblivion.

She was angry with herself for her own weakness, her inability to be steadfast, and to insist on making her own decisions. But she couldn't handle her mother's cold shoulder, so she'd have to come up with something, a little lie. If only she had the courage to tell her the truth. Cleaning every inch of carpet with fury cleared her mind. She would drown herself in housework.

After her laundry tasks, the phone rang. It rang three times. She considered not answering, then grabbed it. She would have to face her mother eventually.

"Glad you got it before Hanna did, your party-line snoop," her mother said. "I wanted to continue our conversation about that job, Marjorie."

Be your own person, a voice within told her. Another voice said, *You'll pay dearly if you don't do what she says.* If she defied her mother, she knew her mother would put her out in the cold again.

Marjorie hid a deep sigh and hesitated, working the ring on her finger. *I think I'm the best judge of what is good for me, Mother.* But the words she said aloud were, "Well, I've thought about what you said. I'm going to talk to my supervisor about it soon."

"That is the best thing for you. A job is just too much for a fragile girl like you. Your dad agrees. It's good you came to your senses about this. I'll call next week to see how things went so you won't have long-distance charges. Bye for now dear."

Marjorie held her head with her hands. How can I live my life with Mother's scrutiny looming over my decisions? Why do I allow her to have such power over me? I should stand up to her. For now, I'll just focus on the moment, do something positive, then talk with Les tonight.

That evening before Les arrived home, Marjorie changed her clothes and fixed her chestnut hair in a different style, the front part sweeping in a wave over to the side and held by hairpins. She would make this a pleasant evening now that her demons were calmed.

"You look nice tonight," Les said as he put his hat on the clothes tree and threw his coat over a chair. "Something's different."

"Yes, your hat made it to the hat rack!"

"I'm getting the hang of it." He chuckled at his word play and stood back, scrutinizing her.

"Practicing a new hairstyle for work tomorrow," she smiled.

"And I thought it was for me." Les turned down his mouth, imitating a sad child.

"Of course it's for you!" She leaned up and kissed his pouty mouth.

As they ate leftover beef stew, Marjorie said, "I've got something I need to discuss with you." She put her fork down and looked at him.

"What's up, honey?"

"Mother wants me to quit my job. She thinks it's too stressful and could cause me to get depressed, sick again. What do you think?"

"I say the invention of the telephone was a mistake. I also say that everyone would be a lot happier if your *mother* got a job! Are you enjoying what you do at Bamberger's?"

"You know I love working there." She smiled, her eyes wide.

"Then you should continue working until you don't want to anymore. Plus, the money you earn is a big help." He caressed her arm. "You can't do everything your mother wants you to. She's trying to control your life. Our lives." He pushed his chair back. "It's time to stand up to her. Take charge."

"I thought you'd agree I should stay," Marjorie smiled. "I know you are right, but the part about Mother is not that easy for me," she said, pulling her napkin tight. "There's something I feel so afraid of that takes over me when I cross her." She bit her lip.

"It's been years of brainwashing. You've been conditioned to obey, or bad things happen." He patted her arm. "You are smart, honey. I know you'll figure a way to ignore her controlling," Les said.

He rubbed the last bit of gravy with a corner of bread. "Is there any more stew?"

*

The next morning, as the bus swayed and bumped down Market Street, Marjorie's stomach felt a bit off. She stared out of the rain-spattered window. She would not quit her job, but to keep things harmonious with her mother, she'd tell her a bigger lie, a coward's way out. She'd say she promised the supervisor she would continue working until they found a replacement for her. And, well, they might have a lot of difficulty finding just the right person. In fact, it could be quite a while.

As she passed the driver to get off at her stop, she heard Bebe's daily sendoff, "And the finest day to you, Ma'am."

"And to you, too, Bebe," she smiled as she stepped off the bus and walked toward the corner, taking comfort in this ritual.

Marjorie arrived a few minutes late. She hurried over to her sales counter and opened the cash register, then adjusted the glove display. Fall felt hats with pheasant feathers and sparkling pins greeted her. She put on her best smile for her first customer, a red-haired woman who asked about green felt hats.

"You sold me my favorite hat a few weeks ago. I knew you could find just the right thing today. You were so sweet and attentive, so I came back."

"Thank you, I'm flattered." Marjorie smiled and her face warmed. "Let's look over here. We just got some new hats in that might accent your lovely red hair." Leading the way to her newest displays, she couldn't help but think how heavenly it was working for this company.

Suddenly, nausea enveloped Marjorie, crept upward, then lay like a crouching tiger in her chest. "Excuse me, please. I'll be right back." She grabbed her purse and dashed across the shoe department and through men's coats, knocking into a shopper, finally reaching the ladies room, her hand over her mouth. She pushed open the bathroom door, bent over the toilet, and threw up. She caught her breath. What on earth was this about? Was it something she ate? Or could it be concern about the lie she'd be telling her mother? This must be why her stomach was giving her strange signals.

The nausea was gone. She flushed the toilet several times. Staggering to the sink, she swished water around her mouth, wiped her face with tissues, and stood for a moment staring at her reflection. She took some calming, deep breaths. Then, she fixed her lipstick, combed her flopping hair into its old style, pinched her cheeks, and made her way back to search for just the right green felt hat.

Deceiving her mother lay heavily on her. She hated lies, but she wanted this job more. If throwing up was going to be the price she paid for lying to her mother, well, that's just what she'd have to do.

*

As soon as she got into the apartment after work, someone knocked on the door. "Hey Marge, open up," Betty called. She almost smacked into Marjorie as she burst into the room. "Sorry, Marge, but oh my gosh, Cal's been shot! This morning, right outside Kresge's. Some men held up the armored truck—and there was Mr. Save-Them-All," Betty blurted, rapid-fire.

Marjorie held her chest. "Oh, no, not our Cal!"

Betty interrupted, "It's his arm. We're waiting to see how bad it is. He was probably playing the hero." Betty dropped to the sofa, putting her head in her hands. "I knew something like this would happen. A brave cop. Who knows what the next time will bring?" Betty heaved a sigh.

Marjorie could see tears in Betty's eyes as she went over to the sofa, sat down next to her, and hugged her.

"Where is he now?" said Marjorie, her voice full of concern.

"In Newark Mercy, just for tonight. He can come home tomorrow," Betty said, tossing the pillow to the end of the sofa. "I only came home to pick up his pajamas and toothbrush, then I'll go back and stay with him."

"You'll have your hands full tomorrow. Why don't I make a spaghetti dinner for us tomorrow?" Marjorie was confident she could not ruin spaghetti.

"Sure." Betty wiped her eyes with her handkerchief. "You guys c'mon over tomorrow night with good Italian pasta and we'll cheer up Mr. Bigshot."

When Les got home, telling him about Cal was top priority. She would wait until later to share what she had decided to tell her mother. She didn't know how he would react to telling her mother a lie.

That evening, when they snuggled in bed, Marjorie's thoughts were whirling. "I've made a decision about work," her words spilled out.

Les got up on an elbow and looked directly into her eyes. "I'm guessing you decided to stay. I see a little smile there." He touched her lips.

"Yes. My job is very important to me. I like working there and helping with our budget. But you're going to think I'm weak."

"About what?"

"Next time I talk with Mother, I'm planning to . . . well . . . to lie to her about the details. I'll let her think that I'll quit as soon as they get a replacement, but then, that won't happen for a very long time because I won't tell my supervisor anything."

Les's brow lines deepened and he sat up. "Marge, you can't keep avoiding confronting her. You can't let her rule over you, treat you like a child, own you like a dog. You have to let her know you are a grown woman and are in charge of your own life." He stood up and began to pace. "All this is affecting me too. You are worried half the time about what your mother's going to say and do . . . . Well, I can hardly stand it."

Tears filled Marjorie's eyes.

Les bent over and gave her a squeeze. "Think about this, honey. Every time she insists on her way, you could say, 'Thank you for your suggestion, I will certainly consider it. I have to make my own decision, but I hope you will support whatever I decide.' "

"That sounds so good when you say it," Marjorie said. "I'm just afraid of the consequences, her being so angry she won't talk to me, or ever call again. That gut-wrenching, sinking feeling over-whelms me—she has a hold on me I can't seem to break." Marjorie rubbed her forehead. "I'm afraid it just has to be like this for now," she said softly. "Please be patient with me. I'll get stronger . . . . I wish I had a different mother."

"Wouldn't that be nice," Les said, slapping his leg with a laugh. "C'mon now, honey, chin up. Things will work out. You'll have to do this eventually, but let's not worry about it tonight" he said, climbing back into bed, kissing her. "Wow! What a day, with Cal being hurt, and the hassle with your mother. It's been a crazy twenty-four hours around here."

"And maybe even crazier," said Marjorie. "I think maybe I'm pregnant."

CHAPTER 8

LES LEAPED BACK out of bed, flipped on the light, and stared down at Marjorie. She squinted, then opened her eyes wide. Her face flushed as if her cheeks had a heat source of their own. She bunched the pillow against the mahogany headboard and sat up in bed, beaming.

"You think you're . . . pregnant?" he asked, his brow furrowing with surprise.

Marjorie nodded her head. "I think so. I haven't had my cycle in over three weeks, and I've felt a little queasy lately. Often, on the bus, I wouldn't feel quite right." She rubbed her tummy. "Today I got sick in the bathroom at work." She pressed her hands against her flaming cheeks to cool them. "I thought my stomach was upset over Mother's insisting I quit my job. But then, tonight, when I couldn't eat that spaghetti, and you know how much I love it, I put it all together."

A grin grew wide across Les's face as he tumbled into bed, kissing her neck and rocking her. "Holy cow! I'm going to be a father. Now I won't be the only guy without a baby picture in his wallet!" Les gave her a loud kiss.

"I still have to go to the doctor to find out, y'know. I'm afraid to be too thrilled until the doctor says all is okay," Marjorie grinned.

"Hey, you're a doctor's daughter. You probably know as much

as they do!" Les said, reaching up to turn out the light. He snuggled, and she giggled.

This is ecstasy! She peered at the slits of light from the moon that filtered between the window blinds. She might burst, spilling golden stars and confetti everywhere.

*

One evening after work the following week, Les called, "Hi Mommy!" as he dashed through the door, waving his hat like a vaudeville dancer, then throwing it on the chair.

"Hello there, Daddy," she said, kicking up her leg like a Rockette and pecking him on the cheek. "I see your hat didn't make it to the hat tree."

"No, it has a mind of its own, but you're pretty good for an amateur. How long will you be able to do that?" Les chuckled.

"Probably another month, then I'll do cartwheels, the doctor said."

Les did a double take. "What?"

"Actually, he said everything was fine. I go back to see him again in a month. I'm supposed to drink milk every day."

"I'm so glad everything is good." He gave her a squeeze. "We can make milkshakes!"

"Sounds yummy. How was work today?"

"I told Hank and Tony we might be having a baby. They want to take me out for a drink to celebrate and give me some tips. Hank said, 'It's important we dads stick together.' Plus, I can compare what they paid for their hospital bills." Les sat down on the sofa, motioning Marjorie to join him. He pulled out a piece of paper.

"We have seventy-three dollars saved up so far that we can use for the hospital. I found out that at St. Michael's Medical Center it's seventeen dollars for maternity service, seven dollars a day for the mother's stay, and two dollars a day for the nursery." Les rattled off the numbers. "It costs fifteen if a cesarean section is necessary, plus the doctor's fee. So I think we're in pretty good shape." He clapped his hands like a little boy who'd gotten his first truck at Christmas.

"Wow, I'm impressed with all that research, and your math professor would be overjoyed. You've sure done your homework."

"Of course, there are a bunch of baby things we'll need, like diapers and baby clothes, then a highchair and playpen to buy later. I'm so glad you have your job, Marge," Les smiled. "I wonder, will they let you work if they know you're going to have a baby? I guess they won't know until it's obvious."

"I'll have to find out. I want to work as long as I can to save for a crib, dresser, the big stuff."

Les turned to face her. "Well, the next part isn't such good news. I figured what we'd need for a two-bedroom apartment, and I'm afraid we can't make it." Les patted her leg. "The baby will have to be in our bedroom."

"Another bedroom would be good, but we'll work that out. You know, Les, since Dr. Alexander said everything seems fine, maybe it's okay to tell people, but I want to let our parents know first, and of course Betty and Cal. I'd hate it if they found out from someone else," she said, walking to the kitchen.

"You worry too much. Hank and Tony don't know Betty and Cal, and they certainly don't know our parents," reassured Les.

"I guess you're right. I'm just a little nervous since it's so early in my pregnancy, and if problems arise, they usually happen during the first three months."

"I'd really like to tell my folks in person. How about driving over to Passaic this weekend?"

"Okay, I'd like that. They are so sweet, and I'm sure they'll be excited! We haven't seen them in over a month. It's too bad they didn't want to learn to drive because that way we could see them more often, and you wouldn't have to pick them up and bring them here."

"Marge, it's because their English isn't good enough to pass the driver's license test." Les shook his head.

"Oh, no, I'm sorry, I didn't think about that."

"Don't worry. It's a shame, but that's how it is. Boy, I can't wait to see Mom's face. I'll call and tell them we're planning a short visit on Sunday, okay?"

"Sure," Marjorie said. "I can make an angel food cake to take. I did fine on the last one! Betty has the pan for it."

Marjorie rubbed her forehead. "Maybe I should call Dad and Mother tonight." She had rehearsed several approaches to telling her parents about the baby. She wanted her mother to know this pregnancy was really planned, not an accident. She hadn't confided their plans to have a baby earlier because she had feared her mother's reaction.

"On second thought, let's tell Cal and Betty first." Marjorie smiled, knowing that their friends would share in their happiness. "We could invite them over for coffee and dessert tonight, just to chat."

"Great idea." Les slapped his leg.

*

"A little dessert with you folks. What a nice treat on a weekday," Cal said as they walked into the apartment and sat down on the sofa. Cal rested his splint on the sofa arm.

"So, what's new with you guys?" asked Betty, pulling her skirt to cover her knees. She smoothed the cushion beside her as she waited for an answer.

Marjorie and Les exchanged looks, and Les gestured to Marjorie.

"We're going to have a baby!" Marjorie blurted.

Cal jumped up and pumped Les's hand with his good, left hand. "Congratulations you sneaky folks—you beat us to it!"

"Oh my gosh, I can't believe it! That is fantastic," said Betty, giving Marjorie a lingering hug. "No wonder you're glowing like Reddy Kilowatt!"

"I just went to the doctor yesterday, so you two are the first to know. Well, Les did mention it at work today to two of his colleagues. But they don't count!"

"Are we unofficial aunt and uncle then?" asked Betty.

"Absolutely family," said Marjorie, pouring coffee into cups.

"This uncle has to have an operation in a few days so he can pick up his niece," said Cal, feigning a clown frown. "I'm not jumping for joy about it, but if it works, it'll be worth it."

"Golly Cal, what do they have to do?" asked Les.

"They're going to stitch up my bicep so it'll connect better to my bone! The doctor tells me it'll give me some strength in my right arm again. I can hardly pick up a fork now."

"I sure hope that works out, Cal. This turned out to be a worse injury than we ever dreamed," Marjorie said.

"Yeah, definitely. They've got me in a desk job now, which I hate. Just can't stand to be inside all day. But what good is a one-armed detective?"

"You miss all those drug addicts, thieves, and murderers, don't you?" asked Les.

Cal sipped his coffee, "Sure do. Better than reports, staplers, and paper clips." But I should be in good shape by the end of next month, about the time they'll have the lottery for the draft."

Marjorie tensed at the word *draft*. She leaned forward in her chair. "How does this draft lottery work?"

"They're putting all the numbers of all the men who registered into capsules, one number in each. Because there are over 6,000 draft boards, many guys have the same number, so everyone has the same chance to be picked." Cal tipped his cup back, finishing his coffee in a gulp. "All these capsules go in a big fishbowl and one of the hoo-ha's, like Secretary of War Stimson, I think, will pull out one capsule at a time."

Les said, "Yeah, and I heard President Roosevelt will call out the number. Then they do it over and over again 'til they have as many guys as they need."

"That's one fishing expedition I could happily miss," Cal said.

Marjorie leaned toward Cal, her clasped hands clammy. "What happens next?"

"All the men holding the numbers chosen are brought in by their draft board to be checked out for service. You get an order to report for induction. It tells you when to go for your examination," Cal explained.

"I heard at work that you could be sent home if you only have half your teeth, or you're less than five feet tall," Les said, showing his teeth.

"I can't do anything about your height, Les, but I could help with those teeth if you wanted." Cal made a fist and laughed.

"I'll let you know about that one, Cal. You're a lefty now. You probably couldn't do the trick."

Cal screwed up his face, laughed, and threw a punch with his good arm.

"The other exemption is if you are in an occupation considered critical to the war effort at home. Unlike Cal, I work for a candy factory, not exactly a resource important to warfare." Les hesitated, "But, seriously, if my country needs me, I'm in. Who knows what's gonna happen, with London being hammered to kingdom come?"

"Yeah, and the U-boats attacking so many supply convoys." Cal shook his head.

Marjorie's eyes darted back and forth from Cal to Les. As she listened to every word, her fear rose. She swallowed hard and asked hoarsely, "What's your number, Les?"

Les said, "Four hundred sixty-seven. I'm sure it's a lucky number."

Betty looked toward the door. "I'm sure this is a good number!"

"Yup, Betty's got this crystal ball in the bedroom. She's won all those sports bets at work, so now they've banned wives playing because of Betty's winning streak." Cal snorted. "I won't wager against her." He poked Betty with his good arm.

The living room was quiet for a moment. Then Cal said, "Hey, why don't you come over to our place on the twenty-ninth? We'll have dinner, then we'll listen to the lottery on the radio. We'll celebrate Les's number not being picked, Marge, so bring a pillow because it might take a while!"

"Sounds good. Good friends, good food, good time," Les agreed. "What do you say Marge?"

Betty reached out and patted Marjorie's arm. "I imagine this will be an uncomfortable evening for you, Marge, so if you—"

Marjorie interrupted Betty. She did not want to be part of this hair-pulling torment, but she knew Les wanted to go. "It's okay, so why don't I bring a Waldorf salad? It goes with anything."

"Nice," said Betty, getting up and blowing kisses. "G'nite Mommy and Daddy! Maybe we can come in a close second!"

"Better get on home then," urged Cal, patting Betty on the behind. "See you later."

After Cal and Betty were gone, Marjorie put the cookie plate and the cream and sugar on a tray. "But you're an engineer. You could help here in a hundred ways."

"They need engineers over there, too," Les said.

The tray almost slipped from her hands. "But not this one." She gave him a kiss.

That night, Marjorie dreamed of babies falling from the sky and exploding. As she tried to catch them, they would disappear in a bright puff of black smoke just as they reached her arms.

*

On Sunday as she and Les drove to the neighborhood in Passaic where Les grew up, Marjorie balanced her best angel food cake on her lap. Many of the houses were only partially painted, and much of the shrubbery was overgrown or unkempt. Empty cars lined the streets like people who had fallen asleep waiting for a parade. But Casper and Catherine's house was painted white with black accents. Trimmed shrubs framed the front door and a flowerbed full of orange and lemon-colored marigolds lined the walk.

As they were getting out of the car, Les's mother hurried over, wiping her hands on her apron tied over a loose-fitting housedress. Catherine's salt-and-pepper hair, frizzy from home permanents, was pulled back in a small bun at the back of her neck. She wore no lipstick, but her lips formed a wide smile.

"Hallo, hallo," she cried, hugging each of them. She clapped her hands just like Les did when he was excited. "Looking so nice." She took the cake Marjorie held out to her. "Oh, special cake of angels. Thanks, thanks. Come, I have *pierogi* for you," she gestured to the door. Casper was in the kitchen pouring drinks of gin and orange juice, adding a little grenadine with a practiced hand that came from managing a small neighborhood bar. His light-blue sweater vest matched his eyes. "So nice you be here," he said, patting each of them on the shoulder. He was a bit shorter and stockier than Catherine, but stood erect, often stroking his receding hairline.

"Sit, sit," Catherine ordered, her face radiating a bright glow. She served the *pierogi* with sautéed onions, slices of *kielbasa*, and applesauce that she had made that morning. As soon as Marjorie said, "This looks wonderful," her stomach rebelled. The morning sickness had stretched to the afternoon. "I'm so sorry. As lovely as this is, I'm afraid I just can't eat much."

"No worry. I give you to take home. Maybe eat tomorrow."

After the meal, Les told his parents their news. Casper jumped up and kept pounding Les's back and chuckling till Marjorie wondered if he'd rub a hole in his shirt. His mother kissed her cheek over and over, urging her to eat for the baby too. Delight filled Marjorie's soul. *What a blissful greeting, just as I wished it might be.*

On the way home, Marjorie held the *pierogi* that Les's mother had insisted they take. "That was such a lovely visit, Les. They are so excited about the baby. I do love your parents and their sweetness." As they drove, she wondered how her own parents would receive the news.

*

On the bus to work Wednesday morning, Marjorie carried crackers with her to nibble on if she felt sick. The diesel fumes made her a bit nauseated, but if she leaned close to the window, the cool air helped.

She would call her parents tonight. She hoped they would be excited at becoming grandparents. Marjorie would simply thank them for any advice, as Les had suggested, then do what was best for her family. Now, she would be the mother in her own family. She smiled at the idea.

Marjorie stepped down from the bus with more care than usual and walked briskly to the store, taking a peek at her reflection in the tall window. She was pleased at what she saw—a tall, slim-to-average-built woman who moved with a graceful stride. *A woman whose profile is about to make a drastic change.* She chuckled.

Marjorie's satisfaction with work increased as her responsibilities widened to training new personnel. Today she was training a new girl, Sylvie, to work in the hat and accessories department. Sylvie had a good sense of style and color, which made everything quite easy when selecting a hat. In the middle of showing her the cash register, Marjorie suddenly felt very nauseous, so she excused herself, grabbed her purse, and dashed to the ladies' room. She nibbled at the crackers and drank water from the faucet. In a few moments the nausea subsided, so she walked back to her counter.

Sylvie asked her what was wrong. She did not want to tell Sylvie, as she wasn't ready to tell her supervisor. She wasn't sure of store policy, and she wanted to work as long as she could to save money for what they needed for the baby. Although she suspected her parents would be generous with gifts, she wanted to feel that she and Les were providing the essentials, that they were self-sustaining, and not beholden to Mother.

"I wasn't feeling well. It must have been something I ate. I'm okay now," Marjorie said with a smile.

"You looked kind of green," observed Sylvie. "Glad you're okay."

She and Sylvie continued to role-play sales where Marjorie coached her in different customer scenarios. Marjorie enjoyed helping her learn the various processes and requirements of the store. Bamberger's specified that certain words be used when giving change, that each transaction end with a smile, and, "May I help you with anything else?"

As she was leaving for the day, Marjorie heard a group of women in the shoe department talking about one of them leaving because she was four months pregnant. Marjorie walked slowly and stopped at the cosmetic counter, pretending she was interested in makeup. One of the women said to the other, "Thank you so much. Hope to see you soon," and walked toward the door. Marjorie timed her leaving to coincide with this woman's departure. Once outside, she excused herself and asked the woman if she had enjoyed working at Bamberger's. She replied she had, but their policy was when you are four months pregnant and showing, you had to leave. It was not proper to continue working as a store representative with the public. Marjorie thanked her and wished her well.

Her face twitched. This meant she had about seven more weeks to save that money for the baby furniture. She would have to be careful about her clothes to avoid showing, and maybe wear a slimming panty to hide her tummy.

That evening, Les heartily gobbled his pork chop dinner, while she spooned applesauce and nibbled on toast. "Okay, I'm going to call Dad and Mother now. Would you time me, and if I'm on the line more than five minutes, yell, 'Betty's at the door waiting for you.' "

"Sure. I'm good at timing, with my time-motions studies I do at work," Les said, puffing up his chest, grinning. "After all, I am the Charms Company's best engineer."

Marjorie dialed and took a long breath.

"Hello," her mother answered.

"Mother, how are you?"

"Well, we're doing just fine. It's good to hear your voice," she said.

"Can you ask Dad to come to the phone, too? There's something I'd like to share with you both."

"All right, if you think it's necessary. Ho, Doc, its Marjorie. She wants you by the phone too," her mother called.

"How are you Marjorie?" her dad asked.

"Just fine. In fact, really well. I'm calling to tell you we have some special news."

"Les has a promotion?" her mother interrupted.

"No." Marjorie paused. "You are going to be grandparents."

There was silence, as if she'd spoken the news in a foreign language. "Hello?" Marjorie said again, puzzled that the call may have been lost. "Hello?"

"My goodness, this is awfully soon. You've hardly had time, what . . . five months . . . to get used to being married, and probably still can't cook. How can you care for a baby? Oh my, and you'll have to move. You can't possibly have the baby in that little apartment. Where would it sleep? Certainly not with you!" She rambled. Her mother's words kept tumbling out, jabbing at Marjorie with her prickly prattle.

Marjorie sat down, her nerves stretching to their limit, just like the phone cord. She had hoped her mother would soften with news of the baby. "I want you to know we did plan to have the baby. I admit we thought it would take a few months longer, but we are very excited, and we'd hoped you would be too." She maintained a calm voice, the sting of her mother's comments burning.

"There are so many considerations. Your health is fragile, and I'm concerned that the stress of caring for a baby would get you down. You'd be up half the night. Of course, we are happy to be grandparents. We're just concerned about you and your situation. We'd like you to come home to have the baby so Dad can oversee the birth."

Marjorie froze.

Her dad chimed in. "Marjorie, I'm so pleased you're having a child. Think seriously about coming for the baby's birth. This would be a special time for our family."

She choked out her words. "Thanks for the idea, I'll consider it. But I want to be with Les when the baby is born. It wouldn't be fair to him to have the baby born so far away," Marjorie said. She beckoned to Les to shout. He was standing in the doorway listening, staring at his stopwatch.

"Don't rush to a decision," her dad said. "Have you been to a doctor?"

"Yes, the other day. Everything is fine," Marjorie said, her right knee twitching.

Les shouted, "Marge, Betty's here for you!" He looked puzzled and angry.

"Oops, have to run, my friend Betty is here, talk to you soon," Marjorie called into the phone. Les reached over, took the receiver from her, and hung it on the cradle. Tears welled up her eyes. "Why can't she ever respect me as an adult?"

Les leaned down and put his arms around her. "I can only imagine what she said to make you so upset. She doesn't see you as an adult, and maybe never will. She needs someone to control. But we are starting a family of our own now. We need to do what's best for us. Marge, you did a good job saying you'd consider their idea. I'm glad you said you wanted to be with me when the baby is born." He poked hard at his chest.

Marjorie warmed at Les's compliment. Well, she hadn't given in to them. She had stood up for what she thought was right. Thank goodness she'd have her chance to really love and cherish her own baby. She would turn this grey around to the light.

CHAPTER 9

IT WAS OCTOBER twenty-ninth. Marjorie was looking forward to celebrating their pregnancy with Cal and Betty this evening over dinner at their friends' apartment. Betty was like a spark of sunlight, and Cal was her perfect playmate, always joking in their time together. After dinner, Cal's plan was for them to listen to the draft lottery on the radio. Marjorie had been convinced Betty's crystal ball would be right, and that Les's number would not be called in the lottery. She could still hear Cal bragging.

Betty had been right so many times before, surely she would be right again. Besides, Les's number was only one of thousands, if not millions, of men in the pool. Marjorie had convinced herself he would be fine.

But today, fear clawed its way into her thoughts about what could happen if Les's number were called. She shook it off. But this thought of his number coming up kept haunting her. Finally, she implored him. "Les, let's not listen to that number pulling, one by one. It sounds like hair pulling."

"Marge, we can't run out right after dinner, that would be kind of rude." He put his hands on her shoulders. "Hey, c'mon, be a sport, ol' gal. We'll just listen to the lottery for a little while, then leave. Okay? Plus, it's a historical event, this peacetime draft."

"Okay, we'll stay and listen. Go get your shoes on."

Les ambled back into the kitchen, tucking his shirt into his pants. "Ready?"

"Almost." Marjorie wrapped waxed paper around the bowl and picked up the salad she'd made. "Okay, ready."

Les knocked on their friends' door, and a moment later Cal swung the door open, grinning at them. "Hello there, parents, look what I've got!" Cal held up a bottle of champagne. "We've been eating eggs and beans for a week, but hey, what are friends for?"

"Cal, you could get a job in the theater," glowered Betty as she took the salad from Marjorie. "Thanks, this looks great."

"Wow, champagne," said Marjorie.

"Les will have to open it, but after my operation, I'll be good as new!" said Cal.

A resounding pop echoed in the room and the cork bounced off the wall. Marjorie jumped. "That's a good bottle, alright," she said.

Cal raised his glass. "To a healthy baby that sleeps through the night within the first week." They all sipped to the toast.

"And to a beloved auntie and uncle next door," Les toasted.

Betty went into the kitchen, returning with a package wrapped in pink paper. "For our new niece," she cooed, handing the package to Marjorie.

Marjorie unwrapped it, carefully saving the polka dot ribbon, and held up a white teddy bear with a bright pink bow. She rubbed its fur on her cheek. "Oh, how soft, how darling! Our very first gift from our very best friends." Marjorie got up to give each a hug.

"What makes you sure it's gonna be a girl?" asked Les.

"Remember, Betty's got that crystal ball in the bedroom. She sees these things. And she's never wrong," said Cal.

"Well, Betty, you don't see my number coming up tonight, right?" asked Les.

"Right. I told you before, I'm sure it won't," said Betty, patting both her legs for emphasis.

"Good. Let's eat," said Cal.

Marjorie ate a few bites, then rearranged the pork on her plate. The potatoes went down easier.

After dinner, they chatted about repairs needed to the apartment entry, the coming winter, electric bills, baby furniture, Hitler, and Cal's upcoming operation. They avoided talk of the draft.

Marjorie kept checking her watch. It was 8:10 p.m., 8:25, then 8:40. The lottery would begin at 9:00. She fought the vision of Les's number, 467, running through her mind. *Please don't let them pick it,* she prayed.

"Hey Marge, you're so quiet," Betty said.

"Digesting that wonderful dinner for the two of us," she said with a smile.

At nine o'clock, the couples crowded around the radio. Les sat closest to the radio to be sure to hear. Cal was right. The capsules were to be pulled by Secretary of War, Stimson. President Roosevelt called out the first number—158.

Cal said, "Everyone with number 158 will get an induction notice. Since every county has its own draft board, a low number like that would draft several thousand men at once."

The next number was 6,126. "Only large draft boards have that high of a number," Cal said. Marjorie crossed her fingers and took a deep breath, cradling the baby bear.

Next was 349, then 816. Secretary Stimson announced that the numbers would continue until they had sufficient draftees. Marjorie saw Les bite his nails, which were already stubs. She fidgeted, crossing and uncrossing her legs, and took long breaths. She would be calm. After all, she was going to be a mother in charge of another human being who depended on her, acting with wisdom and composure in every situation.

Her mind wandered. She pictured Les bleeding, lying in the snow in a field in some foreign country, unable to move, calling for help. Feeling nauseated, she stood up.

"Excuse me, bathroom break." Marjorie smiled without looking at anyone. She rushed down the hall, closed the bathroom door, and gripped the toilet. She shuddered but did not get sick. False alarm. Why was she torturing herself? She had to go home.

When Marjorie returned to the living room, they were all looking at her—Betty's eyes wide, Les's brow wrinkled with concern, Cal's lips in a tight line. The radio droned on. Marjorie felt her face flush. "Gosh, I hate to miss this time together, but I'm afraid I just can't stay up for the rest. I think this mother-to-be is ready for her bedtime."

"Oh, Marge, sure we understand," Betty said, giving her a hug. "This is a lot of tension for you."

Les turned to Cal and Betty. "This was a special night. Thanks so much for inviting us, celebrating with champagne, and sharing this crazy time," said Les.

"Of course. We love having you over," Betty said. "We had a chance to celebrate your baby," Betty beamed. "And Les, as a bonus, your number wasn't even close, and they're almost done."

"Sure am glad for that," Les said. "I want to do my part to get that devil Hitler, but the timing's not best for us just now."

"I can't thank you enough for such good company, and our very first baby gift," Marjorie said, giving them each a hug. "Cal, best of luck with your surgery in a couple days. We'll be praying for great success and a two-armed hug soon."

"If we can help at all, give a holler," Les said.

Marjorie cuddled the teddy as they left.

As soon as they got into the apartment, Marjorie collapsed on the sofa and put her feet up. "I hope Betty and Cal were okay with us leaving so abruptly. I didn't want to ruin our evening."

"You need your rest. I'm sure they understand. You worry too much." He leaned over her and kissed her forehead.

She looked up and kissed him. "Your number didn't come up,

and they're almost finished. I'm so glad no one's taking you away from me."

"I'm here . . . at least for a while, so c'mon, let's call it a night."

Marjorie prepared for bed and snuggled under the covers. Les soon climbed in beside her. "And now I count four in our bed. I see you've brought Teddy," Les said.

"He asked so sweetly, I couldn't resist."

*

The next morning, Marjorie heard a knock at their door a little after seven. She was brushing her teeth. *Who could that be?* Another knock. Les went quietly to the door, grabbing the metal pipe he kept in a nearby corner, holding it behind him. This was an old habit from living in Passaic. She watched from the hall. He opened the door a crack, gripping the pipe, his foot braced against the door.

There stood Cal, with the morning paper in his hand.

"C'mon in Cal," said Les. "What's up?" Les wiped his brow with his free hand.

"Man, what were you gonna do with that pipe?"

"You have a gun, I use plumbers' tools for defense," Les chuckled.

"Gee Les, maybe a little overreacting?" Cal pretended to swing a pipe.

"I grew up in a tough neighborhood. Leftover I guess."

Barefooted, Marjorie moved to the doorway when she heard Cal's name.

"Can't stay, have to get to work, but I need to show you this before I go. Look here at this article about last night's lottery." He pointed to the newspaper listing the draft numbers chosen. Marjorie peered over Les's shoulder. There toward the end of the list, Cal had circled the number 467.

Marjorie leaned against the wall in the entryway, her knees

unsteady. She stared at the news that might dig deep to the roots of their hopes and plans and twist them into tangled knots. Her heart raced.

"I hated to bring this over but thought you should know. We'll talk more later," Cal said, hurrying out the door.

"See you later, buddy," Les said as he closed the door.

Can this nightmare really be happening? Marjorie remembered Cal telling them they wouldn't put an engineer in the infantry. Still, he was being sent to the military. She pushed her panic deep inside and turned to Les. "Wait. Maybe this is a mistake. The paper could have made a printing error with your number," she said. "That kind of thing happens all the time."

"Well, honey, I guess it's always possible. But we still have to assume it's right. We'll wait and see when a draft board notice comes in the mail," said Les.

"You mean *if* one comes." Marjorie stood tall, a half-smile forming on her lips. "I vote for a printing error and no notice." She watched Les's face. His jaw was tight, pulsing as he clenched his teeth.

"I'm going to see what the mailman brings before I say anything about my number at the plant. Maybe your printing idea will bring us luck." He glanced at his watch, "I'd better run now, honey." Les grabbed his hat and coat, shoved his arms in the sleeves, and pecked her on the cheek. "Things will work out, you'll see," Les said.

She smiled and hugged him hard. The door shut behind him. How many more days would she be able to kiss him goodbye knowing he would return to her that same night?

CHAPTER 10

FIVE DAYS PASSED with no draft notice in the mailbox. The faint breeze of hope strengthened. The draft board was supposed to send notices within a week. Marjorie began to accept her notion of a mistake. She and Les avoided conversations of how they might be affected by his being drafted. Each day without a notice meant dinner chats focused on plans for the week, the leaky faucet, how to save on their electric bill, and whether they could afford a new record album. But underneath, creeping low and ominous, was Marjorie's other dinner companion, fear.

At work each day between customers, Marjorie's thoughts slipped to the mailbox and what might lurk there that could turn everything in their lives sideways. The mailbox held their future hostage. If Les were drafted, he'd miss the birth of their baby. Working while caring for their baby would be impossible. She might be dependent on her parents again. When she thought of her mother and the baby, she closed the door in her mind.

Each day after work, she rushed to catch the early bus so she could dash home to see what fate held behind the small metal door in the hallway neatly marked Stoltz. After six days with no notice, she believed she might have been right about a printing error. By today, day eight, she was almost certain the paper had made a mistake.

Please let it be a mistake, she prayed as she opened the mailbox. She ran her fingers along the back of the box to be sure no piece of mail lay unnoticed. Scrutinizing every envelope, and finding nothing from the draft board, she took a deep breath.

Marjorie listened for Les's steps on the stairs. When she heard him, she threw open the door. "Guess what? Eight days now, and no notice! I was right. It was a mistake!" Marjorie clapped her hands and squeezed Les.

"I hope you've got the clear crystal ball this time! It could be that you're right about a printing mistake. Maybe I should call the draft board tomorrow. Don't want to be the fool that rushes in."

*

After dinner Marjorie was preparing coffee and tea for Cal and Betty, who were coming over to play cards, when Les plunked the deck of cards on the table and turned to her. "On the one hand, I don't want to draw attention to myself, yet since Bill at work received his letter a few days ago, it seems like something is up. This may be good news, but I'm afraid to think it."

The doorbell rang. "Gosh, they're here early," said Marjorie. She stopped arranging oatmeal cookies on a glass plate and walked to the door. Les followed her. Mr. Fleckenstein, their downstairs neighbor, stood in the doorway.

"I've been at my daughter's for the last few days and found this in my mailbox when I returned. The mailman must have left his glasses at home." He handed the envelope to Les. Marjorie could read the return address clearly, *Local Draft Board No. 27, Essex County, N.J., Official Business.* It was no mistake. The anguished sound of a wounded animal escaped her lips. She clutched Les's arm and held fast.

"We've been wondering about this. Thanks for bringing it up," said Les.

"I'm sure you wish it had disappeared." the neighbor said. "But they're dogged about finding folks. Best of luck to you."

Les closed the door. He held the envelope for a moment as if looking through it and imagining the words on the inside. He pulled out his pocketknife and neatly slit the envelope across the top as if he were handling a precious document.

Marjorie felt the blood drain from her body as she read over his shoulder.

Order to report for Induction

To Lester Donald Stoltz

Order No. 1764

Greeting:

Having submitted yourself to a local board composed of your neighbors for the purpose of determining your availability for training and service in the armed forces of the United States, you are hereby notified that you have been selected for training and service in the Army. You will therefore report to the local board named above at 7:15 a.m. on the 17th of November, 1940. You will there be examined and if accepted for training and service, you will then be inducted into the stated branch of the service.

Stunned, Marjorie stared at the notice, wishing she could erase his name. Her stomach knotted at her impending loss. It couldn't be true.

"Guess we were wrong," said Les, his jaw tight with tension.

Marjorie jumped when the doorbell rang again.

Les turned to the door and shifted from inductee to host. "Hey there, neighbors. How's that arm doing, Cal? It's been a week since surgery, want to arm wrestle?" asked Les.

"I'm still quite the one-armed bandit, but plan to knock all your socks off tonight with my superb card playing," Cal said. "I've been practicing dealing with one hand. Quite a show. I could be in the circus."

"My socks, shoes, and senses have already been knocked off. Just a few minutes ago," said Les, his face white.

"Marge been after you again?" said Cal, winking at Marjorie.

Cal always gave Marjorie's spirit an upward tug. She made a face at him, working around her anxiety.

"Just got the draft notice. They mean business."

Les's words jolted Marjorie out of the cloud of denial.

"It came, eh?" Cal screwed up his face.

"Yup," said Les. "C'mon and sit down."

"This wasn't in my crystal ball," Betty said, slumping onto the sofa and shaking her head.

Marjorie sat watching Les pace like a caged animal. She squeezed her hands. Her trembling would pass in a minute. Her heart ached for Les as she watched him tread back and forth.

"Y'know, Les, you're really gonna wear out that pretty carpet," said Betty.

"C'mon, take a load off, Les. I saved the comfy chair for you. Listen, I know what I told you before, that you'd be okay, but you really can't count on the army to consider your engineering skills. They have quotas to fill, kind of like cows in a pen for slaughter. They could stick you in the front lines as a radio technician with the infantry."

Betty shook her head and scowled at Cal.

Marjorie cringed at Cal's words, imagining the sound of gunshots and Les in a bloody battle.

"But what choice do I have?" Les swept his hair off his forehead as though it interfered with his thinking.

"Consider this. If you enlist in the navy, they could put you in a design shop for shipbuilding or engine construction, a better place than the front lines. The local draft board gives the okay."

Les stared at Cal. "Suddenly, I could like boats. I was in a canoe once," he said.

"It sounds like enlisting in the navy is the better choice. But you've only got a few days before you have to go for the army physical," said Cal.

"I guess the navy would give me more options, though there probably are no guarantees. It's a crap shoot." Les looked down at the floor.

Marjorie fidgeted in her chair. "Please, let's take the safest route on this scary journey."

"You'd look better in blue than putrid green," said Betty, breaking the tension. "You need a little time to digest it all."

"C'mon, I'm dealing," said Cal, changing the subject, plopping himself at the dining table. "C'mon. It'll work out. How about we distract from this and play a little canasta tonight."

Marjorie bit her lip. She wanted an excuse to not play. Her mind spun in turmoil, but she thought Les needed the diversion. They did play for a while, bantering about the advantages of the navy until the emotional strain overcame the card contest.

"Ok, Marge won, my numbers say," declared Betty, calculating scores. She reached over to give Marjorie a pat on the shoulder.

And Les's numbers say I've lost, in a big way. After Cal and Betty left, Marjorie watched Les rub his forehead. "How are you doing, hon?"

"Aside from being punched hard in the stomach and dragged over hot coals, not too bad. I guess I really believed there was a mistake in the paper." Les shook his head. "We don't know how this war will go. Dad heard they've moved all Jews in Warsaw into a ghetto. I want to do what I can to get rid of that madman Hitler." Les shook his head. "Since my parents have sacrificed so much for me to go to college, I know they'd want me to help in as safe a way as I can." Les started pacing again. "So how about you, honey?"

Marjorie recoiled. "Like I've been pressed between the rollers of Mother's old clothes wringer at slow speed. Squashed and spit out a different person. I . . . I can hardly believe this is true. We've just begun our life together after waiting for so long. Right now, I'm heartbroken and dog-tired. Let's talk more in the morning, okay?"

*

The next morning at breakfast, Les dunked his toast repeatedly in the yolk of his soft-boiled egg, but he didn't take a bite. "Think I should go to the navy recruiter today and do my appeal, see what they'll do for me, like Cal said?"

Marjorie rubbed the tension knot in her left shoulder. Her sleep had been interrupted by visions of arms and legs flying through trees and landing in mud until she woke up in tears. She tossed for hours afterward.

"For sure, it's worth a try. I don't want you in the infantry. You can tell them all about your engineering skills," Marjorie said. "Tell them all the electrical stuff you've done, except the radio trick! They'll see how valuable you are and how you can fit in with what they need."

"Maybe I could mention I graduated top honors at school. I think I'll go right after lunch."

She straightened his tie and kissed him. "I'll say a prayer, honey. Can you come home early?"

"I'll try. You take it easy today. Need my gal healthy and strong." He hugged her.

She knew she couldn't take it easy. Since this was her day off and she wouldn't have work at the store to distract her, she poured her nervous energy into household tasks—scrubbing the kitchen floor, scouring the bathroom, doing hand laundry. By afternoon she was drained, but she had had less time to dwell on what might be in their future, like their home disrupted with Les far away.

As she was stirring the soup for dinner, a finger appeared in the pot, then an eye stared up at her. She jumped back and screamed. After a moment she dared to look again. Potatoes and beef. Her mind was playing tricks—just a consequence of her pregnancy and overdoing it. She lay down to rest for an hour.

At four o'clock, she decided to iron her yellow dress that Les liked so well. With the last bit of energy, she pressed the bodice and puffy sleeves. It was a cheerful dress, and she would welcome him home in a crisply-ironed favorite.

Les walked into the apartment at five, an hour earlier than usual. Marjorie rushed to the door to give him a kiss. His shoulders sagged as he came in the door.

"Don't you look like Miss Sunshine! A feast for sore eyes," Les said, nuzzling her neck.

"Come and tell me all about it." Marjorie dropped into a chair and leaned toward him. He pulled his chair close to hers.

"Well, I have some good news and some not so good news. What do you want first?" Les asked softly, his eyes looking away.

"The good news," Marjorie said with curved lips and a pounding heart. She watched his lips and focused hard on his words. She would not interrupt him.

"I went to the navy recruiting office and told them I wanted to serve my country, that I was an electrical engineer, and I was interested in working in a munitions factory nearby if I could." Les rubbed his forehead. "I was pretty nervous. The petty officer said I'd have to do an appeal first to change to the Navy. A munitions factory assignment might be a possibility. There are torpedo factories in New York. He couldn't guarantee anything, but they need engineers. If I pass the physical, I'd go to boot camp with a rank of E-1 Seaman Basic, then I'd get an assignment, hopefully one I asked for, then a promotion with a small increase in pay." Les paused, forcing a weak smile. "So, I could be nearby."

Marjorie heard all his words, but *hopefully, could,* and *might* rang loudest in her ears. "Did he say anything more?"

"Jim said it was possible to have liberty some weekends. I checked on the munition's factory. There's one in Tarrytown, New York, about an hour from here, so if I got lucky, I might be close. That's really it," he sighed.

She wiped off beads of perspiration that had formed on her brow and forced a smile. "That seems pretty good. Wish they could guarantee you a factory nearby."

"Are you ready for the bad news?"

"I guess so." Marjorie pursed her mouth.

"The bad news is the pay is fifty dollars a month. Ninety dollars less than what I get now. That throws a giant monkey wrench in our plans." Les shook his head and stroked her hands. "I just can't believe this is happening. Our plans for a good life here together." His hand swept around the living room.

Marjorie felt the dampness under her arms soak her dress. Her starched linen frock was melting, even though it was November. "We'll have the extra expenses with the baby, and I probably can't work much longer." The wrinkles in her brow deepened to furrows. "It seems like we'll have to give up the apartment. Where will I go? I don't want to go home to my parents." She was working herself into a lather. She forced her shoulders back knowing she had to be strong, then fought the tears that began welling in her eyes.

"I've been thinking about that too, honey. What about living with my parents for a while to see how things go with me? What do you think? You'll need help with the baby, and Mom would be there," Les said.

Marjorie fidgeted in her chair. No, she didn't want to live with his parents, or her parents. She wanted her own apartment, and to make her own decisions without worrying about having to please someone else. "Do they have room for a baby too?"

"Mom has a small sewing room that would hold a crib. She would be a help to you and wouldn't interfere with what you wanted to do. You'd have the car. If I'm lucky, we could be together some weekends. Seems like the best we could make of this damn dilemma."

"It's a sweet idea to offer your mom's home," Marjorie whispered. "I just wish I could stay here in the apartment until we know where you're going to be. Betty and Cal are right across the hall." She sighed her eyes heavy with fatigue. "Let's talk more tomorrow. All this is happening so fast." She would figure out a plan. Her thoughts ricocheted in her head like startled birds in a cage.

CHAPTER 11

THE NEXT MORNING, Les moved his spoon back and forth on the tablecloth, tracing the flowers printed on its surface. Uneaten oatmeal hugged the inner rim of his cereal bowl.

"I couldn't sleep much last night worrying about all this," he said.

"I know. Every time I slipped out to go to the bathroom, you sat up and called out my name," Marjorie said.

He grabbed her arm as she walked by him. "I had a dream that you were gone."

Concern seemed to cloak him like a cape.

She gave him a kiss. "Just to the bathroom," she smiled. "I hardly slept either, thinking about us and this little one." Marjorie opened the blinds in the dining alcove to reveal the pre-dawn darkness beyond. She sat down to sip her morning tea. Nibbling her toast, she stared wide-eyed at Les, memorizing the line where his whiskers met his cheek, and the curl at the top of his hair. He would be leaving soon for some place unknown to them. She envisioned his arm missing, jagged scars on his cheek, him in a wheelchair. She shuddered. Waiting for the future was like galloping blindfolded toward an abyss.

"The recruiter said it was possible I could work in a munitions factory nearby. So if I get my appeal from the board accepted, I think I should enlist like we talked about yesterday. They said it would be fine."

"It's better than the army," she sighed, reluctant to firm up any decision that would take him away and risk his life. She wanted to tuck him away and keep him safe so he could be near her when the baby was born in just over five months. "Y'know, maybe it would be good to talk to Cal one last time before you enlist."

"I don't know what else he could tell me. The navy was his idea." He bit his bottom lip and looked at her. "Okay, I can't resist those pleading brown eyes. Cal's always up early, so I'll go knock on his door. Then we have to figure out what you'll do," he said over his shoulder. Marjorie followed him. Les knocked on their neighbors' door. Cal stood in the doorway, his eyebrows raised. His eyes darted from Les to Marjorie.

"Hey buddy, what's up?" Cal said, dressed in his police uniform, his jacket loose.

"Can you come over for a quick cup of coffee? Marge wanted me to talk with you before I go and enlist. Ask Betty if she'd like a cup."

"I can come, but Betty's running late for work," said Cal. He called to Betty that he'd be right back.

"Your arm doing better?" Les asked as they moved back into their apartment.

"The doctor gave me some exercises, but they hurt like hell. Betty still has to button my jacket for me," he flicked the loose jacket with his good hand. "The job's getting better, though. I'm learning to use the Dictaphone, and someone else types the reports. I'm in charge of the lineups too. Don't need two good arms for that. So, what's going on?" Cal sat down and leaned back in the chair, tapping his fingers on his bad arm.

"I was going to enlist today with the navy since my time is running out to report to the army. Wondered if there was anything more than my engineering I should mention."

"Did they talk to you about Officer Candidate School?"

"Nope," Les said.

Cal moved forward in his chair. "Well, gosh, then yeah. Glad you asked. If you just enlist, you'd be a Seaman Basic, skills or no skills. With your college degree, you can apply for Officer Candidate School and eventually be an engineering or munitions officer. Then after graduation, with a commission, you'd get a bunch more money. The recruiter should have told you this. But sometimes they have quotas they have to fill and don't tell it all." Cal stood up. "I just found out my cousin graduated OCS last month, and you're a lot smarter than he is." Cal slapped Les on the back.

"Wow, that could make a big difference for us," said Marjorie, a flash of hope gleaming in her eyes. "How long does all that take?"

"Phil said it was two months. I think you go through basic training while you go to school," said Cal with a smile. "It's your best bet, Les. Gotta run now and master that Dictaphone. Good luck. And let us know how it goes."

"I can't tell you how thankful we are for you in all of this," said Les as he patted Cal's back and walked him to the door. When Cal was gone, Les grabbed Marjorie by the shoulders. "Marge, you have good intuition," he said, kissing her. He sat down at the dining table to drink cold coffee.

"There's hope here after all. Before you have to leave for work, let's talk about what I should do with the apartment. During the night, I kept thinking about our choices." Marjorie sighed and her thoughts gushed out. She rubbed the back of her neck as she paced in the small dining area.

"Your suggestion of living with your mother is a nice idea, but what about all our furniture? Where could we store it?" She threw up her hands. "I really wish I could stay here in the apartment for a few months till we see where you're going to be stationed. Especially since there's a good chance you could be earning more money as a commissioned officer." Her words flew like steam from a kettle. "Our savings is for doctor bills, the delivery, and the hospital." She paced silently for a moment, then stopped and looked at Les. "I hate to say this, but maybe Dad and Mother would loan us some money just for a few months. Then, when you become an officer, it seems like we might have enough to keep the apartment. Oh, Les, I love living here . . . and with such good friends next door."

"I know you want to stay, Marge. But I don't want you squirming under your mother's thumb. I don't like owing them anything. Your mother has given you such a hard time over so many things." Les hesitated and blew out a breath. "It's kind of a matter of pride, too, I guess. I should be able to provide for you." He waved his hands. "This is such a lousy situation. I worked so hard to do well at school toward my goal to have a good job and earn the money I needed to provide for my family, to be able to buy things I never could, go places I've never been, and . . . now a step back for who knows how long because of a maniac named Hitler."

Marjorie pressed her lips together. "It's not fair."

"Never mind my babble of self-pity. I am so grateful for you, and I just have to trust that it will all work out." Les hugged her and patted her tummy. "And I'm so happy about our baby."

"Come home as soon as you can after work so you can tell me what the recruiter said. I'll be home by three."

*

After Les left, Marjorie had a sense the world was spinning without her and she was trying to grab ahold to climb on. She could not get through the morning at work without some resolution, some tad of a plan for where she would live in the coming months. It would be good if she could speak to her father, as he was likely to be sympathetic to her situation. He saw patients in the afternoon today, so he would likely be able to talk to her this morning. But then, Les didn't want her to ask for money. So, she wouldn't ask for a handout, just a temporary loan.

Maybe she should wait until tonight and try to persuade Les that it was okay to call for a loan. But if she were going to have a chance to speak with her dad, she needed to call this morning. Her mother usually went to town Friday mornings, so it was a good time to talk with her father alone. Her thoughts oscillated like Les's fan. She went to the kitchen to wash the breakfast dishes, then threw the dishtowel down.

She bit her nail and sat down near the phone. Shifting in her chair, she wondered if the phone would be an instrument of ill or of joy. The heartache of the last call, when her parents tried to talk her into coming back to Pennsylvania to have the baby, was still a tender wound.

Picking up the receiver and holding it for a few moments, she put it back down. Don't disappoint Les, a voice admonished. Find another way. She picked up the receiver again, indecision playing havoc with her mind. She swallowed hard. Then her fingers made the decision. She dialed. On the third ring, her mother answered.

"Hello, Mother. How are you?"

"Well, we've had a little accident, but we're fine. Your dad distracted me when I was driving and the car went off the road, up a hill a bit. I have a cracked rib, but they don't do anything for that anyway. Your dad wasn't hurt, but he used some loud words, so that's the end of my driving. I *won't* have him yelling at me."

"Oh, my, I'm so sorry. I'm glad it wasn't worse." Marjorie paused and bit her lip. "That must have been upsetting." She roused her empathetic self. "Don't do too much so that rib has a chance to heal."

"I send the sheets and Dad's shirts out, so it's just the towels and little things I hang in the basement, nothing heavy," her mother said.

"Is Dad there?"

"No. He took the car in to have the oil changed."

"When do you think he'll be back? I wanted to talk to you both."

"In about an hour. How are you doing?"

"Things are kind of crazy right now. Les got a letter a few days ago. It was a draft notice for the army."

"Oh no!" her mother said.

"After talking with a friend, he decided to apply for Officer Candidate School in the navy. Perhaps he'll have a chance to do ship engineering or work in a munition's factory. Maybe close by in New York. But his pay will be half of what he earns now, for the first few months," Marjorie explained.

"Well you should just come home then, and we'll store your things in the attic and the basement," her mother interrupted.

Marjorie's chest tightened. "Mother, I really want to keep the apartment until we see where Les will be located. He has a chance to be nearby, and he'll have a good pay increase once he's commissioned. Uprooting everything is the last thing that I want to do. It wouldn't be good for me or the baby." She dug her nails into her leg.

"Well what can you do?" she asked.

Marjorie stared at her shoes. *Why is this so difficult?* She inhaled deeply. "I wondered if you and Dad would be able to give us a loan for two months' rent? We would pay it back this year."

"Don't you have savings?"

"Not enough to cover two months' rent. We've saved for the hospital and doctor, though."

"If you came home to have the baby, you wouldn't have those expenses," her mother retorted.

"Les and I want to be together when the baby is born, if possible. And we have good friends next door."

"Well, I guess you made your bed, and now you have to sleep in it. You don't have any assurance about where Les will end up, and you'll be faced with moving when you're nine months pregnant, or with an infant." Her terse tone left no room for discussion.

Marjorie flinched as if stung by a wasp. The air grew heavy. A tear fell on her shoe. She shouldn't have been hopeful. Why had she called?

"Marjorie, are you there? I want what is best for you. Living in that apartment alone is not the best thing for you, or the baby. Anything could happen, and you'd have no family to turn to. It's not safe to be moving when you're very pregnant. It's better to make the change now, dear, when you're just three months along."

"I wish you could understand," she whispered.

"What did you say?"

Marjorie shook her head to regain her composure. "Les and I have a lot of decisions to make. Now, I have to get ready for a doctor appointment," she lied, not wanting her mother to know she was still working.

"We'll talk soon. Take care, and remember, we want what is best for you. Always."

Marjorie dropped the receiver to the floor. Beaten again. Her chin trembled. Why had she thought her mother would agree with her? Only crazy people maintain hope for change when someone behaves the same way over and over. Maybe she was crazy.

She rocked and caressed her tummy. *Honey bunny, don't you worry. I won't be a mother who insists on having her own way every time. I'll believe what you say is important, and I'll help you make your way in the world. I'll be a good mother, you'll see.*

The time on her watch jolted her back into the moment. She might miss her bus. She quickly powdered her nose, grabbed her jacket, and dashed out the door. Rushing down the stairway, she caught her heel and fell down the last three steps. She landed hard on her hands and hip. Shocked and breathless, she rested a few moments, then drew herself up slowly.

Her hands stung and her hip hurt, but everything else seemed to be working. She eased herself to a standing position. It hurt to put weight on her leg, but she moved forward. This fall couldn't have hurt the baby, could it? She remembered her dad's stories of pregnant women who'd fallen off hay wagons and bicycles and had no harm come to their baby. "God made women sturdy," he'd said. She hoped she was one of those sturdy women.

Marjorie brushed off her skirt, glad her stockings weren't torn. She limped along, favoring her hip, praying her father would be right. She hurried as much as she could so she wouldn't be late for work. The bus hissed to a stop just as she arrived. She pulled herself up the steps and collapsed into a seat. *Thank goodness the fall wasn't worse.* She'd had quite enough trauma for one day.

What could she do to earn more money? Perhaps she could tell her supervisor about Les being drafted, and that she needed additional work. She would have to explain her pregnancy, risking immediate layoff. Then their money situation would be even worse. But it was worth the chance. Mrs. Dowling had complimented her work before. Besides, she couldn't think of other options. If she could work full-time for another six weeks, and if she was very frugal with food expenses, it could mean another month that she could stay in the apartment. If she could hold on to the apartment until Les found out about what he'd earn as a commissioned officer, his salary might be enough for them to keep it. She could continue to be her own person, and not be beholden to anyone. Especially not to her mother.

In the ladies' room at work, she ran cool water over her sensitive palms, fixed her hair, and rehearsed what she would say to Mrs. Dowling. She made an appointment with her for 11:30 that morning. At her counter, she dove into tasks that would occupy her mind. She unpacked some new hats, helped a clerk rearrange all the hat displays, and organized the gloves and scarves to blend with the color of the hats. Finally, it was 11:25. Marjorie headed toward her supervisor's door and knocked. She was greeted with a smile and sat down. She told her story.

"I am glad you came to see me," grinned Mrs. Dowling. "We have been delighted with your work here. I want you to know I will do everything I can to persuade our store manager to offer you a full-time position for as long as you are able to work, perhaps three more months. We are shorthanded with receivables and billing. With your degree in home economics and your demonstrated skills in training others, you could do well in a position in the back offices."

Marjorie was stunned. Mrs. Dowling's words showered her with possibilities she could hardly believe.

"I don't think your pregnancy would be an issue since you would not be face-to-face with the public." She nodded her head. "I personally believe we need to look out for our military wives."

Marjorie, glowing with delight, reached across the desk and locked her hands over her supervisor's. "I am truly overwhelmed. Being able to work the next three months or so means so much to me, to our family. Thank you. Thank you for your understanding, and for your confidence in me." Her spirit soared. They valued her. Life was looking up, way up. She might be able to stay in the apartment until Les knew where he'd be.

"We won't know for sure until Mr. Banks agrees, of course. I should know by Tuesday or Wednesday. We'll keep our fingers crossed," said Mrs. Dowling.

If it weren't for her hip, Marjorie would have skipped out the door. She was light-headed, almost giddy. This arrangement was so much better than she ever dreamed. She beamed. A sense of pride filled her heart. They wanted her for her abilities. She couldn't wait until two o'clock to go home and tell Les.

*

Unable to keep her mind on more complex culinary efforts, Marjorie stirred sauce for spaghetti. It was after four, and Les was still not home. He probably had to go back to work. No phone calls. Finally, near five she heard Les's familiar, "Anybody home?"

Marjorie limped to greet him, threw her arms around his neck, knocked off his hat, and kissed him hard.

"Wow, what a welcome! Let me come in again and see what happens then," he laughed. "Why are you limping?"

"Oh, nothing. Just tripped on the step and twisted my hip. I'm dying to tell you what happened today. Of course, I'm anxious to hear your news with the recruiter too. Who should go first?" They sat down in the living room.

"You go first," Les said, clearing his throat.

"I decided to tell my supervisor about my pregnancy and asked to work full-time for six weeks so I might stay here in the apartment until you knew where your commission would be. She was so kind and offered me more—a full-time job in the offices doing training, and also billing and receiving work," Marjorie grinned. "That should make up for your half pay, shouldn't it?"

"You are something! On the loose, you might win the war alone! You should be proud honey. We'll figure out the details."

"Now tell me about your news."

"It's a really mixed bag," Les said, his voice wavering. He pulled a folded paper from his jacket pocket. "This is my life for almost the next five months. First, he said the appeal to enlist in the Navy wouldn't be a problem. I do have to start out as Seaman Basic after all. I go for six weeks of basic training at Great Lakes Naval Training Center—"

"Where is that?" Marjorie interrupted.

"Near Chicago," Les grimaced.

"You mean I won't see you at all for more than a *month*?" Her brow wrinkled.

Les sighed and shook his head no. "So, during that time I'll apply for Officer Candidate School—OCS. Petty Officer Willis pretty well assured me that, with my schooling, I'd get in. Then it's twelve weeks of OCS at Newport, Rhode Island. If I do well, I'll get a commission. I'll know later what leave I'll get during that time. After the commission I may get some choice, especially if I do really well." Les scrunched up his mouth. "I hate all this. But what else can we do?"

The words *twelve weeks* resonated loudest, echoing in Marjorie's head. "All that would end right before the baby is due. And you'd be nowhere near here most of that time," she sagged in the chair.

"Hey, there is some good news. I'll have leave for up to thirty days after the commission."

She sat up. "Finally, something that might work out. Sounds like maybe you could be home when the baby is born?"

"I'll try my damnedest. This is all so much, so fast. Now, for the other part." Les sucked in his cheeks and stood up. "I have to report on Wednesday."

"Wednesday?" she shouted, stunned, her eyes wide. "Oh no! That can't be."

"I have to bring my marriage certificate. Nothing else."

Marjorie jumped up, wringing her hands. "That only gives us four days together before you're gone for nearly five months," her voice choked.

Les hugged her and kissed her neck. "I may get leave in between. Plus, I'll write to you every day. Your job is to take care of yourself and our baby."

Marjorie pushed him back a little and glued her eyes on him. Her world was about to collapse, and she couldn't do anything to stop it. Her eyes slowly moved down from his head, to his chest, to his long legs. Her hand followed. "I just want you back the same man you are," she whispered. She squeezed him tight.

"We'll get through this, one day at a time. You'll see."

She blinked away tears. "Well, honey, come and eat one of

your last suppers." She put her arm through his. "I need a potty break first, though."

Marjorie shut the bathroom door and took some long breaths. *I will be strong. I will manage. I have to.* Then she paled. Her panties were stained with blood.

CHAPTER 12

I<small>F SHE HADN'T</small> made that call to her mother, and hadn't rushed afterward, she never would have fallen. Guilt rose in her throat and deposited a lump. She swallowed hard. She couldn't lose her baby—her very own sweet one. Her thoughts raced. *First, Les going to war, now this.* Then she realized it was probably good that she didn't have any pain. From the back seat of the car, where he had insisted she lie down as he drove to the hospital, Marjorie asked Les, "If it were a miscarriage, I'd have pain, wouldn't I?" Desperate for reassurance, she would have asked the question of anyone within earshot.

"I remember my sister talking to Mom about women spotting when she was in nursing school," Les said. "Women had a little blood, but it wasn't a miscarriage. So that's what we'll think."

"Yes," Marjorie muttered.

"We're almost there, Marge. I'm going to drive right to the door. Now, wait here until I go inside and tell a nurse what's going on."

Please let the baby be all right, she prayed while she waited. She swept her hand across her forehead to wipe her brow. From her position in the back seat, she could only see the top of the doors to the hospital. As she waited, she took deep breaths and told herself to be calm.

The car door opened. Les bent over, poking his head in above her. "I've got a nurse who will help you, honey."

"It's best if you don't walk," said the nurse, wearing a starched white dress and standing beside a wheelchair. We'll get you taken care of very soon. I'm Miss Watkins, but you can call me Sara," she said, patting Marjorie's arm.

Sara? Mother's name? Is this an omen? I'm not calling her Sara. "Miss Watkins, I'm almost fifteen weeks pregnant and found blood in my panties this evening. I missed a step this morning and fell down pretty hard on my hip. My fall might have hurt the baby. I'm so worried something is wrong." Marjorie grabbed the arm Sara extended and held tight.

The nurse smiled at her. "We'll get you checked in and have the doctor examine you. Everything may be fine. A little blood may not mean something is wrong with your pregnancy."

Les rolled the wheelchair inside a brightly lit waiting room filled with people crudely bandaged—some hunched in pain, one man's foot twisted at an unnatural angle, and others in obvious states of misery. She was used to seeing injured and sick people, having been to her father's hospital many times. But tonight, this waiting room seemed ominous. She squinted at the brightness of the lights. While Les talked with the intake nurse, Marjorie squirmed in the wheelchair, wondering if the bleeding had increased. She had stuffed a wad of toilet paper in her panties just in case.

"Where do you want to wait, honey?" Furrows were deeply etched on his brow.

She pointed to the end of a row of patients. The only empty chair was beside a woman with disheveled hair and a roughly bandaged arm. The woman craned her neck to look at Marjorie.

"Pretty lady, what are you here for?" The woman grinned, revealing several missing teeth.

Les answered for Marjorie, "We're going to have a baby. A checkup."

"Worried about a miscarriage, huh? I had five before I could keep one." The woman punctuated her comment with her index finger.

Marjorie felt her skin crawl and swallowed hard at the lump in her throat. This baby meant everything to her. If she lost their baby, there'd be no time to get pregnant again, and if something happened to Les, everything would be lost. She began to sob, resting her face in her hands.

Les stood up. "Going to get some water," he said to the woman, quickly wheeling Marjorie across the room.

"Don't pay any attention, honey," he said quietly. "Looks to me she's had too much to drink and doesn't know what she's saying."

"I'm crying about so many things. I'm so worried I could lose the baby, and I'm worried about you leaving, how much I'll miss you, not knowing when we can be together again. All this and more. What can we do?"

Les's eyes scanned the room, as if searching for his words in the air. "We stay strong and trust each day will be okay."

Marjorie heard their last name mispronounced over the speaker and wiped her eyes with a hanky her mother had always insisted she keep in her purse.

"Let's go now," Les said, wheeling Marjorie to the double doors that led to the inner workings of the emergency room. A different nurse took Les's place behind the wheelchair.

"I'll be right there in the waiting room." He ran a jerky hand through his hair.

The nurse pushed her into a long room. On either side, there were compartments divided by yellowed curtains hooked onto metal rods that hung from the ceiling—a bit of privacy.

"I'll help you onto the bed, just lean on me," said the nurse.

Marjorie climbed onto the bed and lay back on the pillow.

"The doctor will see you shortly."

After what seemed an eternity, a doctor pushed aside the curtain that separated her bed from the next patient. "I'm Dr. Long, Mrs. Stolz. Just about fifteen weeks along, and you fell earlier today, eh?" he said, consulting his clipboard. "We'll have you checked in no time. Try to relax now."

Marjorie held her breath as the doctor completed the examination. He reminded her of her dad, who had a kind, business-like manner, was balding, and had a grey mustache. *Please give me good news.*

The doctor helped Marjorie sit up. "This amount of bleeding is not unusual, and your cervix is not dilated, so everything seems fine. I hear the heartbeat."

Her hand flew up and covered her mouth. "Oh, thank goodness!" A flood of relief coursed through her. She wanted to hug the doctor.

"We want to be on the cautious side, though, so I want you to lie down and rest with your feet level with your head for about three hours each day for a week. No lifting. The baby should be fine. Your fall may not have had anything to do with this spotting. It's quite common."

She would still be a mother. They would be a family. "Oh, thank you, Dr. Long, this means more than you know." Her prayers had been answered. She couldn't wait to tell Les.

*

The fear of losing her baby had jolted Marjorie into realizing that even if she could work another three months and keep the apartment, she would probably have to move after that time. Then she'd be moving when she was very pregnant and alone. Her dream to stay in the apartment was vanishing, but it was best to move now while Les was here to help. She began planning to live with Casper and Catherine.

Marjorie was heartened that over the last few days there had been no more spotting. She had been careful to rest while preparing for the move, just as the doctor suggested. Her first task had been to search for boxes. The grocer, who had always joked with her, unpacked canned beans and peaches so he could give her boxes with lids. She would miss his friendly banter. Luckily, she found more boxes at her shoe store.

All their furniture as well as their kitchen items, lamps, bedding, tablecloths, towels, and Les's clothes would have to be stored in the basement of the bar Casper managed. Les could pack the books, records, his electrical equipment, his clothes, and personal things while she focused on the endless kitchen items.

Thankfully, Cal had found more boxes at the drugstore, and on Sunday Betty had insisted on helping her pack pots, pans, and bowls, carefully labeling each box. Marjorie packed the good china they had received as wedding presents, cushioning each piece with dish cloths, hand towels, washcloths, or potholders. By the last night, she was out of boxes and energy.

Monday morning Marjorie ventured out to the post office while Les took a load of taped boxes to Passaic. On her way back home, she was careful to hold the banister as she climbed up the stairs to her apartment. Changing her address from 214 Salem Court, Elizabeth, to 875 Fourth St., Passaic, had not been easy. She longed to stay here, in her own home. But until Les knew where he would be stationed, moving in with Les's parents was the only choice she had.

As she walked into the apartment, the contents of the room emerged into view piece by piece—the Duncan Phyfe style sofa, the wingback chair, the fluted brass floor lamp—all the evidence of their precious few months together. The furniture, for her, was a sign of the independence she had so long yearned for and achieved. These tables and chairs would now be stored in the attic of her mind, as well as the basement of her father-in-law's bar in Passaic.

She looked around to imprint the happy times they'd enjoyed in this room—meals with Betty and Cal, playing cards, cozy times listening to phonograph records. Their wedding album lay on top of a box. She paged through it, gently caressing the pages. A smiling couple looked back at her, their faces registering excitement, delight in starting a life together. She closed the book. Now, reality and her dreams were fighting their own battle.

It was time to lie down again, so she lay on the sofa with her stockinged feet propped on the curve of the sofa arm. Tears filled her eyes. *I don't want Les to see a sad, miserable woman during his last days at home.* Her job was to stay strong, Les had said, and she would do her best.

The doorbell rang, so she got up, wiped her eyes, and padded across the room. Betty stood in the doorway holding a bakery box.

"Hey Marge, I thought we could use a treat after all that packing yesterday." Betty smiled, opening the lid to reveal four puffy pastries. "Tea and crullers, just you and me? I guess Les is out since your car is gone."

"Oh, how nice! Right, Les won't be back for a while. He took a load of boxes and his electrical stuff over to his parents."

"Good, then we can finish our talk from yesterday. I'll make the tea, then, while you lie down, I'll do some packing. You can supervise!"

"Betty, you are such a dear friend, taking the day off from work to help." Marjorie expelled a loud sigh of relief.

"My boss is a pretty good guy. He knows I don't ask often," she said, carrying the bakery box into the kitchen. "Hey, I see that Les made a lot of headway packing dishes last night," Betty called from the kitchen.

"I can't believe how much he got done. I wrapped most of the glasses and cups, then fell asleep while he was still working. Liquor boxes and orange crates sure are a blessing." *And a curse if they are to carry away all your treasures.*

Betty came back into the living room balancing two teacups on saucers, put them on the coffee table, left, then returned with the teapot. "So, what about going back to work from Passaic? You said you wanted to. But it means you have to change buses to get to the store."

"Yeah, I know."

"The station where you have to change is not in a safe area of the city. Cal's always talking about crimes there, robberies and such. I would worry about you having to wait there. Could you take the car to work instead?"

Marjorie sat up. "I will have the car now, but parking downtown is impossible."

"Wouldn't it be a really long ride from Passaic by bus?"

"I was going to check the schedule to figure out how long it would take. I've got a schedule in the phone book over there."

Betty pulled the bus schedule from the drawer of the phone table and they studied it together.

"It looks like it takes nearly an hour with all the stops, even though it's only about eleven miles from Passaic to downtown," Marjorie said with a grimace.

"Yikes! That's two hours a day to get to and from work. Are you sure you want to go through all that?"

Marjorie grimaced. She couldn't afford to sacrifice her health, but maintaining her job was so important. She was a whole person at work, happy there. She would not let herself sink down at 875 Fourth Street, Passaic, under the well-meaning scrutiny of her mother-in-law all day long. She had to keep her job. They needed her.

"I know it's inconvenient. But at least something will stay the same after Les leaves and I move to his parents." A long silence followed, and Marjorie's voice caught. "I love my job, and I need the money for the baby." She paused again, her thoughts slowing to a drip. "I don't care how long it takes me to get to work." She bit her cheek. "I guess I need to cling to a sliver of my normal life here."

Betty pulled a chair close to Marjorie and patted her arm. "I understand, I just wanted to make sure you knew the bus situation. It will work out. Now, here's something else for you to cling to. Cal and I were talking last night, and we want you to come over on Friday nights and have dinner with us. You'll have the car, and parking won't be a problem here. It will be fun."

Marjorie's mood lifted. "Oh, goodness! I couldn't put you out every Friday like that! That would be too much of a commitment for you both, I—"

"Whoa there, Marge. If something comes up for us, I'll just call you. Don't worry. Cal goes with the boys once a month, so those times, it will be just you and me. I'd love that! We could even go to a show!" Betty said, grinning.

Marjorie cast off the leaden shackles that weighed her down She got up and threw her arms around Betty's neck. "I'm so glad I'll have a chance to spend time with you here. It really means so much to stay connected." She picked up her cup and raised it in a toast to Betty. "Here's to Les's safety, Cal's regaining his arm strength, and our future fun."

"*Prosit!* Okay now, you lie back down and tell me what I can do. I refuse to pack Les's underwear, however!"

"If you could pack some more things in the kitchen, that would be wonderful. There's a stack of newspapers in the dining room you can use to wrap around stuff. I feel like a darn invalid."

"Do what the doc says. Who knows, one day you may be helping me move!"

"Oh, Betty, don't pack my silver coffee pot and teapot 'cause I want to take them with me to Les's mom's. Also, leave my meat grinder."

"Well aren't we the chef now!"

"Les likes me to buy chuck and grind it at home." Marjorie

put her hand to her head. "What am I thinking? Les won't be there. Never mind my goofiness." Would Les's mother even allow her to prepare meals? She had no idea.

*

She and Betty chatted from separate rooms for over an hour. They compared jobs, discussed Cal's disappointment with the slowness of regaining the use of his arm, and where to buy a crib. Talking with Betty was a much-welcomed distraction from the gloom that invaded her spirit, taunting her about the little time that she and Les had left together. Marjorie heard the door open.

"Hey, honey, I'm home with more boxes. Mom said she wanted to make dinner for us tonight. I thought that would be a help." Exhaustion resonated in his voice. Les dropped the boxes he was holding and reached into the hallway for more.

Disappointment dampened her spirit. "I thought we could have dinner together at the diner down the street. Just the two of us. I know your folks want to spend time with you too, but all this has happened so fast. I want us to have time alone before you go."

"I know . . . can we go out for dinner tomorrow night, our last evening together?" He looked at her with pleading eyes.

"I'm having a hard time sharing you with anyone right now." Marjorie got up to hug him. "I guess it has to be this way, but I wish we could stay here tomorrow night."

Betty poked her head from around the kitchen door. "Hi, Les. We've been packing. Pretty well finished the kitchen."

"Actually, Betty has worked like crazy, while I loafed." Marjorie said, grinning at Betty.

Les walked over and gave Betty a hug. "You're a savior, my dear. I can't thank you enough."

"I have to get home and prepare the palace for my prince!" Betty walked to the door. "See you tomorrow."

Marjorie closed the door. "What would I do without Betty?

And what am I going to do without you?" asked Marjorie, her back to Les, fearing if she looked at his face she might cry.

"So it's okay if we have dinner at Mom and Dad's?" His tone was hesitant.

"If we don't stay long afterward. There's still so much to do, like packing most of my clothes in boxes. Well, I guess I can manage that tomorrow."

"I can finish all the rest of my packing tomorrow. I have to," said Les with a frown. Suddenly, he pulled Marjorie to him, pressed her against him, and kissed her with fervor. She responded with her own intensity. They would be late for dinner.

*

Marjorie was anxious to get back to the apartment to be alone with Les. There was so much packing to do, and it was already 7:30 in the evening. She could only eat a few bites of the tasty dinner of *kielbasa* and cabbage that Catherine had made for them. Anxiety was also their dinner colleague. She glanced at her watch again. Time, as well as a soldier, was marching on. She raised her eyebrows at Les, conveying the *how about it?* pleading look.

"We better get going, Mom, we've got a lot of packing to do tonight before Dad, Tony, and his friend come back with the truck tomorrow." Les stood up from the oilcloth-covered kitchen table.

"Here, take," Catherine said, thrusting a package wrapped in butcher's paper into Les's hands.

"Good, *pierogi* for our breakfast!" Les grinned.

"We can warm them up in the morning. I still have one pan I didn't pack," Marjorie said, moving toward the door. Catherine's gift of food was her way of showing love.

As they reached the front door, Catherine wrung her hands. "I don't like you going. War is no good. First Russians come, then Germans. And now here they take you and maybe you go for war." She took a hanky from her apron pocket and wiped her eyes.

Les turned to her and held his mother by her shoulders. "I'll be fine, Mom. I'm probably gonna be in a factory right here. New York maybe."

"We pray that," said Casper, patting his son solidly on the back.

Marjorie blinked back her own tears and forced a smile. "We will comfort each other while Les is away." She hugged Catherine, then Casper. "Thank you so much for the dinner, it was very good. You're a wonderful cook."

"You are my family. Like fingers on my hand." His mother wiggled her fingers on one hand, then she squeezed Marjorie's hands between her own.

"I'll stop by tomorrow when Tony and Dad bring our first load of furniture," Les said.

"Wait. Don't forget blankets I have for you. Wrap around so no scratch tables," she gestured. "I borrowed from Milly, too," Catherine said, nodding with approval of her own idea.

Les and his dad loaded the blankets in the car. As she closed the car door, Marjorie looked back at the house. Catherine stood in the doorway, wiping her eyes with one hand and waving with the other. In one more day, Marjorie would be taking her place with this family. Somehow, she had to fit in, to find her niche where she could be independent, yet not be intrusive on this couple with well-worn habits. She bit her lip. *Would it be an easy fit?*

*

"I'll drop you off at the apartment, then I'm going to make a quick stop at the liquor store for more boxes. They stack them out back. That way, you'll have enough for whatever we don't get finished tonight and tomorrow," Les said.

"Hurry home, please," she rubbed his arm, trying to memorize the terrain under her fingers.

Unlocking the apartment door, she glanced at the disorder that had replaced the tidy living room before hurrying to the bedroom to do the very thing she dreaded—separate her belongings from his. The closet revealed both their clothes hanging side by side, pressed together in a unity representing the physical closeness they would not have for some unknown time. She slid her hand down his jacket sleeve over and over while chiding herself to be the strong woman he needed her to be, not the sentimental, sappy one she really was. For his sake, she would do her best to shoulder the situation like a good military wife. *Focus on making this evening a nice one to remember. Smile, so he remembers you that way. Get busy.*

She would pack the clothes that she needed for work for the next two weeks in their two suitcases. Les could leave with only his marriage certificate. When she opened his suitcase to place her blouses and skirts inside, she found a bottle of Old Spice aftershave left at the bottom. She picked it up and stared at the sailing ship on the label. She smelled the cap. A flood of memories coursed through her. She tucked the bottle tenderly into one of her socks and put it back into the suitcase. A bit of him saved for the future. She jumped when she heard his voice.

"Hey, honey, I could only get four boxes with lids," Les called.

"I'm in the bedroom sorting my shoes from yours!"

"I didn't know you learned so much at Bucknell. Holding out on me," he teased.

Her mind raced to find a response that would move the evening away from overwhelming sadness. "Why don't you work in here with me? Let's put on some Glen Miller, and we can make this crazy task more enjoyable." She chuckled, "How about "In the Mood," Les?"

"Now there's a great idea. I'll plug the player back in. Glad I didn't pack it up yet."

Since there was not much room at his parents' house for more than her clothes, toiletries, and a box or two, she repacked one box. In it she placed their wedding album and honeymoon photographs, her jewelry case, her 1939 Bucknell University year-book, and a few favorite records, including Hoagie Carmichael's "Stardust," Glen Miller's "Stairway to the Stars," "Blueberry Hill," and Frank Sinatra with Tommy Dorsey, "I'll Be Seeing You."

He hummed out of tune and she sang while they packed. The music soothed. Marjorie insisted they dance to a few of Frank Sinatra's songs, and she took several records back out of her special box. They fell into bed about midnight after slow dancing, pressed together to "I'll be seeing you." Marjorie wrapped her body, heart, and soul around him.

*

As each piece of furniture was carried out, a fragment of Marjorie's spirit followed it. Life as they knew it had disappeared from the apartment within five hours. What remained was an empty shell. Her voice echoed in the bare bedroom as she called out, "Hey, Les." She lay on the bedroom floor, her feet resting on her suitcase, prone, as the doctor had ordered.

"Coming," his weary voice answered. Les flopped down on the floor beside her, grabbed the other pillow left behind, and folded it under his head. "Well, I guess I've finished the first half of boot camp, after lugging that heavy dining room buffet and those mahogany dressers down. I'm so glad your mother chose solid furniture and not the cheap, lightweight stuff."

"Yeah. You can count on Mother to make things easy."

She snuggled up to him. Checking her watch yet again, she realized they had only fourteen more hours before she had to take him to the bus. Time was not an ample resource. She wouldn't fall to pieces and have him worrying about whether she could cope without him. Nor would she show him how unsure she was about her move to his parents' house. She would gather every bit of her resolve and put the bits in a basket to be doled out as needed.

Marjorie's eyes blurred with tears. She pretended to rub her tired eyes, and yawned. *Chin up.* She couldn't reveal how essential he was to her very well-being. The mystery of what the future held pulled down on her like a dead weight.

Les propped himself up on an elbow and faced her. "Would you be okay if we got some more blankets and stayed here tonight?"

Marjorie turned toward him and wrapped her legs around his. "It'd be better than okay. Let's sleep right here in our own bedroom on this nice floor." She patted the oak boards. "We still have the bedspread here, and I'll borrow blankets from Betty." Marjorie bolted up, her eyes opening wide, her sadness dissolving into a moment of delight.

"Our heat is on till Friday, so we'll be good," Les said.

"I have a feeling we'll make our own heat." Marjorie chuckled and gave him a kiss.

"Glad you don't mind kissing a grimy guy." He pulled her close.

"I'll love you always, any way you are, covered in dirt, grease, or slime."

"And I will love you every moment of every day. You will be in my mind always, my love, my beautiful wife. And you too, my precious baby." He gave her tummy a gentle pat.

"We'll be waiting with bells on," She added, forcing a lilt in her voice.

"Now, dinner at the diner, then cozying up here. What a great plan we have! You rest and I'll take a quick shower. Do we have any towels?"

"The maid left only an embroidered pillowcase, my dear." She pulled the pillowcase off her pillow, folded it neatly, and presented it to him as a handmaiden might. "Just for you, my love." She smiled her very broadest smile.

He stood up and turned to her as he reached the bathroom door. "I already put my favorite picture of you, one from our honeymoon, in my wallet so I can see you every day."

She caught her breath. "And in the night when I look at the moon, I'll be seeing you coming home to me again."

"Just as soon as I can." He stared down at the floor, pressing his lips together in a tight line, turned away, and closed the bathroom door. She heard the water run in the shower, and her tears flowed unseen, dampening her pillow.

CHAPTER 13

MARJORIE WATCHED LES wave with gusto, then climb into the military bus along with a dozen other young men. Standing in front of other wives and girlfriends, she waved with exaggerated motion as the bus lurched into gear, rumbled its way down the street, and disappeared until it was a speck where the pavement met the trees. He was gone. The world around her seemed to move in slow motion. Tearful families hugged, automobiles eased past, people's mouths moved. But she heard no voices. It was as if she were deaf and alone, treading water with no sense of how far it was to the nearest shore.

A horn blared, startling her. She realized she was still standing near the middle of the street. She jumped to the sidewalk, grabbing a woman near her for support. Her heart pounded at the near collision. She apologized, shook her head to clear her dizziness, then began navigating her way back to the car through the narrow streets of Passaic. She fumbled with the keys, started the car without flooding it, and tried to retrace the route Les had taken. If only she had paid closer attention when he had repeated the street names for her as they drove to the bus.

After moving slowly down several streets with the same simple row-style houses that made a landmark difficult to find, she turned the car around. Disoriented, she circled past a familiar group of houses twice until she finally found her way back to his parents' house. But now this was also her house, rather, her home. She parked on the street in front, by the sidewalk, and sat in the car to compose herself.

Weaving through a maze of thoughts, she finally found her path. She would focus on making the best of living with Catherine and Casper, and not interfering with their routines. She'd devote herself to becoming the most congenial, supportive daughter-in-law his parents could ever imagine. It was important that Les be proud of her, and perhaps he might hear directly from his parents how well she fit into the family. Maybe they'd even mention in a letter in Polish how helpful she was. With all the energy she could muster, she would be sweet and generous to make his parents feel comfortable. She smiled. This was her mission. She would make this all work out. She had to. There was no way she would return to her parents to have every move dominated by her mother.

She walked up to the house and touched the door handle, then knocked on the front door. Casper opened it immediately, standing in the doorway with a big grin. He must have been watching for her.

"No knocking. You are family. Walk in, say, hello!" Casper chided her.

"Okay, I will." Marjorie felt a warm glow rise up to her face. "Les sends you another hug and tells you not to worry." Marjorie gave her mother-in-law a tender embrace as she met her in the kitchen. Casper and Catherine had wanted to say their goodbyes to Les at their home. They said seeing him go on the bus wasn't good, that they liked to have their memory of him at home with them together.

"I say Rosary for him." Catherine held up her rosary beads. "Father Mulligan says say Apostle Creed, one Our Father, three Hail Marys, and after, ten more Hail Marys, every day to help him."

"That is beautiful," Marjorie smiled, reserving a special place in her heart for this devoted woman. She hesitated. Her eyes met Catherine's. "Maybe I can learn this too."

Catherine nodded with enthusiasm. "Yes, I teach you. You not Catholic, but you smart gal. I have extra rosary. Pope is happy for me do this. I know."

"Come, Margie, take off coat now, and sit. Have apple cake. I make tea. After, put up feet and take a rest."

"That sounds good. I will rest for a few minutes, then maybe Casper could help me bring in my cases and the phonograph player later. Les loaded them into the car this morning, but they're a little heavy."

"Yes, yes we do that."

"I have some work to do in the apartment and several things left there to pack up. I want to sweep the floors and clean the stove so we can get our deposit back from the manager." Marjorie smiled. "May I borrow a dishrag and some soap? I left the broom there."

"Yes, I get for you. But first, tea and cake." She served both to Marjorie, paused, and said in a tentative tone, "Maybe I come help?"

Marjorie grinned. "That would be lovely. It would make me happy if you came with me to the apartment. I'd be sad there alone without Les." Marjorie savored the sweetness of her cake. "Could we go soon? I'll rest later. I am fidgety to be busy, to do something."

"Yes, yes I get dustpan and cloths," Catherine said, clapping her hands. Perhaps she was also eager to be distracted from her loss.

After several hours of carrying odds and ends to the car, cleaning every crevice of the stove, mopping the kitchen and sweeping the oak floors, Marjorie and her mother-in-law stood in the doorway a moment before closing it.

"God close one door, but open another, yes Margie?" Catherine gave the broom handle a tap on the door.

"Yes, I know you are right." Marjorie would make this come true. She locked the door for the last time and did not look back.

Once they arrived home, Marjorie decided to rest for half an hour. As she was lying down, she wondered how near Chicago Les was in his travel.

Afterward, she got up, scrubbed her face with a rough washcloth, and joined Catherine in the kitchen.

"I have *golumpki* I make special for you," Catherine said, holding a platter close to Marjorie.

"That is very special, thank you." Marjorie looked at the cabbage stuffed with meat, rice, and onions, topped with tomato sauce and sauerkraut. She knew she loved it, but she also knew that with her pregnancy, the cabbage would give her gas pains. She put a small serving on her plate.

"Oh, not enough! Eating for two now." Casper scooped another cabbage onto her plate, beaming. "Want big, healthy baby."

Marjorie nodded, returning his smile, and began taking slow bites. With the emotional storm of Les's leaving still blustering in her head, she had little appetite. She did not want Catherine to feel she was ungrateful, or that she didn't like her cooking, but she couldn't possibly eat both rolls of cabbages. She wanted them to have a good first impression of her, and she knew food was important to Les's mother. Maybe if she ate very slowly, they would get tired of waiting and busy themselves away from the table. Then, she could sneak a big chunk into her napkin and hide it, as she used to do when she was a child.

After finishing his plate, Casper got up to turn on the radio. This was her chance. Marjorie pointed to her silver teapot on the buffet. "I brought my little teapot and I thought maybe we could make tea."

Catherine got up, turning away toward the buffet.

Marjorie grabbed a chunk of her dinner in her napkin, and crushed it in her left hand, glancing over at her father-in-law to be sure he could not see. How childish she was. "And every night, we can pour tea from this pot and say a toast to Lester's health and safety."

Catherine carried the pot as if she were handling the queen's jewels and brought it to the table. "I make you toast, if you like with tea."

"Oh, no toast, thank you. I meant we can make tea and say a prayer for Les each night."

"Yes, we can say Rosary now, if you want."

She struggled with what to say, to be agreeable, yet do what she needed to. "Maybe a little later? The doctor said I must lie down three hours each day, but for only a few more days." She held up two fingers. "To keep the baby safe." She smiled.

"Maybe girls today not so strong. Now, not much working on farm." Catherine chuckled. "This fancy pot needs polish, see dark here?" She pointed to several tarnished places. "I don't have this kind polish. Maybe we use my red pot?"

Marjorie wanted so badly to use her own teapot, a ritual she and Les enjoyed together at her urging. "Maybe when I get more polish, then we can use mine. I like it because Les and I used it a lot." She paused and smiled again for emphasis. "Happy times. Now, I will help you with the dishes. After, I'm afraid I must do what the doctor says."

Catherine waved her hand across her chest, signaling *no*. "No dishes for you. I do them. We have tea when you get up. Take care of baby. Do you want lie on sofa, or bed?"

"Maybe I'll rest in bed now." Marjorie brought her plate to the sink with a small portion left.

Catherine pointed to her plate. "Not so hungry, eh? Sad day, Les going."

"Thank you, the *golumpki* was delicious. You are such a good cook. We'll have a lot of time together tomorrow to talk. I don't go to work tomorrow."

"Yes, and I can help you with so many boxes."

Marjorie smiled and closed the door to her tiny bedroom. The room was stacked full of boxes. She tucked the food-stuffed napkin into her purse so no evidence of her misdeed would be found and she dropped down onto the bed. Exhaustion filled every pore.

She awoke in the dark to discover someone had put an afghan over her. Groping for the light switch, she couldn't believe her watch said it was 11:48 at night. She had slept almost five hours. There was no sound in the dark house. She stepped softly to the bathroom, returned to the bedroom, unfastened her bra, and climbed under the covers in her clothes. The Rosary would have to wait.

*

Marjorie awoke to the whistle of a teakettle. She lay for a few moments feeling the vacuum of Les's absence, wondering where he had slept, how he was managing. She would write to him as soon as he wrote to tell her his address. It all had happened so fast.

She threw off the afghan and stood up, her skirt a wrinkled mess. Marjorie chuckled at how shocked and disapproving her mother would be at her having slept in her clothes. She'd have to call her parents today to let them know Les had left, and that she had completed her move. She would phone them later, after she had created some order in her life. One challenge at a time.

Gathering fresh underwear and a dress from her suitcase, she headed for the bathroom. Today was the only day she had to organize her little room, to unpack and iron her work clothes. Fortunately, Mrs. Dowling had suggested she take these few days off. Tomorrow she would go back to work full-time. Most importantly, though, it was her first day living with Les's folks. She would cause as little inconvenience as possible.

After a quick sponge bath, she joined Catherine in the kitchen. "Good morning."

Catherine wiped her hands on her apron and turned to her.

"You have good sleep? Dad go to work. Come drink tea and have bread and cheese. I make farmer's cheese myself. You like?" Catherine's eyes begged for approval.

"Yes, I'd like to have some. Thank you."

Marjorie ate the white, salty cheese with a slice of fresh bread and a smile, wishing she had her usual toast and jam. She grinned at Catherine and nodded. "I like it." She took her plate to the sink and had begun to rinse it when Catherine came rushing over and nudged her away.

"No, no. I do cleaning."

Marjorie acquiesced. "Thank you." She had to allow Catherine to do what she wished to, even if it meant accepting that her mother-in-law was waiting on her.

"My home, you home. Eat anything you like. Now, I help you with boxes? Closet is small, but many hangers."

Marjorie could not imagine where she could hang all her work outfits. As they began unpacking the first box, the closet filled quickly.

Catherine threw up her hands. "Not enough room. So many dresses and skirts. Can make a store here!"

"I can buy special hangers to put over the doors of the closet and the bedroom and hang more clothes on them. Then I'll have one place for my blouses and the other for my skirts."

Catherine wrinkled her brow and gestured using a hammer.

"No nails, just put over top of door." Marjorie cupped her hands over the top of the bedroom door to demonstrate. She realized she was beginning to omit parts of speech and express herself like Catherine.

"Maybe Dad can make for you tonight?"

Marjorie looked down, anxiety building. She needed to get her things ironed and hung up for the workweek today. If she waited until tomorrow and had to deal with her clothes after work, she'd be drained. She didn't want to seem unappreciative to Catherine, so she weighed her words carefully.

"Thank you, but it's easy for me to buy at Woolworth's, so I can use them today when I iron. Then I'll have a place to make my work clothes ready."

Catherine touched her head. "So, maybe good idea for today. No rushing tomorrow. You iron clothes in sewing room." She started to leave the room, then turned back. "And maybe have time for Rosary later? To protect Lester."

Marjorie swallowed a sigh, forcing the corners of her mouth to curve into a smile. "Yes, I'd like to learn how to say the Rosary."

She hurried to Woolworth's, grateful to find the door hanger quickly, then went directly back. She heaved a sigh of relief when it fit over the door. She suddenly realized Woolworth's would have had the silver polish for her teapot. Next time. She gulped down a banana, bread, and glass of milk for a quick lunch while Catherine was in the basement doing laundry.

She had just begun to iron when Catherine came to the bedroom doorway and peeked in.

"Hangers looking good. Have place for clothes. Maybe soon, come have poppy seed cake and tea?" Catherine implored.

Marjorie was anxious to finish ironing and didn't want to stop. There was so much else she had to find a place for. She juggled her thoughts. "Oh, that sounds very nice. I'll just take a little break when I get a few more blouses ironed. Is that okay?"

"Ya, ya." Catherine nodded.

It was two o'clock before Marjorie felt she could take a short break. Catherine cut two pieces of the cake for her and stood silently waiting for her reaction. Though the cake was not very sweet, it was filled with a tasty paste of poppy seeds inside a delicate pastry. "It's delicious." Marjorie smiled and Catherine beamed.

After the snack, Catherine brought two Rosaries to the table. She offered one with amber stones to Marjorie. Marjorie recited the prayer in phrases after her mother-in-law. As she repeated the Our Father and Hail Mary, Marjorie sensed a calm, a blanket of peacefulness cover her. She hadn't realized how tense she had been, or how comforting the prayers would be.

Marjorie said she would like to help prepare the dinner, but Catherine insisted they were having beef that was already cooking. Another night she could help. When Marjorie said that she would do the dishes, Catherine said, "You have your work in that room. No worry for dishes. I like to do."

She returned to her room to unpack and create some order for her jewelry, hats, gloves, and shoes, arranging and rearranging in the small space, working until she heard Casper come home.

"Hallo Margie. Come, I have present for you." He handed her a small paper bag. Inside, she found a jar of silver polish. "For teapot," he grinned. "We drink at night like you and Lester. Make everybody feel good."

Marjorie threw her arms around Casper, a hero, hugging and thanking him. She was at home.

*

After dinner, Marjorie asked if she might use the phone to call her parents. She could not put off calling them any longer. She was tired, so she knew it was not the best time to talk with her mother. How could she prepare for disdain and rejection? She simply didn't have reserve to cope with these today. *Please let this call go well*, she asked God. She inhaled deeply and dialed.

Her mother answered.

"Hi Mother. Is Dad there too?" She heard the tremor in her voice.

"No, he's at his card game."

"I wanted to let you know that I have finished moving into Les's parents' home. I know you have the address, but I wanted to be sure to give you the phone number that I didn't have the last

time we spoke. Les left yesterday, but I was too exhausted to call."
She tapped a pencil on her knee.

Silence. "Mother, are you there?"

"Yes, I'm just listening. Well, dear, take care of yourself. It
would be a lot easier if you were here with Dad and me. But you've
made your decision to stay there.

"We're hoping that Les will have leave sometime in the next
four months, and when he is done with his training, he will know
where he will be stationed. Hopefully nearby."

"If you change your mind, you know where we are," her
mother said.

"Thanks. Give my love to Dad. Oh, the number here is
Clifford 6-2207. I'll call again soon. Bye-bye." She put the receiver
back on its cradle and sighed with relief. The call was over and had
not put her into a tailspin.

Casper came over and patted her shoulder. "That is good, you
call your family. Family very important. Come sit." He walked
back to the sofa and patted a cushion on a chair across from him.

"You lucky family here in US. My family in small town—
Spie, Poland near Kraków. I have two brothers and Catherine have
two sisters and one brother. We have farm. Ten cow, ten pig, and
two horse. Everyone have name! Sell milk and cheese, onion and
cabbage. Now, Germans take many cow and pig, kill for meat.
Can't make milk." He shook his head. "Don't have food. Germans
take all food for soldiers."

"That is so terrible. I am so sorry for both of your families,"
Marjorie said. These invaders were destroying the basic livelihood of
the people. His family was under siege by foreign attackers, and she
was under siege by her family. "It must be so sad being so far away."

"My one brother is priest. Others say Germans take him. We
don't know if he die or in prison. They take many priests and
teachers and officers and put in prison. Kill many, too. Very bad.
We pray every day for them."

Marjorie stood up and gave Casper a hug. "I will pray for your family, too. I am learning how to pray the Rosary. Catherine is teaching me."

"Thank you, Margie. You very nice gal. Lester pick good. Prayers all we have. Mother sent coats to family, but they never got. Letters sometime." He wiped his eyes with his handkerchief. "Maybe we have tea now? Say prayer for Lester."

Marjorie agreed, and began to apply the creamy polish to her teapot. As Casper talked, she rubbed until the teapot gleamed.

"We want Lester go to college. Education important for good living. We have only six grades." He pointed to Catherine. "Catherine sew clothes many nights very late to earn money, and I manager of bar, we save and save for him go to college," Casper said, lifting his head with pride.

"Now, he is a wonderful engineer. You can be *so proud* of all your hard work, and of his too," Marjorie said.

"Yes, he is good boy. So smart."

Catherine had been sitting in the kitchen, sewing and listening. She got up, put the kettle on, and brought four delicate teacups to the table. "Use special cups."

Marjorie looked at the four cups decorated with tiny pink flowers, then asked, "One for Lester?"

Catherine grinned. "He is here." She put both hands over her heart. "So, we pour him tea."

Marjorie poured tea from her shiny silver teapot into the three cups, plus one for Lester. They raised their cups and toasted, their eyes reflecting the harmony of the moment. Would Les be proud of her today? She hoped she wouldn't falter in the days that lay ahead.

CHAPTER 14

IT HAD BEEN almost three weeks since Marjorie moved into Les's parents' home. At first, she'd been a guest, a visitor tiptoeing on eggshells not wanting to interfere with their household habits. Much sooner than she imagined, though, she became a welcomed member, at ease in this family—so different from her own.

Though she felt cared for, even loved by Les's folks, in a dark corner of her mind there was a void where joy had once blossomed. She had still received no letter from Les. She longed for a word, some news about what he was experiencing, his regimen, or any little tidbit of his life in boot camp. But most of all, she wanted to know he was okay.

It was dark when Marjorie got home from work. "Is there a letter from Les today?" She held her breath, as she did every evening.

"Nothing." Catherine shook her head. "Maybe tomorrow postman will bring."

Marjorie's spirit sagged. It seemed so odd Les wasn't given an address before he left, and even more peculiar was that he hadn't written. She decided she would call the navy recruiting office to inquire. Surely, they would have his address. She would call on her lunch break.

She could hardly eat her dinner. Her schedule was wearing her down. 5:45 in the morning arrived like lightning. She had to leave the house promptly by seven to be sure she made the bus connection. That way, she could arrive at Bamberger's and be at her desk by 8:30 to be ready when they opened at 9:00. At 5:00, she would reverse the trip, arriving at home around 6:30.

"I'm afraid I can't listen to the radio with you tonight. I'm going to go to bed early," Marjorie said, her eyes at half-mast. She had been listening to world news most evenings and explaining to her in-laws what was happening with the German advances.

"Margie, you working too much," Casper shook his head in disapproval. "No good for healthy."

"Margie, before bed, you like drink *herbata*? Special tea from flowers no keep you awake, and some love knots? Maybe relax?" Catherine motioned to Marjorie to come.

"You know how to tempt me. No tea tonight, thanks, just a couple delicious cookies."

Catherine opened the lid of the cookie tin and placed a mound of delicate pastry covered in powdered sugar on a plate, offering them to Marjorie. She bit into one. The flaky pastry crumbled and melted on her tongue. "Thank you. You know I love these. I want to learn how to make these angel wings."

"Real name we call *chrusciki*."

Marjorie repeated the name several times, accompanied by Catherine's chuckling. After giving Catherine and Casper each a small hug, she scuffed to her bedroom. How could she maintain this grueling schedule? She simply had to. She needed the money for the baby's furniture and supplies. She felt so happy in this training job, helping new employees discover clever ways to assist customers choose just the right scarf or accessory, sweater or suit. It was so satisfying to see the smiles on her trainees' faces when the customers carried away their perfect purchases. She also loved to see their smiles when they were praised by the supervisor. She would persevere.

She stared at her closet. Last week, Marjorie had begun

preparing her clothes for work before bedtime so she could get dressed quickly in the morning without creating any more noise than necessary. Now, she seemed to be thinking in slow motion. She opened her closet door and stared at her clothes. Maybe she would wait until morning to decide what to wear. But she knew she would pay tomorrow if she didn't force herself to take the time now.

She had only been working full-time a little over two weeks, but she was questioning whether her stamina would hold or not. With her independence at risk, she would not ask her parents for help. And she certainly would not move back under their roof. She would have to figure out what she could do.

Marjorie grabbed her brown tweed suit and beige blouse and quickly draped her brassiere and slip straps over the top of the hangers. She laid her underwear and stockings on the table. Deed done! She reset her alarm's unwelcome wail for 6:00 adding an extra fifteen minutes of sleep, and fell into bed, too tired for night cream or prayers.

She was startled awake by her alarm, as usual. She grabbed it quickly to avoid waking the family. In her bleary mind, she realized the clock said 3:15. She stared at it. Her eyes were right. She must have accidentally changed the time. She turned on the lamp and set the alarm for 6:15. She fell back on her pillow and curled up in the down comforter.

Knocking woke her.

"Margie, Margie, you sick? You okay?"

Marjorie jerked herself up. The clock read 7:10. Her heart leaped.

"Oh, no, I slept through my alarm, or it didn't go off," she wailed.

She would never make her bus.

Usually, in the mornings she would creep barefooted into the bathroom, wash her face, fix her wavy hair in the tiny mirror, and powder her nose. She'd put on her garters, straighten the seams of her stockings as best she could without a long mirror, and carry her shoes to the front door to slip on just before leaving.

Breakfast was always toast, jam, and farmer's cheese. Then she would shuffle back to the bathroom, apply her lipstick, slip on her shoes, and leave.

This morning, there was no time for any of that. She ran to the bathroom, pushed a wet washcloth over her face, threw on her slip, her suit, pulled up her stockings, ran a comb through her hair, brushed her teeth, shoved a banana in her purse, and dashed out the door at 7:33. She left Catherine standing near the door holding a cup of tea for her.

"I'm sorry, no time!" she called out. She just might make her bus if it came a few minutes late.

She bolted down the street as fast as her heels could take her without risking a fall. She was beginning to feel the weight of the baby adding awkwardness to the front of her body as she trotted. Worries stung her. She had to be on time. If she were late, Mrs. Dowling might see her as lazy. No, she couldn't lose her job.

Dashing down the street, she arrived at the stop just in time to see her bus pull away. The next bus wouldn't be there for another half an hour, so she wouldn't get to work until 9:00, or later. She couldn't be thought unreliable. She needed this job.

She was alone at the bus stop. She looked around for a place where she might catch her breath and sit. An older woman left her house opposite the bus stop and ambled up the street, so Marjorie walked over and sat on a step leading to the woman's front stoop. Her heart stopped its pounding. She pulled out her banana and ate it, putting the peel in a hankie. Then she put on her lipstick as best she could without a mirror. Thank goodness her skirt was tweed and wouldn't show any dirt from sitting on the step.

For the next twenty minutes, she worried that the next bus might be late, what her supervisor might say, and practiced what response she could give. Oh, how she missed Les. Then she thought about what Les would say to her. He would convince her that since she hadn't been late before, this one time she would be forgiven. She climbed onto the bus with a bit of hope. From boot camp, without knowing, he had helped her.

At the connecting bus station, Marjorie surveyed the area like she usually did. Only a few passengers were waiting. One man wearing a dirty jacket and a cap pulled down to his eyes clutched a brown paper bag. Two other men in dark jackets were arguing as they smoked their cigarettes. An elderly woman with a cane hobbled over to a bench nearby. Marjorie studied the men for any movement that could be threatening. These were just ordinary folks. She pressed her purse close, feeling a bit silly. Her purse never contained more than five dollars, but this was a significant amount toward a baby basinet. The baby would sleep in a bassinet in Catherine's sewing room, which was too small for a full-sized crib.

As soon as she got to work, she put her purse in her desk drawer and was heading to her supervisor's office when Mrs. Dowling met her in the hallway.

"Marjorie, what happened? I was planning on a meeting of all the trainers this morning and you weren't here."

"I'm so sorry. I missed my first bus this morning. My alarm had a mind of its own, I'm afraid," her tone apologetic.

"You take two buses to get to work?" Mrs. Dowling looked at her wide-eyed.

"Yes, unfortunately, since I moved."

"That does make it hard. And with your pregnancy, it seems a bit difficult to do every day." She hesitated. "Maybe this job is just too much. I noticed how tired you were yesterday."

"I really love the job, Mrs. Dowling. I believe I can make a contribution to the store. I'm looking into some transportation alternatives that should shorten my day," Marjorie fibbed. "A friend and I are going to work something out."

"Good. We appreciate your work, and you have always been on time in the past. I just worry that this is too hard on you. We'll have our meeting this afternoon at two instead."

Marjorie smiled, but relief and concern collided in her mind. Then a light shone. She would call Betty. She was the friend who might listen to her dilemma.

*

Mrs. Dowling's words preyed on her mind all morning. On her lunch hour, Marjorie decided to call Betty at her job, hoping to catch her at her desk. Though she rarely made private calls on her work phone, Marjorie wanted the privacy she didn't have at home. She dialed.

Betty answered. "Hey honey buns, how are you?"

Marjorie fought back tears when she heard Betty's voice. Betty immediately invited her to dinner on Friday—her sweet promise of Friday dinners together would be kept. Marjorie would wait to discuss her work problem until they had dinner together.

All week, Marjorie looked forward to visiting with her chum, to chatting with a confidante who had no problems speaking English.

At work on Friday, the clock slowed, creeping its way to five. She checked its progress every few minutes. Unable to concentrate on creating training schedules for the next week, she shuffled delivery receipts on her desk. Finally, it was five o'clock. To have the most time together possible, they had planned for her to take the bus to Betty's apartment, and Betty would drive her home.

As the bus neared the apartments, she steeled herself against feeling homesick when her building came into view. It had only been three weeks since she had to leave her cherished home. She bit her lip. She couldn't look back and revisit memories in that apartment with Les. As the bus got close, the bare trees gave the street a stark appearance. The windows on the second floor of the building, where her apartment had been, appeared to frown. Marjorie looked away and made her way up the familiar stairs, stepping over the old crack on the third step, eager to see Betty. A wave of nostalgia washed over her. She avoided looking at the door that used to be hers.

She bit her lip and knocked. Betty flung the door open and hugged her neck. "Well, if you aren't a sight for sore eyes! Come in and tell me everything." She crushed Marjorie's shoulders in another embrace.

They peered at each other and laughed. "Yup, same Marge."

"Did you think I'd grown another head, or a beard?" she asked.

"I really meant you still look good, in spite of all that's happened—Les leaving, moving in with his parents, starting full-time work," Betty retorted. "C'mon and sit down. I have a little glass of sherry with your name on it!"

Sitting across from Betty, Marjorie picked up the dainty glass half filled with amber liquid. Sherry was new to her.

"To best friends," they clinked glasses and sipped.

"So, how's it going, Marge?"

"Pretty well, considering," she fibbed. "Well, I'm really worried about . . . " Marjorie began to blurt her work problem, but changed her mind, reluctant to reveal the work issue before they had a chance to catch up. "Why I haven't heard from Les." Marjorie threw up her hands.

"So that's why you sounded kind of upset on the phone."

"He promised he would write immediately, and it's been nearly three weeks. But still nothing! I need the name of his unit to write to him. Can't just write Lester Stoltz, Naval Station Great Lakes."

"If you added number-one handsome engineer, it might get there!"

"Sure, that's what I'll do. Betty to the rescue!" Marjorie chuckled.

"Seriously, you could call the recruiting office. I can't imagine they didn't give him that information before he left. And it's not like he doesn't know his home address."

"I planned to call them all this week. It was difficult to have privacy at work. I will definitely call them Monday at lunchtime." Marjorie slapped her leg for emphasis. "I should have called sooner."

"So, how's it going, living with his folks?" Betty said.

"It's been a bit of a whirlwind, but his parents have been sweet. They're both trying hard to make me happy. Catherine even offered to make me some maternity tops. She sews a lot. I'm afraid I might not like the old world style she creates, but I'll wear them anyway. Aren't I awful?" Marjorie turned down the corners of her mouth and stared at Betty.

"I'll go get Cal's handcuffs right now. He'll take care of someone like you when he gets back from his card game," Betty said in mock seriousness.

Marjorie laughed out loud, something she hadn't done in what seemed like months. Her spirit lifted through the veil of clouds covering the looming issue of possibly losing her job.

At dinner, Betty filled her in on Cal's progress with his arm. It looked like a desk job for him for a long while. Marjorie also learned that they were still trying to conceive and might see a specialist.

Marjorie shared the latest with Betty. She told her about Casper and the teapot, about Catherine teaching her how to pray the Rosary, and how the Germans were overtaking their hometown in Poland, stealing their crops, and possibly killing their relatives. Though she missed cooking food she loved, she was grateful for Catherine's potato soup and *kielbasa*. She also shared with Betty how tired she was at the end of each day.

"I knew that bus schedule would drive you nuts," Betty said, shaking a finger at her.

Marjorie sighed. "You were right, Betty, about the buses. I had to try to make it work, though. I need the money for the baby, and to buy a few groceries to help out Catherine and Casper. But I have to get up so early to catch the first bus, worry about my safety at the connecting station, then get the second bus, all to be at work on time. Then I don't get home until after six thirty, by which time I'm pretty exhausted." She slumped back in her chair.

She told Betty about setting her alarm clock wrong, and her supervisor's comment that perhaps the job was too much.

Betty put her hand on Marjorie's arm. "You can't keep this up, Marge—it's not good for you, or the baby."

"But I *really* want to keep my job."

"Well, I think your supervisor is right. It's not a good idea for you to continue like this. You are wearing yourself down to a shred. It's not healthy. Les will be sending you money soon, so the finances will get better."

Hardly able to speak, Marjorie cleared her throat. She'd been so sure Betty would support her. Right now, the job was her salvation. She would not quit and become a burden to Les's parents. What else to do? She couldn't bear the idea of crawling back to Mother.

"Betty, this job is really important to me. It means so much to be on my own, and helpful to others. I love teaching the new employees how to interact with the customers." She paused. "I need this for my sanity." Marjorie twisted her napkin and rested her chin in her hand.

"Sure, but you have to think of your precious baby, and what might happen if you continue to be exhausted."

Marjorie exhaled a deep breath and looked at her napkin, wondering, *Am I not a good mother-to-be?*

"You're right, Betty. The way things are, it *is* too much."

Betty leaned toward Marjorie and spoke more softly. "Marge, I want you to be happy, but you are my good friend, and I care about you and your family. Maybe you need to change your job, perhaps back to part-time."

"If I'm to keep my training position, I can't work part-time." Marjorie could feel her face flushing. She had to calm herself and try to think. There was no way she could be emotional and convince Betty. *How can I get Betty to see my side?*

They sat in silence a few moments. Marjorie tried counting to ease her discomfort. She focused. The problem was not the work.

"It's the transportation that's the real problem," Marjorie said. Betty's brow wrinkled. "It sure is."

"If only I could drive to work, I could get up later, get home earlier, and avoid the stress of the bus schedules. But it's the darn parking situation in Newark that keeps me stuck."

"You'd need a wizard to figure that out," Betty said, raising her eyebrows.

Marjorie hesitated, and stared at the table as if to eke out an answer from the linen cloth. There had to be nearby parking somewhere. Could she possibly ask Cal for his help locating a place for her to park? She struggled with the thought.

She plucked a small bit of audacity from her storage of unused mettle and looked up sheepishly at Betty. "I wonder if Cal might know of a place I could park, and maybe walk three or four blocks to work?"

Betty thought for a moment. "Maybe. Hey, nobody knows Newark any better than his highness, my cop, Cal!" Betty smiled. "I bet he could find somewhere you could park near your store. I have faith he knows the Newark streets." Unable to contain a chortle of joy, Betty added, "Then you could keep your job!"

Marjorie jumped up and hugged Betty's neck. "That would be wonderful, if it's not too much trouble for him." Marjorie sensed a heavy load lifting and warmth radiating through her body.

"Heck, no! He'd love to help you. He likes a challenge. We've got a plan, my dear," Betty said.

"Betty, this would be the answer to a prayer. Cal's already my hero from helping Les with advice to enlist in the navy. I thank you both so much. It's so great to spend time with you, and, of course, to have spaghetti again."

"You are so welcome, dear gal. I'll call you as soon as Cal figures something out. Don't you worry, Marge. He'll work on it first thing tomorrow."

Later that evening as she walked down the stairs arm in arm with Betty, Marjorie felt almost jubilant. She might be able to keep her job after all. She thought of herself dressed in her tweed suit, a professional woman teaching and coaching new employees, delighted as they succeeded in pleasing customers. She had a place in the world.

CHAPTER 15

MARJORIE TURNED THE key in the lock to the front door and waved goodbye to Betty. It was almost ten o'clock, and she didn't want to chance waking Catherine and Casper by knocking. As she entered the living room, tall shadows loomed on the wall from the side table lamp, giving the room a menacing feel. She stared at the shapes. Taking a closer look, she saw a man's profile. He was wearing a fedora, and a cigarette seemed to dangle from his mouth. Her imagination was running wild as her mind whirled and questions loomed.

What if Cal couldn't find a parking place? If only she could talk to Les. She ached for him. What would Les say? He would tell her to be strong, to take one day at a time. That is what she had to do. She turned off the lamp, slipped off her shoes, and padded to her bedroom.

On her pillow lay two white envelopes. Les's handwriting jumped out at her. Her heart leaped. She dropped her pocketbook and scooted to the bed, unsure if the envelopes were ones created by her hopes and imagination or if they were real. She ran her fingers over the onionskin paper. They were real. The postmark on one was blurred, and the other was postmarked four days ago. She sat down on the bed and opened the one with the blurred postmark, thinking he must have written it first.

Dear Marge,

Hi honey. I hope you and our baby are doing well, and that you're getting used to my folks. I know it's a big change for you. I miss you so much and wish I could hold you close.

You would not recognize me now. They gave us buzz cuts, so my curls that you liked fell with the other guys' hair to the floor. We had to put all our clothes in a box and send it home. You should get it soon. We stood naked, shivering, while they issued our uniforms. My pants are too short, but they don't care. Then we got our sleeping gear. First a hammock. Can you believe that? Then a thin mattress, a pillow, and two blankets. It all gets rolled up a certain way and goes in a canvas sack. Everyone had to stencil their name on their bag.

My life goes like this. Up and at 'em, drop 'em for push-ups any time of day or night. The chief petty officer seems to enjoy harassing us. I'm sure not used to the calisthenics and lack of sleep. Muscles hurt that I didn't know I had. I'll write again as soon as I can. We don't have ten minutes to ourselves.

I can't wait to hear from you. Write me often! I love you.

Always,

Les

P.S. Only five weeks and four days more till I am done here and have leave to come home!

P.P.S. I left my address stuck on the box with your hats. I was already on the bus when I remembered. I found it in one of the papers they gave us just before I left.

Marjorie's mind took turns jumping from relief to joy to annoyance. He had written three days after he reached Chicago, but the letter had taken eleven days to get here. She wanted to throttle the navy postal staff *and* the mailman. Yet, Les was okay, so she could live with the navy or post office delay. She jumped up to look at the box of hats. There it was, a paper sticking out of the cardboard top. She shook her head. Why hadn't she finished her unpacking?

She grabbed the second letter but used a hatpin to slice open the envelope more neatly this time. Les always opened mail with a trim slice.

Dearest Marge,

I still haven't received a letter from you. I miss you so. Did you find my address? I was so distracted the morning I left I forgot to tell you where I put it the night before—on your box of hats. Did you get my letter? I hope so, dearest. I'm worried that I haven't heard from you. Please tell me you, and our baby, are okay.

Life here isn't easy. I'll have a lot more respect for soldiers after this! And I thought my class in differential calculus was tough! Some nice guys here, though. We look out for each other, which keeps things tolerable.

I think of you every moment. Please let me know how you are.

Your hubby always,

Les

Marjorie sank onto her pillow. At least he was okay. Pangs of loss flowed through her, followed by a wave of sadness for him. Tonight, he would still be wondering how she was. She reread the letters. Afterward, she put them up to her nose and inhaled to see if his scent might be there. Nothing.

Fatigue consumed her. She would get up early and write to him. *No,* she scolded herself. *He hasn't heard a word that we are all right. I have to do it now, so I can finish it and get it ready to mail first thing in the morning.*

As she sat up, a sharp spasm in her tummy shocked her and she had to lie back down. *Oh, no, something's wrong with the baby. Please, no . . . .* After a moment, she stretched her back and rubbed the area gently. The discomfort eased. She waited, lightly circling her fingertips on her tummy as if to send a soothing message to her baby. She lay a while to see if the pain would return. It didn't. Maybe just a muscle cramp. After a few moments, she rolled to her side and eased out of bed. She breathed a sigh of relief. All was well.

It was almost midnight when she finished writing Les's letter. After she kissed the last page, she folded it and slid it into an envelope. She checked his address several times to be sure she had written it correctly. No more mistakes. If only he could know *now* that all was fine, and not have to wait days more.

The room seemed to spin as she put on her nightgown. She pulled back the covers and collapsed onto her bed. Grateful it was Friday, she had no need for an alarm the next day.

She drifted in and out of sleep, dreams muddied with the same anxiety that bled through from her waking hours. She found herself in a hospital searching from room to room for Les, then for her baby. No one had seen them, no one knew where they were. Morning brought relief when she realized it was a dream, but a fuzzy fog filled her head. She felt her tummy. The baby was safe. Her treasure.

"Margie, Margie, did you see letters from Lester? Come and tell us." Catherine knocked on her door. Her voice was pitched two octaves higher than usual, as excited as a child at Christmas. Marjorie hurried to the kitchen in her robe with the letters in hand. Catherine greeted her with coffee and potato latkes. Casper pulled her chair out for her. They sat watching her eagerly as she read.

"At least Lester is safe. Hard work, but safe." Catherine offered to walk to the post office to mail her letter.

"Let's go together. I want to buy some more stamps, too," Marjorie said. She had to see this letter drop into the slot at the post office for her peace of mind. "Do you want to write one too, while I get dressed?"

Casper hung his head and shuffled more than usual as he moved away from the table. He thought a few moments, and said, "No, thank you. Not now. You take your letter. We talk more later."

Catherine stood fumbling with her apron. "We don't write very good. Maybe next time, you can write for us what we say to you? We don't want his friends see letter in Polish."

Marjorie blanched with discomfort at her own ignorance. "Of course, I'm happy to do that. We can write together later today if you like."

Catherine nodded and smiled. "Yes, please. Now you go post office. Maybe you like go to store, too. I go next time." She looked at Casper and said something to him in Polish.

Marjorie hadn't realized the extent of their limitations with English, or perhaps, even in Polish. Les had told her reading was a problem for them, but she had assumed the difficulty was the vocabulary. She sympathized with their desire to maintain dignity regarding their inability to communicate with their son. They had done so much with so little education. She would make this day a good one for Les's parents in his absence.

*

Marjorie decided to drive to the post office since the car needed to be run regularly. Les had reminded her several times before he left, but she'd neglected this duty. She climbed into the car and tried twice to start the engine, taking care not to press the gas pedal too far down and flood it. On the third try, the car choked, bucked, then rumbled to a smooth rhythm. *Thank goodness.* She released her vice-like grip on the steering wheel and gave the dashboard a pat of love. She was off. If all her angels were lined up, she'd drive it to work every day.

At the post office, she asked if airmail would get there faster. The agent said it would be a waste of a stamp in the United States. She handed him the letter, as if it were a precious gem, and breathed relief that it was one step closer to Les.

"How long will it take to get there?" she said, hoping he would say two days.

"Tomorrow is Sunday, so he should have it Wednesday or Thursday."

"Oh dear," she said, frowning.

"Sorry Ma'am, no magic elves working here. They don't start 'til December." He looked at her over his spectacles.

"I'm sorry, I didn't mean to be rude."

"You just want your military man to get your letter tomorrow. I know."

"Yes sir." Marjorie smiled and gave him a little wave as she left.

At the grocery store, she chose some apples, bananas, carrots, onions, and a quart of milk. This weekend she wanted to cook a dinner for Catherine. Any woman who sewed late into the wee hours, night after night, to enable her son to attend college, surely deserved a dinner prepared for her. She and Casper never ate in restaurants. Catherine believed it wasn't healthy. Les had explained this belief was a result of a bad experience with food poisoning in Poland.

Marjorie drove the extra miles to her favorite butcher shop in Elizabeth, where she knew the grocer would cut a tender chuck roast for her. Marjorie knew better than to attempt to cook in her own mother's kitchen, which was ruled with an iron apron, but she hoped that Catherine would allow her to make this dinner. She hadn't yet agreed that Marjorie should do much in her kitchen. Though Catherine expressed definite preferences, she was not intractable.

As Marjorie lugged the groceries out of the car, Casper came shuffling out to meet her. "Hallo, Margie. I can help." When he bent down to get her bag, he wavered, almost losing his balance. "Big melon in there," he laughed. "Betty, your friend, call for you. She call back in afternoon."

"Did she say anything else? Maybe about a parking place?"

Casper stopped a moment. "No, nothing."

Maybe she'd find out Cal's news today. She closed her eyes and willed a parking place to appear. She should pray with her rosary.

"You buy whole store, Margie?" Catherine chuckled, looking at the purchases as Marjorie pulled them from the bag.

"I want to buy some groceries every week. But today I would really like to make a dinner for us."

"Oh, no. Too much work for you. You relax on day off. Maybe different day." She turned away, her back punctuating her decision.

"But I very much want to do this for you . . . for us." She paused. "It would make me happy."

Catherine turned part way around, folding a dishtowel on the counter. She looked up at Marjorie. "I want you be happy. But no need cooking. I make *golumpki* tonight. You take nice bath, read book. Let baby have quiet mother."

Casper sat near the kitchen table, drumming his fingers on his lap.

Marjorie wanted to give her this gift, but she didn't want to thrust it into unwilling arms. It wasn't praise she was seeking. It was to gain the satisfaction of helping.

"I thought it would be nice to have a dinner I cooked that was Les's favorite, so you could taste what he liked at our house."

Catherine refolded the towel.

Marjorie persisted. "Kind of a celebration of getting his letters. He would like it. He's told me your *golumpkies* are his favorite. Maybe we could have them tomorrow? And I would like you to show me your special way of cutting an onion."

Marjorie noticed Casper give a slight nod.

"Maybe talk more after you take bath?" She looked at Casper. After a moment, her face cracked into a slight smile. "So, okay, we do you dinner. For Lester."

"And after dinner, we will write your letter to him." Marjorie's spirit sang a sweet tune. She would take that bath Catherine suggested now and soak in the joy of giving back to Les's parents.

*

Refreshed from her bath, Marjorie began to work in the kitchen. Catherine handed her an apron.

"Catherine, where do you keep your potato peeler?"

"What?" She squinted at Marjorie.

"Potato peeler." Marjorie gestured peeling.

Catherine opened a drawer and took out a paring knife. "Here." She handed it to Marjorie. "I say knife. Okay?"

"Yes, good. Thank you." Marjorie chuckled to herself. She felt tenderness toward Les's mother in a way she never had with her own mother.

Before Catherine could show her the special method she used to cut onions, the phone rang.

"Maybe Betty." Casper said to Marjorie. "You go."

Marjorie answered the phone, and Betty's voice boomed, "This is our lucky day! Cal has a friend who owns a liquor store and he has a place for you to park. It's just three blocks from Bamberger's, just what you wished for. Can you believe it?"

"Betty, oh my gosh! There aren't words for how thrilled I am. Oh, thank you, and thank Cal so much for me."

"You can thank him yourself tomorrow. We want to pick you up and show you the parking space, so on Monday you'll have no problems. Would twelve be okay? You can have a bite to eat with us."

"Perfect. I promised I would go to Mass with Les's folks earlier in the morning. See you then."

"I can drive the car to work on Monday," Marjorie shrieked, restraining herself from jumping up and down. She gave Catherine a big hug.

"So good. You can go later, get home early," Casper said.

"I pray for that," Catherine said. "Now cut onion!"

"Peel come off easy after cut onion in half. Cut this way." Catherine sliced the onion between the ends, sliced the very ends off, and pulled off the skin in a few deft strokes. "Now, put open side on table. Cut maybe eight times for skinny pieces. Keep place at end so hold onion together like fingers on hand." Catherine then demonstrated how to cut across the "fingers" to make diced pieces.

"That is such a good way to make diced onion, or perfect slices to put over the meat! Thank you," Marjorie said. She copied Catherine's instructions and put the onion slices on her roast.

Catherine beamed. The women continued dinner preparations. While the roast cooked, Marjorie got her rosary and prayed for this family and for tender meat.

"Taste so good," said Casper, after taking a bite of the pot roast.

"Soft. Cut with fork. I know why Lester like it," Catherine added.

Marjorie beamed, basking in the pleasure of the moment.

After dinner, Catherine and Casper dictated their thoughts and advice to Lester. "Keep your feet warm. Wear socks to sleep. Marjorie make very good meat, one you like. We eat some for you. We say Rosary you are safe."

Marjorie glowed at the thought that Les would be pleased how well she was getting along with his parents. She noticed how much Les's smile was like his father's. Casper smiled with his lips pressed together. Les had told her that in the countryside of Poland, many believed that if someone saw your teeth, and they could count them, that was how many years you had left to live. They would be living a long time, she guessed!

Casper interrupted her thoughts. "Margie, can you listen to radio and tell me what they say about war?"

"Of course, I will." Marjorie positioned her chair closer to the radio.

"Many words I can't understand. He speak very fast. BBC hard to hear." Casper had difficulty understanding other evenings, and she had helped him at those times too.

She was able to tune the radio to NBC News of the World. Marjorie explained to Casper and Catherine about the British bombing of Berlin, and the German's heavy bombing of London and other English cities. Then the announcer said that all Polish Jews living in Warsaw ghetto were prisoners in that area. Marjorie cringed. The war was getting so much worse. The fear she had buried deep within crept to the surface, clawing at her. How long would Les be safe from this war? She fought giving in to her private dread, chewed the inside of her cheeks, but said nothing.

"So bad. We have many friends, Jews. Very bad time. We are here and cannot help them," Casper said, shaking his head. He put his head in his hands.

Catherine crossed herself. "Next time you go to store, Margie, buy two big bags of sugar. In war, hard to get."

Catherine's request triggered Marjorie's fear that the chances of another war involving the United States increased with each week's news. On the news, she'd heard that Jews were crowded into the ghetto that was sealed off from the rest of the city with a high wall. They could not leave, and only had what food was given to them by the Nazis. But Marjorie didn't tell this detail to Casper. Hitler's aggression in Europe was worsening. Would Roosevelt be convinced to enter the war? Sugar was not her worry, Les was.

CHAPTER 16

SUNDAY WAS DAMP and chilly, the wind catapulting from every direction. After lunch at Betty and Cal's apartment, they hurried to Cal's car to drive to downtown Newark.

"The store manager said it was fine for you to park in his lot," Cal said. "It's really close to Bamberger's. We're lucky this manager is a good guy. I told him we'd keep an extra eye on his place." Cal slowed, turned into a liquor store and eased to an empty parking space. "This one's yours, Marge, except after five and on weekends!"

Betty laughed. "And she can stop in and have a short one on a bad day!"

"Thank you so much for bringing me to see my new parking place. I can't tell you enough how being able to drive to work will make my life so much easier! Plus, I loved having a chance to visit with you both over such a delicious lunch."

"Hey, I'm so glad it worked out. It gave us a chance to relax and hear about Les's shenanigans at boot camp," Cal said. They neared the turn-off to her street in Passaic when an ambulance passed them, its light flashing.

"Their place is down about ten houses on the right." Marjorie peered from the back seat. "Oh my gosh, the ambulance stopped near Catherine's. Maybe it's a neighbor. Oh no! It's at their house," she cried. The moment Cal slowed to a stop behind the ambulance, Marjorie scrambled out of the car and dashed to the house, just behind the doctor and his assistants. They were heading to Catherine's front door, their white uniforms and caps a blur. Marjorie's heart hammered.

Catherine stood at the door, pointing to the living room, her face distorted in panic. "He is there, I don't know. He fell and can't talk good. He can't get up. Oh please help!"

Marjorie put her arm around Catherine's shoulders and froze. Did Casper have a heart attack? He lay near the radio, his eyes open. The doctor felt Casper's pulse, listened to his heart, asked if he hurt anywhere. Casper tried to answer, but he slurred his words. She suppressed a cry, *Not him! Please, God, don't take this gentle soul. Let him live to see his son again, and his grandbaby.*

The ambulance driver asked Casper to squeeze his hand. One hand squeezed, but the other didn't. *Oh no, a stroke.* Marjorie shuddered. Her father had told her many stories of similar symptoms. Suddenly, she missed her own father, his calm approach to medical events. He would know what to expect, what to do.

The doctor's assistants lifted Casper onto a stretcher. His face was ashen, and his eyes darted back and forth. He struggled to lift himself as the men buckled a strap around him. His left side seemed lifeless.

"It's okay. This strap keeps you safe while they drive," Marjorie assured Casper. She wasn't sure how much he understood, but she had to try to comfort him. Marjorie patted his leg.

"Casper, you are going to the hospital, where they can help you get better. I'll be there with . . . Mom . . . right away. Close your eyes if you understand me."

His eyes continued to move around like a wild animal's.

Marjorie's strength dissolved. How fragile life could be. Such a narrow distance between brightness and dark. Casper always worried about his relatives and friends in Poland being struck down by the Germans. Now he had been attacked too, but by his own body.

Cal and Betty stood by Catherine at the front door as the men carried Casper outside and lifted him into the ambulance. For a moment, Marjorie thought of jumping in with him. But there stood Catherine, shaking her head, sobbing, and shivering under her shawl as the December wind whipped and tore around them. She needed Marjorie's help too. Betty stood beside Catherine, hugging her.

Catherine called out in Polish to her husband, repeating the same phrases. She suddenly quieted. "Maybe he not coming back. Hospital can kill him. Need pray now." Head bowed, she looked toward the house.

Betty caught Marjorie's arm. "I'm so sorry about your father-in-law. Is there anything we can do to help now, Marge?" Betty asked.

"Thank you. There's really nothing to do but wait. I'll call if things change."

"We could follow you and stay a while."

"Really, no. I'm going to call my dad and Les when I get there. There's really nothing to do but wait," she said, her voice cracking. "Thank you so much for offering. I'll let you know if things change."

"We'll check on you tomorrow morning then, and please, don't forget to take care of yourself too." Cal and Betty each gave Marjorie a hug.

As the ambulance drove Casper away, a slice of Marjorie left with him. He'd been a rock to her. This loss deposited itself like ice in her heart. She put her arm around the woman she called Mom, and together, in silence and in tears, they stepped back into the house.

*

St. Mary's Hospital was only a ten-minute drive from their home, but the ride seemed to take hours. She knew Casper would be frightened, so she drove as fast as she dared. She had not expected to return so soon to the same hospital where she had been a patient just weeks before, when Les had brought her there fearing for their baby. She crossed her fingers. Maybe this time, too, all would be well. She would see that Casper had the best care. She would do all she could to help him recover.

Les would be devastated to hear of his father's illness. *Should I call his emergency contact number now?* Pondering what she should do, she wavered. No, she would wait until she had more information about Casper's condition so Les would know what leave to ask for. First, she would ask her father for his advice.

A nurse told them that as soon as Casper was taken to his room, they could go see him. In the harsh light of the waiting room, Catherine sat repeating Hail Marys and Our Fathers on her rosary while Marjorie prayed Casper would live and recover.

Marjorie counted coins to see if she had enough to make a long-distance phone call to her father, anxious for his advice. His voice would be reassuring. She picked through to the bottom of her purse for every spare coin, hoping she had as much as she needed. Marjorie walked over to the desk attendant.

"I'll be at the phone booths for a few minutes, so please let me know when you are ready for us to see Casper Stoltz."

The woman nodded and went back to her paperwork, licking her fingers to separate pages.

Both phone booths were busy. Marjorie stood close, without being rude, so she would be next. She looked at the desk attendant and checked her watch every few minutes. Her father would likely be home on a Sunday afternoon. Neither person exited their phone booths. Against her sensibilities, she moved closer to the first booth. She had to reach her father before the hospital sent her upstairs so she would know what to ask the doctor, what to expect, how to help.

She dreaded the thought that her mother might answer or insist on talking. She had to prepare herself in case they pressured her to come back to Pennsylvania. She wavered. Perhaps talking to her father wasn't the best decision. Could she stand firm against their demands if they insisted that she come back? She had to—for Casper, for Catherine, for Les. She braced herself.

After a few more minutes, she waved to the caller in the first booth. The door soon opened. She apologized to the portly fellow and entered the booth, choking on his lingering cigarette smoke. She dialed 112 for long-distance, told the operator she wanted to make a call to Homer Hill in Johnstown, Pennsylvania, and gave the number. A general call would waste valuable time if her mother answered. After several routing operators forwarded the call, she finally heard her father's voice and deposited most of her coins. She exhaled a sigh of relief.

"Dad, I'm so glad you're home."

"Are you alright?"

"Yes, I'm fine. I don't have long to talk, but we think Casper probably had a stroke this afternoon." She filled him in on Casper's symptoms. "I'm at St. Mary's Hospital, waiting. What's likely to happen?"

"I'm so sorry to hear this. Much depends on the extent of the bleeding or blockage, and how much damage was done in the brain. I'm afraid it may be weeks before they can give a decent prognosis."

"Oh no. What can I do now?" Marjorie agonized.

"Marjorie, I'm concerned that this is too much of a burden for you to deal with. I hope this won't get you down . . . with your pregnancy." He hesitated, and his voice softened. "When you have his doctor's name and phone number, let me know, and as a courtesy, we can talk together about Casper's case. In the meantime, when you're talking to Casper, assume he can hear you, though he might not look—" The operator interrupted, asking for more coins than Marjorie had. The call ended abruptly.

A mix of emotions tugged at Marjorie. Talking with her father eased some of the helplessness she had felt. Though his message didn't include a miracle, she trusted him. He was a good doctor. But if Casper made it through today, it might be a long time before there were answers about his future.

*

The nurse, her stiff starched cap perched high above her red hair, beckoned to Marjorie. She said that Casper would be in room 214. They could go up now.

Marjorie guided Catherine to the elevator. The operator smiled and closed the gate. Catherine grabbed Marjorie's arm, anxious eyes peering from under her hat. Marjorie took her arm as the elevator jerked to a stop, and they walked out onto the second floor. Catherine almost hopped over the space between the elevator and the floor.

"I like to walk on steps," she said.

"Then we'll go back down the stairs later," Marjorie said as they reached room 214.

Casper's frame appeared so frail under the bed covers, as if his struggle had left him empty. He muttered something. His breathing seemed shallow.

Marjorie held his hand and spoke in reassuring tones that he would be better soon. She gently rubbed his arm and told him rest would be best now, and exercise would help later.

Catherine spoke to him in Polish, tenderly hugging and patting him, trying to soothe him as he squirmed and tossed in his bed. She adjusted his blanket, smoothed his forehead, and caressed him, her tears spilling down her face. He calmed down and spoke with Catherine in Polish. At long last, he slept.

When Catherine finally sat down in the hospital room's tiny, straight-back chair, she nodded off.

Marjorie studied Catherine, who sat with her chin resting on her chest, her hat held in her lap. She had given so much for so long. But this tough woman had her limits.

After a knock on the door, a doctor and a nurse walked into the room, the nurse keeping a few paces behind. "I'm Dr. Shields." A young man with curly brown hair wearing a crisp white coat held out his hand. As Marjorie shook his hand, the doctor added, "And this is nurse Penny."

"Hello, I'm Marjorie, their daughter-in-law." This is Casper's wife, Catherine," she gestured to Catherine in the chair and to Casper in the bed, both sleeping. "How do you think he's doing?"

The doctor frowned. "I'm afraid we don't know much at this point, which is typical of patients who've had a cerebrovascular incident. Over the next ten days of observation, we should know more. Right now, the gentleman just needs rest," the doctor said, a tone of authority in his voice and a smile on his face. "Shall we wake his wife?"

Marjorie put her hand on Catherine's shoulder and quietly called her name. She jerked awake. The doctor spoke to Catherine about her husband. She nodded, her head bobbing to the rhythm of his words. "Thank you, thank you," Catherine called to him as he left the room.

Nurse Penny stayed. She covered Casper with another blanket and closed the window blinds to preserve the room's heat. Her starched uniform showed not a wrinkle. Moving to the end of Casper's bed, she turned to Marjorie.

"You have both been here with him so long today, and he is asleep now," she said, her tone firm. "It's best for you to go on home. This will be a lengthy recovery, and family must stay fortified." She stiffened. "The doctor will be here again in the morning between eight and nine." She turned to leave, but then said in a softened tone, "We will watch him through the night. Don't worry."

Marjorie was grateful for the suggestion to leave. It was after eight and her back ached. They had been comforting Casper for quite a while. She wanted to get home and call Les, to tell him about his father while she still had a fragment of energy left. It would be too difficult to reach the training center in Illinois from the phone booth here at the hospital. Besides, she couldn't be sure of the name of the commander that Les had given her to use in an emergency since the lettering had smeared on the copy in her wallet.

Catherine stood up and placed her hand lightly on Casper's leg. "For thirty-six years we are always together at night." Catherine stifled a sob, finding a hanky in her coat pocket. Marjorie couldn't do any more for Casper now, but perhaps she could console Catherine.

Marjorie helped her mother-in-law with her coat and guided her down the steps, then out through the labyrinth of hallways. Catherine shook her head as they walked.

"I afraid of doctor. Maybe he give Casper shot like doctor give my first baby boy, before Lester. Then he die. They say maybe dirty needle." Catherine wrung her hands.

Stunned, Marjorie stopped to face Catherine, and took both of her hands in her own. "Oh, I am so sorry, how awful. But please don't worry now. That bad thing doesn't happen anymore. Believe me, everything is always sterilized . . . made very clean."

"You think okay now?"

"Yes. My father says so. He knows. He is a good doctor."

"I believe you, Margie." Catherine gave her a hug. "But I going to pray too," she added in a quiet tone. "Okay, we go now."

As Marjorie opened the door to the parking lot, a blast of winter wind whipped through the doorway. She wrapped her scarf around her head and helped Catherine pull up her coat collar as her mother-in-law hung on to her hat. They huddled together, the freezing gusts stinging their faces while their hearts ached for Casper.

As soon as they got home, Marjorie found the emergency

number and Commander Ellis's name in her jewelry box. She quickly ate the bowl of cabbage soup that Catherine placed before her, then walked over to the telephone.

Catherine pulled a chair beside Marjorie and sat down. "You talk, Margie," she said, hunched over, wrapping and unwrapping her hands in her apron. "Then I call daughter Emilie. First, I put water on for tea." Catherine stood up and hurried to the stove.

Marjorie stared at the base of the telephone. She hated to give Les this terrible news. She knew thinking of his family gave him the comfort and stability to deal with the strain and uncertainty he faced daily at the camp. Closing her eyes for a moment, she collected her thoughts. How much should she tell the commander? If she were too vague about the emergency, and Les couldn't come to the phone, he might needlessly worry about her, or the baby. Yet she wanted Les to hear about his father's stroke directly from her.

Marjorie's hand trembled as she pulled the receiver from its base. She asked the operator to make the long-distance call. When a man answered, she requested to speak to Commander Ellis, the officer in charge. He said he would find the commander.

A shroud hung in the air, thick and leaden. Marjorie glanced over at Catherine. She was striking one match after another trying to light the gas burner. Marjorie could smell the gas odor. Suddenly, in a poof and burst of flame, the burner caught. Catherine jumped back, her eyes bulging.

Marjorie leaned over and whispered hoarsely, "Are you okay?"

"Oooh, no good fire . . . but okay now. I put kettle on."

Marjorie's heart pumped almost as loudly as the static in the receiver. A man's voice finally broke the crackling.

"Commander Ellis. How may I help you?"

Marjorie cleared her throat and explained that she needed to speak to her husband because his father had to be hospitalized. She avoided mentioning his stroke. The commander told her Les was in the barracks now, but he would have Les call within the next hour.

Marjorie thanked him and replaced the receiver. She looked over at Catherine, who was staring at her with eyes wide open, eyebrows raised. Marjorie patted her arm and explained that Les should call in the next hour.

"Oh, poor Lester. No family there for bad news. So sorry for him alone." Catherine hung her head and shook it back and forth. After a few moments, her face became resolute. She began running her hands down her apron, as if to brush off her emotional outcry. "Enough," she announced, as though willing her strength to emerge. "Now," Catherine ordered, unwavering in her new tone, "come, lie down and rest, Margie." Catherine prodded her toward the sofa. "This too much for one day. I fix tea and poppy seed cake." She left to busy herself in the kitchen.

Marjorie was grateful to lie down. The day's events weighed heavily on her. She gently rubbed her tummy. Her watch said 9:20, but it seemed like midnight. She prayed she would be able to talk to Les, and that they would allow him to come home. She wanted so badly to hold him, to feel his strength.

Her thoughts drifted to her work responsibilities for tomorrow, and what to do about them. She could finally use her car to get to work, but she couldn't go. She had to go to the hospital to see Casper and work out a schedule with Catherine for visiting him. And she needed to rest. Fatigue took up residence in every fiber of her body. She would call her supervisor in the morning and ask for the day off.

Marjorie checked her watch. It had been thirty minutes. She stared at the phone, willing it to ring. It did. She grabbed it on the second ring.

"Hello, Les?"

"Hey, honey. What's happened? I just rushed to the phone. Are you okay? Is it the baby?" His anxiety flowed through the phone.

At the sound of his voice, tears welled in her eyes. She swallowed hard to regain her composure. "We're both fine. It's . . . it's your dad, Les."

"Dad? Oh, gosh. I just heard *hospital* and ran to call you. What happened?"

Marjorie spilled out her words. "Honey, he had a stroke. His left side has some paralysis. I'm so sorry. Dr. Shields said he would watch him in the hospital for ten days or so. During that time, another stroke might be possible, but many patients have only one incident. We'll pray it's just one. The paralysis could also improve with exercise, later on."

"So, he might improve, or he might not. Jeez," Les's voice cracked. "I can't believe it."

"I know. It's such a terrible shock."

"How's Mom doing?"

"Bless her heart, she's doing as well as possible. I'll give her the phone in a minute."

"So what happens after the ten days in the hospital?" Les asked.

"We don't know yet how much help he'll need to sit up or get out of bed. In the beginning, when he's home, he may need a bed that cranks to sit him up, like the hospital has."

"Yeah, but where could Mom put that? Their bedroom is too small for another bed."

Marjorie swallowed hard. Her thoughts raced. She might need to offer her room. Her dreams for the future began taking on distorted shapes. Marjorie shook her head to try to stop runaway thoughts and dug her nails into her palms. "We just don't know anything yet. We have to hope and pray that he will improve."

"Yes, of course," Les said. "I want to talk to him."

"Honey, do you think you can come home?"

"I'll sure try. I'll ask the commander." He paused. "One of the guys had his boot camp graduation delayed because he took time off for a funeral." Les lowered his voice. "Then he missed his scheduled entry into Officer Candidate School."

"Oh no!"

"Marge, I'm going to do everything I can to come home. I'll let you know what Ellis says tomorrow night. I'll try to call around the same time." His voice cracked. "Please tell Dad I'm praying for him to get better. I love you and can't wait to see you."

"I love you and miss you. I'll be here waiting." She hoped he couldn't hear the tremor in her voice. The tension that had held her back so stiff eased, and she slumped down. She must not crumble. "Your mom wants to talk to you." She handed the receiver to Catherine, who grasped it with both hands.

"Lester, Lester," Catherine cried, and she began speaking in Polish between her sobs, gesturing with her free hand. After a few minutes, Catherine hung up and stared at the phone.

Catherine's grief for Casper resonated deep in Marjorie's own heart. Marjorie hugged her. "Let's sit and have our tea now," Marjorie said.

Catherine walked to the stove, wiping her eyes. "Yes, we have nice hot tea now."

"I will call my supervisor in the morning and explain what happened so we can both go to the hospital tomorrow."

"Thank you. Thank you. So sad for Casper."

After sipping their tea, Marjorie guided Catherine to her bedroom.

"You go to bed too, Margie." She stood in the doorway for a moment looking at her bedroom, twisting her hands. Their bed would only hold one tonight. Her strength had buckled.

Marjorie went to her room and sat on her bed. How long would she have this room? This family? She sat down on her bed and put her head in her hands. Today, she had done all she could. Tomorrow, she'd figure out what she could do to preserve her place in this home.

CHAPTER 17

"Try to push my hand a little more," Marjorie urged Casper, as she had every day when she visited him in the hospital after work. Marjorie propped her arm against the hospital bed rail to provide resistance to Casper's effort. Her mind willed his arm to push back. If he could use it to help himself sit up and eat, he might not need a nurse's bed. If he could sleep in a regular bed with Catherine, Marjorie could stay in her room. That arm was his independence and her salvation.

Casper tried to push against her hand, but he had little control. "This one is sleeping. He won't wake up," Casper said, slurring his words. He grabbed his left arm with his good right hand and shook it as if to awaken it.

"We'll keep working those muscles. They will get stronger," Marjorie smiled. Every time she said things would get better, voices inside her head argued, "Mercy no, they will not." But she wouldn't give in to those voices. They were dark. She would fight them with every ounce of her being and she would not give up exercising Casper's arm.

Marjorie wondered how Les would react when he saw his father's paralysis. It would be a shock. But Casper's mind was sound, and Les would find that to be a consolation. She could hardly wait until seven to pick him up at the train station. Thinking of Les and their baby gave her comfort as she thought of the three of them cuddling together, faces bright with love.

Tomorrow, she and Les would have their only full day together since travel would take up two of his three days of leave. Commander Ellis had told him he needed to stay first in his class if he wanted to have a choice in his assignment as an officer. To remain first meant taking only a short leave this weekend. Keeping his leave brief would help his chances of being stationed nearby when the baby was born.

Marjorie lifted Casper's hand up to his shoulder and back, hoping to increase the blood flow and strengthen his arm muscles. "Les will come and visit tomorrow. Let's show him how you can push that arm," she said, encouraging him with a big grin.

Casper pushed until his face glowed red.

"That's good," Marjorie praised, realizing there was little change in his strength. Maybe tomorrow would be better. Recovery takes time, her dad always said.

"Catherine is cooking all day for Les, an early Christmas dinner. So we'll bring something special for you tomorrow!"

"Les is special." Casper grinned a crooked smile. "Bring him. Margie, thank you. I practice with arm for you, later by myself."

Marjorie hugged Casper, feeling a love like she had for her father, yet a compassion even deeper. She was counting on this gentle soul to rebound, to improve.

*

Marjorie walked into the grand hall of Newark's Penn Station thirty minutes before Les was due to arrive and searched the arrivals board to find the track number where his train would pull in. She passed rows of wooden seats where passengers sat, some reading, others sleeping. Perhaps some folks came just to rest in a warm place away from the frigid cold outside.

She made her way downstairs and waited by the dimly lit

tracks, hoping Les made this train. A moment after the arrival time, a bright light appeared at the end of the building and the train roared into the station, brakes squealing. It coughed a cloud of steam and screeched to a stop. A woman and her child stepped down from the first passenger car, followed by two men dressed in suits, whose ties were visible at the top of their overcoats. Then, two smartly dressed women bundled in furs stepped off. No one else followed. Had Les made it? A moment later, her heart quickened when she saw Les smiling as he helped an older lady down the steps with her case. When he finally reached Marjorie, he dropped his bag and engulfed her with his eager arms.

"You are a sight for sore eyes."

"And look at you in your uniform! Sharp and handsome!"

They stared at each other, kissed, then walked arm in arm up the platform steps and through the spacious station.

"Y'know, I've imagined seeing your handsome face so many times. I even walked up to a man wearing a hat like yours in the grocery store and peered around to see his face, so sure it was you. Embarrassing! I forgot you no longer had much hair!"

"I look at your smiling face every night, honey. You're the last thing I see before I sleep, and the first when I wake up. But I sure do like you better in the flesh," Les said, giving her a squeeze.

They reached the parking lot, breathing out puffs of frosty air, and Marjorie started moving toward the driver's side of the car.

"Whoa there, honey, I may have had orders drilled into me, and crawled through mud holes, but I haven't forgotten how to drive."

She laughed, feeling almost lightheaded being with him. "Or how to hug or kiss. I'm so glad you're home, even for just a day." Marjorie's spirit soared like a bird catching an updraft, a momentary bliss.

She slid into the front seat, thrilled to be a passenger again.

"Hey, you are lucky. Your mom has been preparing a feast for you, an early Christmas dinner."

"That's Mom. Has she talked to Emilie?"

"Yes, but I don't know if she's coming, what with her job and all. Today is the first day your mom didn't come to the hospital. She wanted to cook for you. I usually take her up to be with your dad in the mornings before I go to work. Then, Mrs. Nelson brings her home after lunch, most days. A few times she was there all day." Marjorie put her head on Les's shoulder and brushed her lips on his coat, inhaling his scent and soaking in his strength.

"She's one determined woman," Les smiled.

Marjorie felt Les's shoulder muscles tighten.

"So, how does Dad seem?"

"He's very alert, but seems to tire easily, so he naps a lot. His left side is still quite paralyzed. I visited every day this week after work, helping him strengthen his arm."

"It's been a heck of a long week worrying about him. Can we go see him first thing in the morning?"

"Yes, of course. He's so excited you're coming."

Les took a deep breath. "Did the doctor say how much longer he'll stay in the hospital?"

Marjorie squirmed in her seat. Wanting to preserve the bit of quiet intimacy and togetherness a little longer, she had hoped to avoid discussing the dilemma of Casper coming home until they'd had a chance to relax at dinner.

She bit her lip. "They plan to release him in about ten more days. The doctor says exercising at home may help him improve. I'm happy to keep helping him do that. He's so sweet."

Les patted Marjorie's leg. "Thanks, honey, for helping him. I know this is going to be tough on everyone. Do you think Mom can care for him at home? I know they can't afford a nurse." Les stopped the car in front of the house, but let the engine run to keep the heater going.

"She can do the bedpan, and she can pull him up when he scoots down too far in the bed. She insists she can manage, but so much depends on how much stronger he can become. You'll have a better sense of things tomorrow," Marjorie said, giving him a kiss on the cheek.

Les turned the car off and stared out the window. "What a predicament."

"C'mon, honey, lets enjoy the wonderful dinner your mom has made for you."

Taking her face in his warm hands, Les leaned over and kissed her. He always had warm hands.

*

The next morning while they visited Casper, Marjorie mused about how little time she and Les had alone. Though Catherine had insisted that she and Les sleep in her bed during Les's visit, their intimate time together was short. Marjorie wanted his body against hers for much longer, but at least they were together for most of one day. When would the next day be?

In the hospital, Marjorie watched as the furrows deepened in Les's brow while he visited with his dad. Casper's face shone as he talked with Les. Now, while Catherine fed Casper his favorite stuffed cabbage, cut into small pieces so he wouldn't choke, Marjorie and Les took advantage of the opportunity to leave his room so they could talk.

They sat huddled together in a corner of the hospital waiting room. Les told her that he didn't expect her to come to his boot camp graduation. He was admitted to OCS training that would begin just two days after graduation, so he would go directly to Rhode Island. This plan would allow him to get his commission as soon as possible. Marjorie agreed that not taking some leave time now so they could be together when the baby was born would be the best plan.

Les clasped his hands together. "Mom keeps insisting that she can have Dad sleep in their bed when he comes home." Les shook his head. "That just won't work. He needs a narrow bed so she can stand on either side to reach him, help change his clothes, reach from behind and pull him up. Luckily, he's not a heavy man."

"I think you're right about a narrow bed," Marjorie sighed.

"A special bed would be best if it's possible to get one. One that has rails so he can't roll out, and a crank to sit him up. He doesn't have the strength to help himself sit up yet."

"Well, there's no room for that kind of bed except in the living room." She paused. "Or my room, of course," Marjorie said in a low voice, looking down at her feet.

Les grimaced, his hand searching for the missing hair on his head.

"He couldn't really nap in the living room with your mom bustling in the kitchen so close by, and the radio on." Life for Marjorie was shrinking into something small and hard. She pulled a thought from her frantic search for a solution. "But, if he had my room, I could sleep on the couch. It's comfortable." She smiled at Les.

He frowned. "Oh, honey, you're five months pregnant. Sleeping on an old couch in the living room sounds really crummy. Mom gets up so early you'd be woken up on the weekend with her banging around in the kitchen. Not sleeping well and having to go to work every morning, well, it's not a good arrangement."

"It would just be for the time being, until your dad improves," Marjorie insisted. The doors to her plans were closing fast. She had to prop them open. "I could keep my clothes in the little sewing room and change there so I'd have privacy. I could help your dad exercise and help your mom when I got home from work. I'm sure your dad will be better in a month," Marjorie urged.

They sat in silence. Les fidgeted, then took her hands. "I hate to suggest this, Marge, but I think it might be good for you to visit your folks for a little while. I'm afraid your job and Dad's illness combined are just too much. I want you and our baby in a comfortable place where you can get decent rest." He squeezed her hands. "It might mean asking for some time off from work. Your boss likes you and will probably agree."

Marjorie clenched her teeth. She would not go home. She would not be stuck there with her mother's eyes and ears in every corner. She knew Les wanted what was best for her, but this was not it. She made a decision. She wouldn't argue. Not now. She forced a calm response, not wanting to reject his idea outright or cause him more worry before he returned to boot camp.

"Sure, that's a possibility, Les," she said. "Let's see how things go after your dad is settled at home. We'll figure out the best thing."

"This is a damned-if-you-do and damned-if-you-don't situation. Promise me you will consider going home, just for a month. You could take the train directly to Johnstown. Mom will be okay. After all, Mrs. Nelson has been such a great neighbor, and Mom says she's offered to come over every day. I know Dad loves to be with you, but—"

Marjorie interrupted. "He tries hard to exercise for me, to please me. I'm afraid he won't keep working at it if I'm not there encouraging him." Her voice rose and she caught herself. She stopped, then hugged him. "Yes, I'll consider asking for time off from work and going home for a bit. Please don't worry."

They walked hand in hand back to Casper's room. But Marjorie swore to herself she wouldn't go home to her mother.

*

The following morning after lingering hugs and kisses, Les boarded the train at the Newark station. The ache in her chest intensified as she watched the wheels of his train turn slowly at first, then gain speed until there was just the silhouette of the caboose framed by the light outside the station. She held onto a post near the tracks, watching as the train took a curve and vanished. Les was gone.

CHAPTER 18

MARJORIE AWOKE TO the tinkle of a bell. Ringing the bell was Casper's signal that he needed assistance. The clock on the coffee table registered 5:12 a.m. It had been three weeks since Casper had come home. Christmas had come and gone with quiet celebrations focused on prayers and hopes for the new year.

Muffled voices told her that Catherine was in Marjorie's old room helping Casper. She adjusted her pillows to cover her ears. *Please let me sleep a little more.* This seemed to have become a recurring wish. At 5:45 she had to get ready for work. She pressed her back against the sofa cushion, tucking her legs up as she lay on her side. She could still hear their hushed voices.

Since Casper had come home from the hospital, Marjorie was awakened two or three times a night. She heard him trying to clear his throat, or choking on a sip of water, or ringing the bell for the bedpan. She felt such sorrow for him being so dependent.

Sometimes she lay awake for an hour before being able to get back to sleep. Catherine almost always tended to Casper's needs when he rang the bell. But sometimes, in her own exhaustion, Catherine didn't hear it, so Marjorie would get up to help him. She might prop a pillow behind his back, refill his water, or pick up the tissue box that had fallen. If he needed the bedpan, he'd ask her to wake Catherine.

When Casper first came home, Catherine had offered Marjorie the double bed she and Casper had used, insisting it was better that *she* sleep on the sofa in the living room so she'd be closer to the kitchen. But Marjorie wouldn't hear of it. After all, Catherine was the main caretaker, so she needed her rest. Catherine had more than a full-time job of managing Casper's needs, as well as handling all of the washing, ironing, house cleaning, and most of the cooking.

Then Catherine suggested they share her double bed. Marjorie was reluctant but agreed to give it a try. After several nights of being kept awake by Catherine's snoring, Marjorie told Catherine she'd be more comfortable on the sofa, using the excuse that Catherine could move around during the night more freely and not worry about disturbing her bed partner. Marjorie had been sleeping on the sofa for over two weeks now.

She turned to lie flat on her back, then soon twisted to lie on her side again, adjusting her pillow. Something had to change. So tired from lack of sleep, she found it was almost impossible to keep up with her job and still help Casper and Catherine in the evenings. Marjorie had tried very hard to make it work so she could stay with the family she had grown to love. But in spite of her diligent efforts to help him strengthen his left side, Casper's condition was almost the same as it had been in the hospital.

She could hardly stay awake at work in the afternoons, struggling to meet the deadlines for the weekly personnel scheduling, billing, and timesheets that now seemed to take her twice as long. Her supervisor, Mrs. Dowling, had always been supportive, but lately Marjorie detected tones of impatience. The other day, Mrs. Dowling had even expressed concerns.

"Are you all right, Marjorie? You've seemed very tired lately, and you've not shown your usual spirit."

Maybe she had reached the limit of trying to stay with Casper and Catherine. Marjorie's thoughts raced. Maybe she should ask her supervisor if it were possible to work part-time. After all, she had saved $105 from her pay, so the essentials for the baby were covered. She had enough for a crib, blankets and sheets, and newborn items, as well as a winter maternity outfit for herself, with a little left over. Les's pay had come in, which covered gas, food purchases for the family, doctor visits, and a little for savings.

Marjorie jumped when the alarm went off. It was 5:45 already. She sat up, her head swimming.

"Do you want tea or coffee, Margie?" Catherine asked, stopping near the sofa on her way to the kitchen while Marjorie folded her bedding. "Coffee sounds good this morning, thanks. It will help me stay awake better than tea! Is Casper awake?"

"Ya. He waits for cream of wheat. It goes down easy."

Marjorie padded into the room that was now his, her first stop every day before getting ready for work. Most of her clothes were still in that closet. "Good morning, Mr. Sunshine." Marjorie smiled at Casper, whose rumpled fringe of white hair stuck out in all directions, circling his baldness above.

"Good morning, my lady nurse. I hope you sleep good." He reached his good arm into the air. "Today, I am like soldier shot in war. No good anymore. But I have no honor here." He patted his heart. "I didn't fight for save my family or friends in Poland to finish like this."

A pang of sympathy tore into her heart for this kind, selfless man. Marjorie bent over his bed and put her head on his chest, hugging him. "You are my hero," she said. "You are my man of honor and courage."

He smiled. "You are good nurse."

She hugged him again. "You are always my hero."

As she walked out of his room, one thing had become clear. She would talk with her supervisor about working part-time. She could be more helpful to Catherine and Casper. It might even allow her to nap when Casper took his.

*

It was almost time for her appointment with her supervisor. Marjorie combed her dark waves in the mirror of the women's bathroom at Bamberger's. She had washed her hair the night before to look fresh for today. The rouge she had rubbed on her cheeks this morning was still visible, giving her the appearance of being more vibrant than she felt. She wanted to present herself positively, from a position of strength, even in the smallest of ways.

She trembled with a sense of impending loss. Besides needing the income, this job made her feel like she was contributing to a larger world. When she was at work, she felt like a smart, competent woman, not the cowering little girl her mother saw.

A change to half-time work was the only reasonable solution, even though asking for reduced hours might mean losing her job altogether. Marjorie hoped Mrs. Dowling would be flexible, at least until Les became an officer, which would bring an increase in pay.

It was time to go. Marjorie smoothed her dress, took a long slow breath, and walked into Mrs. Dowling's office.

"Marjorie, come in," Mrs. Dowling gestured to a chair, "and please have a seat."

Marjorie sat erect on the front half of her chair. She was determined to present a confident, polite figure—no slouching, no crossed legs.

Mrs. Dowling stacked a few papers on her desk, then looked directly at her with a smile. "How may I help you?"

"Thank you for seeing me. You have already helped me so much by giving me this position after my husband was called to military service, and even after I told you about my pregnancy. I want you to know how very much I appreciate that, and how I have loved every part of my work here."

"And I have enjoyed having you as a conscientious employee. Also, your colleagues have always spoken so well of you."

Hope rose. "That means a lot to me." Marjorie shared a smile and paused. "But now my life has changed once again. As you know, my father-in-law, with whom I live, had a stroke a little over a month ago. It left him paralyzed on one side. I have been helping him and my mother-in-law on the weekends and evenings as best as I can, but I have reached a point where it's become very difficult. I feel I need to be able to help them more during the day."

"I'm really sorry to hear that he hasn't improved."

"Thank you. I've given a lot of thought to this request, but I would like to ask you to consider changing my work schedule." Marjorie floundered, barely able to formulate the words. "If I could reduce my hours to work half-time, I believe it would work well for me to be more available at home, and I could focus my energies on the most critical of my duties while I'm here."

Mrs. Dowling leaned back in her chair and uttered a sigh. "Oh, I was afraid you would ask for a leave of absence, which I couldn't do because we need the personnel scheduling to continue. It would be very difficult for me to add these tasks to my duties. Half-time. Well, Marjorie, that is how you began with us in hats on the first floor. Let me think a moment about what we need to do," she said, resting her chin on her hand. "I want to help you, of course."

Marjorie's head began to throb. She willed a positive answer. A few minutes passed. A noose was tightening around her neck. She watched Mrs. Dowling's every expression, how her lips pursed, her brow wrinkled, then she tapped her pencil on her desk. Tap tap. *Should I say something more?* Marjorie ventured a comment. "Half-time would be a true help to me and, if I may make a suggestion, I could continue the scheduling and time sheets, as those seem to be the most urgent on a daily basis."

"Yes, you're right, those are most important." Mrs. Dowling leaned forward in her chair. "The problem is that since you'd only be able to work here another month or so, because of your pregnancy, I would need to find someone to replace you soon anyway."

Panic stabbed at her chest. Marjorie had thought she would have another eight weeks to build more savings. Her eyes darted around the room, searching for words hiding behind the chair. "I . . . I . . . didn't realize . . . I only had another month," she uttered.

"Marjorie, I'm afraid that the manager has gotten stricter about employees revealing more advanced stages of pregnancy. I had been planning to discuss this with you very soon. But if you feel like you can't work full-time for another month, could you at least work full-time for another two weeks? During that time, you would train a current employee to be your replacement. Then you could focus on employee scheduling and time sheets, plus employee training."

Oh, no, I'm losing my job early. How can I possibly work full-time for two more weeks? Marjorie's heart raced. Stunned by this news, she could barely think straight. Marjorie stammered, "Would working half-time for the next four weeks be possible if I could do the scheduling and time sheets, plus train my replacement? That would be the same amount of time on the job as two weeks full-time."

Mrs. Dowling shook her head. "I'm afraid not, because we have to offer the replacement a full-time position. If you were here just half-time, she wouldn't have work to do the other half of the day."

Marjorie sunk in her chair. Suffocation was making itself at home in her chest. "Oh my."

Mrs. Dowling rubbed her brow. "Well, would it help if you worked half days next two weeks, just doing your scheduling duties, then finish your last two weeks full-time? That would give me over a week to find your replacement, and you could spend a bit more time with your folks."

Marjorie felt numb. She choked out, "Thank you. That should be fine." She heard her own words but wondered where they came from.

CHAPTER 19

MARJORIE HAD BEEN sure that part-time work would be the salve she needed for her constant fatigue. But she was wrong. Though she only had to work half-time the week before, the nightly interruptions continued.

She knew Catherine was trying to be quiet at night as she ministered to her husband in the nearby bedroom, whispering to him. But because of his impaired hearing, Catherine had to repeat her words louder and louder. She tried to creep through the living room where Marjorie slept as she moved from the kitchen to Casper's room, but she couldn't soften the brightness of the light in the nearby kitchen when she warmed milk for Casper or cut some bread. A cup would clatter, the icebox latch would snap, and Catherine would whisper, "Tsk-tsk, sorry Margie."

Marjorie's attempts to nap on her time off were nearly futile because of the noise of daily tasks that continued around her—preparing meals, washing dishes, and doing laundry. The day before, Catherine had offered her own bed for Marjorie's nap. She would take her up on her offer today after work.

As she drove to work downtown, she replayed the conversation she'd had with her mother, who had called two days before. For once, Marjorie had been home to answer the phone. Catherine was spared the discomfort of covering for her absence.

Catherine had agreed that if Sara called when Marjorie was working, Catherine would say "Sorry, Marjorie not here right now." As
far as her mother knew, Marjorie had stopped working long ago.

"You are six months along and still able to travel," her mother
had announced. "But you shouldn't wait much longer, Marjorie.
Traveling after this is a risk, to you and to the baby. The worst of
winter is almost here, and you know the roads get icy and the snow
builds up here in Southmont."

"I'm sure you are right, Mother, but I'm really needed here
to help with Casper. There is so much to do. I must be here for a
while anyhow. It's a critical time for them."

"Well, you've made your bed, so I guess you have to sleep
in it!"

Her mother resorted to this expression whenever Marjorie
did not follow her advice or when she challenged her mother's
idea. Little did her mother know the irony of her homily. Marjorie
wished she had a bed to sleep in.

She parked the car in the space that Cal had found for her
behind the liquor store and navigated through the sidewalk slush
to the store. She forced a bright smile for her colleagues and
walked to her office.

The time sheets on Marjorie's desk mocked her with their missing calculations. She shuffled the schedules. *Put pencil to paper. Put
pencil to paper.* It didn't help. She stared at the names but couldn't
concentrate. Fog clouded her brain. This was work she had so
enjoyed, but now it had lost its joy, its importance.

Marjorie forced herself to look at the work schedules again.
She stared at the calendar on her office wall until it blurred, then sat
peering through the spaces between her fingers, her hand pressed
to her face. Her mind wandered. Going home might sound easy
to others, but having every move controlled by her mother—what
to wear, what to eat, how to fix her hair—*no.* She couldn't do it.

A deep loneliness crept through her, a heaviness settling in her chest. She had no answers. But imagination grows in the loneliness of the soul, and now it sparked an idea that surfaced through her fog. She picked up the phone and dialed Betty's work number. The sound of her friend's voice pulled tears from Marjorie's eyes.

"Betty," she said hoarsely, "I know it's last minute, but could we possibly get together for a little while after work today or tomorrow? I have something I want to talk to you about . . . in private, if we can."

"Has something happened with Les?" She sounded anxious.

"No, Les is fine. I just got a letter from him yesterday. He said OCS is better than basic! I want to talk to you about work."

"Tomorrow is fine. Sure! Can't wait to see you, hon. How about we meet at the diner on Oakland Street for coffee or tea at 5:30?"

Marjorie released a powerful sigh. "Oh, I'm so glad you are free. Yes, the diner would be good. At 5:30."

A weight had lifted. She wasn't alone.

*

By the time she reached the diner from her parking spot just after five-thirty, her coat was dotted with snowflakes. She brushed herself off and pulled open the restaurant door. Scanning the room, she saw Betty waiting in a booth.

Marjorie took her coat off and hung it beside the others. Betty stood up and greeted her with a huge, welcoming grin. They hugged.

"I'm so glad you could meet me."

"Sure, Marge, what's up?"

Marjorie cleared her throat and slid into the booth across from Betty. "I want to tell you about my darn predicament. It seems like I only visit with you when I've got problems."

"I'm always glad to see you, no matter what. I ordered us tea and some pound cake. Is that okay? His majesty expects dinner served tonight."

"Yes, that's fine, thanks."

"So, tell me what's going on?"

"I'm trying to figure out what to do, Betty," she murmured, twisting her napkin into a linen rope.

Marjorie explained her situation at Les's folks, her sleeping on the sofa, unable to function at work due to loss of sleep, and her supervisor telling her she had to quit working in a few weeks.

"I haven't written to Les about this yet. I didn't want to distract him from the demands of OCS training. He has been urging me to go home to my parents for a while, but I was waiting until we saw how his dad improved. But I just can't go back." Marjorie paused. "I'm afraid I'll be stuck there."

Betty looked at her, wide-eyed. "Stuck?"

Marjorie hesitated, and blew out a sigh. "Truthfully, getting married was kind of like escaping a prison whose warden watched over and judged my every move." She wrapped her arms protectively around herself. "Ugh. I feel guilty saying that."

"Jeez."

"I haven't told you a lot about my mother. It's hard for me to talk to anyone about it, but now I think I should, so you can understand my situation." Marjorie took a deep breath. "For example, when I was little, if I had a nightmare, I would go to our housekeeper, Lonie, in the middle of the night for comfort, not to Mother. Lonie would take me into her warm bed and snuggle me until I fell asleep. I always felt calm and safe with her." Marjorie looked off in the distance. "When I was about four and threw up all over my good dress. Mother was annoyed, but Lonie scooped me up and told me it was okay over and over. She rubbed my back and washed me."

"Well, y'know, they say you can't go home, but I don't think they mean it the way you describe it."

Marjorie shook her head. "Everything had to be Mother's way. The dresses I wore, parties I could attend, the college I went to, not wanting Les's parents at our wedding. She even wanted to pick the kind of vacuum cleaner Les and I should have. I could go on for days." She paused and squeezed some lemon into her teacup. She looked up, her lips forming a frown.

Betty had been gazing at her, brow wrinkled.

"Anyway, I can't risk going home for a month and then being pressured into staying for the baby's birth. That's what would happen. I want to be near here, where Les can easily come to be with us when he has his commission." Marjorie shrugged. "So, I thought you might help me come up with a magical idea."

"Golly, Marge, I sure wish I could wave a wand. I also wish we had a second bedroom. I'd love to have you with us, even to get through the next few weeks of work. Our darn sofa isn't long enough to sleep on. Do you have to finish these next weeks?"

"I'm supposed to train my replacement. I feel I owe my supervisor that. Plus, I really need the money. I need to stash away as much as I can for any emergency that might come up." Marjorie slumped in her seat. "I can't afford a hotel."

Betty frowned. "This is not a good situation, Marge. You're really in a tough place right now." Betty shook her head and drummed her nails on the table. She hesitated. "Marge, you're my dear friend, and I want what will make you happy."

"Thank you. But I have a feeling you're going to say more."

Betty brushed her hair back from her face and hesitated. "As your friend, I have to tell you honestly what I believe." Betty took a deep breath and sighed. "I know you feel an obligation to finish your job and you want to stay to help care for Casper. But your health, and your baby's health, come first." Betty moved forward on her seat. "I think you should quit your job and go home for a while. Let your parents take care of you. Rest and get ready for your baby."

Marjorie stared at her friend in disbelief.

"Can't you tolerate your mother for a few months?"

Marjorie had hoped Betty would have some clever solution. She bit her tongue. A voice in her head said, *No, don't go back there. You'll crumble. Betty just doesn't understand. She couldn't know what it was like to be a pawn under her mother's thumb, powerless.*

Marjorie collected herself and forced a smile. "Betty, you're probably right," she fibbed. "I just have to get used to this idea."

Betty reached across the table to touch Marjorie's hand. "I sure wish I could help you with a solution you'd *rather* have. I hope you're not mad at me for not coming up with some ingenious idea."

Marjorie clasped Betty's hand between hers. "Betty, of course not! You'll always be my dear friend. I'm afraid there's no miracle solution, or perfect answer here. Not even in the tea leaves."

Betty sipped her tea and nibbled her pound cake while Marjorie continued to dunk her tea bag in her cup over and over. They sat for a while sharing fond memories.

As they left the diner together enduring the sting of a raw January wind, Marjorie's feet felt too heavy to lift. The knot in her chest gave way to a determination to keep charge of her life. She would not go home.

Marjorie reached her car. The windshield glistened from the ice that had begun to form a crusty layer. She pulled down her coat sleeve and wiped the driver's side with it, her warm gloves left at home. Once inside, she turned the key and pressed the gas, forgetting to pull the choke. The carburetor was flooded. She rubbed her arms and put her fingers inside her collar to warm them while she waited to try to start the engine again. She huddled in the car, trying to think of a plan. She would get a nap in Catherine's bed next weekend, then take one day at a time.

After ten long minutes in the freezing car, she tried the engine again, praying for success. It whined to a start. She drove home hunched over the wheel, her foot gently tapping the brake so she wouldn't skid on the thick layer of snow that was already piling up on the road.

*

"Hallo Margie," Catherine called as Marjorie opened the front door.

Welcoming heat and the delicious smell of cooking greeted her. Marjorie realized she was starving. In the kitchen, Catherine was bent over a frying pan, sautéing *pierogi* in butter and onions.

"Oh, my, the *pierogi* look so good. After I visit with Casper a bit, I'll set the table," Marjorie said. She loved being with this family.

Catherine put the wooden spoon down and looked at Marjorie, her brow wrinkled. "I afraid you drive in snow. Danger of cars and ice." Catherine shook her head.

Marjorie took off her coat, pulled off her boots, and eased down on a kitchen chair with a groan, rubbing her fingers.

"Oh, Margie, your mother call two times. I say what you tell me, but I hear she not happy. Maybe you call her?"

Marjorie couldn't bear to talk to her mother again. Not today. She nibbled on a fresh slice of bread. "Thank you. I'll have to call her soon."

Marjorie got up, hung her coat in the closet, and placed her boots on some newspapers to dry. She went into the bathroom to wash her hands and glanced at herself in the mirror. Her nose was red from the cold and her hair windblown into tufts. Suddenly, she felt a rumble in her tummy, a sensation she hadn't felt before. She had felt something similar the other day but had thought it was a gas bubble. There! She felt it again, stronger. And again! It must be the baby moving!

She hurried into Casper's room, excited to tell him. "Hello, my hero," she said as he lay propped up on a pillow. He was rubbing his bad arm.

He was turned toward her. "How are you, my dear nurse?"

"I'm fine. How are you?"

"I have much time for thinking." He kept rubbing his arm. "Sometimes feeling sad. When I think of baby, my heart is so happy. Baby doesn't know sickness, war, bad feelings. Here is chance baby can make world better. New eyes and kind heart. Heal bad things we know happen. Start again fresh. Baby can do that."

Marjorie melted. "That is so sweet. I'm glad you feel good thinking about the baby." She patted his shoulder. "I have some news for you. You are the first to know."

Casper smiled. "Tell me quick."

Marjorie leaned close to him. "I just felt the baby moving. I think he wants to talk to you."

"Good! Good. I tell him he has nice mother and father. He will be fine boy, or gal." He laughed. "Maybe he is good-looking, like Mama."

"And strong, like his Daddy." Marjorie pumped her muscles and chuckled. Then she heard Catherine calling her. It was time to eat.

Marjorie hurried into the kitchen to share her news with Catherine, who insisted they have a toast to the baby. She poured some clear liquid from a special bottle into a juice container and shook it, then poured a small amount into two glasses. They touched their glasses. "May baby smile be bigger than baby feet. *Na zdrowie*—meaning blessings! Now we do again with Dad, then dinner." Marjorie clung to this moment of joy.

After dinner, Catherine suggested Marjorie go lie down. She dragged herself over to the sofa, exhausted. She still had to tackle the phone call to her mother, but first she would rest for half an hour. Betty's advice replayed in her mind.

*

"Margie, sorry. Are you going to call Mother?" Catherine was bending over her.

Marjorie looked at her watch. She had slept an hour. It was almost eight o'clock. Her parents would be finishing the evening paper, so it wasn't too late to call. She didn't want Catherine to think she was a bad daughter. Perhaps she would tell her parents the news of the baby moving.

Marjorie sat by the telephone table. Her mother answered, as usual.

"How is it that you're hardly home? I can barely understand Catherine since her accent is so strong." She paused, and added in an accusatory tone, "Are you still doing work at that store?"

Marjorie considered lying, but she had hidden the truth long enough. "They asked me if I would train some of the new hires to work with the customers. I'll be done in two weeks."

"I can't believe, with you being pregnant, that they would want you there. I've never seen a woman who was showing in our department store."

"I'm upstairs in my office, not with customers. I was promoted."

"I never thought a daughter of mine would be working, especially not when she was pregnant. How are you feeling? Exhausted, I imagine."

How right you are, Mother. "I'm doing fine. Tired at the end of the day. How are you and Dad?"

"We're fine. I had the sniffles, but I'm over it now. Dad gave me some cough syrup. Have you thought more about coming home? You know your dad and I still think that would be best. If you can work, you surely could manage a train ride!"

Marjorie kept her tone soft in spite of her mother's comment. "It's a hard decision, Mother. But I'm helping Catherine with Casper, grocery shopping, and staying with him when she goes on errands. He really counts on me."

"You are wearing yourself out."

"You know I want to be here when Les gets his commission. He's doing really well, first in his class, and he hopes to apply for his choice of assignment."

Her mother peppered Marjorie with more questions about what would happen when Les completed his training. Marjorie was explaining, making excuses, and presenting a rosy picture of what in reality was gray and uncertain. She guessed she wouldn't tell about the baby moving.

"You can't count on anything with the military. They dragged your dad all over Europe during the war. Anyway, Marjorie, I hope you'll reconsider. You could be home here, with us caring for you until the baby is born, then make your move to wherever Les is stationed." Silence hung thick in the air. "We miss you."

For a nostalgic moment, Marjorie missed her home, the comfort of her own room, even her mother's cooking. But the moment quickly passed. She knew that on the other side of home she would be a puppet, dangling from the strings her mother pulled.

"I miss you both too. I'll call soon." Marjorie hung up the receiver, weary from the charade. She wrapped her arms around her belly to hold herself together. She staggered to the sofa, arranged her sheets and blanket, and lay down, too tired to think.

A few moments later, the telephone rang. "Hallo, Emilie," Catherine answered, her voice rising. Marjorie knew Emilie was anxious to visit her father. Catherine spoke back and forth between Polish and English. "You finish job? No more working there? You sleep with me . . . I know, snoring. No, Marjorie sleep on sofa. I know, but she—" Catherine finished her conversation in Polish as she padded into the kitchen.

Marjorie sat up, her heart pounding, the air thick with this new dilemma. When Catherine hung up the phone, Marjorie asked, "Catherine, when is Emilie coming?"

"She finish her nurse job in California now. Coming soon, maybe next week. Maybe find new job here."

Marjorie reeled. Emilie was coming to be with her father and to help. Marjorie knew how hard it was to sleep with Catherine's snoring. Emilie needed the sofa. Waves of distress battered every fiber of Marjorie's being. There was no longer a choice about what she could do. She would have to leave to make room for their daughter, a real nurse who was coming to care for Casper. She went limp. She had nowhere else to go but home.

CHAPTER 20

MARJORIE CALLED HER parents the next morning after hearing that Emilie was coming home to help. She smothered a sob that escaped from that tight place below her throat and choked out that it was best for her to come home. She reflected on how hard she'd worked to prevent this, but she knew the failure wasn't hers. It was life. Sometimes it provided joy, other times a grueling challenge. Maybe planning for the future only worked well in the scope of one day, or perhaps an hour, before new challenges arose unexpectedly from the depths and knocked hard on your door.

"I'm glad you came to your senses. It will be nice to have you home," her mother said.

"I will come to pick you up next Sunday after lunchtime," her father said. Marjorie knew he would arrange his schedule to come for her as soon as he could. When she said she wanted to drive her car, he would have none of that. "It is not a good idea for a woman, a pregnant one at that, to be driving on the turnpike with all those trucks through the mountains hundreds of miles alone in the winter!"

He was right. But she would miss the independence her car provided. Hearing her father's voice made her anxious to see him—a safe mooring in an unpredictable sea. During the drive with him, she would have a chance to talk to him and maybe ask for his help with her mother, hoping he would be the bulwark that would shield her in a storm.

*

When Marjorie thought about telling Mrs. Dowling she would have to leave her job, she bit the inside of her cheek to keep from tearing up. She hated to let her supervisor down, especially after all the support Mrs. Dowling had given her. Marjorie loved her work at Bamberger's and she loathed leaving the one thread of independence she possessed. To make her last week as helpful as possible for Mrs. Dowling, she would make an appointment to talk to her first thing on Monday.

At their meeting Monday morning, Marjorie told Mrs. Dowling how much she appreciated her help and how grateful she was to have had the opportunity to work under her guidance. She explained her family situation and why it was necessary for her to leave.

"Marjorie, you have had your share of burdens to carry, but I believe your intelligent approach to your work and your earnest desire to help others will help you throughout your future. I'm happy to give you a letter of recommendation. Perhaps we'll meet again someday." Mrs. Dowling smiled and walked around her desk to shake Marjorie's hand.

"Thank you so much for understanding. I dreaded letting you down. Now I'd like to devote this week to doing all I can to prepare my replacement for the scheduling process and the training plans."

Mrs. Dowling opened the door for Marjorie. "I'm really going to miss you."

Each day for the rest of the week, Marjorie worked hard in spite of her fatigue. She wrote detailed notes for her replacement outlining the procedures for scheduling, giving tips for training, and making notes for billing and other accounting duties, always checking her progress with her supervisor. On Friday she was summoned to Mrs. Dowling's office.

After she knocked and was told to enter, Marjorie opened the door and was stunned by shouts of "Surprise!" Staff she had trained and colleagues from the accessories department where she first worked had gathered to wish her well. Marjorie almost exploded with joy. One of her colleagues, Irene, passed around hats that she had made from papier-mâché and decorated. Everyone wore a hat claiming Marjorie had sold it to them, making fun of the colors, style, or feathers and buttons.

"You started selling hats, but never had one of your own, and now you do!" a colleague said.

After enjoying her surprise party and saying thank you to everyone, Marjorie floated to her car with her heart full and her bag of seven papier-mâché hats in her hand. She would put a hat on both Catherine and Casper when she got home, crowning them king and queen. Tomorrow, she would begin packing.

*

On Sunday morning she sorted her things, preparing for her father's arrival. Thirsty, she took a break and walked into the kitchen. The table was set for three, where she had shared so many meals with Catherine and Casper. She stifled a ragged sob—how she would miss them! Reminding herself this was a temporary move, she got a drink of water and walked back into the little sewing room to finish boxing up the suits and dresses that would be stored. She folded her three maternity outfits and placed them with her sweaters, nightgowns, lingerie, and shoes into two suitcases. As she gathered her clothes, she reflected that not long ago, she and Les had been packing the last of their things in the apartment as they prepared for her move here.

Now, the clock seemed to unwind. She was going back to her parents, still unsure about her future. But she wasn't alone. Her baby was tucked close, and she would keep her focus on this little treasure. She would reject any unreasonable demands her mother might make. Her baby would come first.

She wanted to keep control of her emotions before she left, to present a loving memory that indicated she was happy to be going home so Casper and Catherine would not feel they were forcing her out. Her father was due to arrive within the hour. Catherine came over and stood beside her. Tears welled up in Catherine's eyes every time she looked at Marjorie. Seeing her tears, Marjorie's eyes pooled too. They sniffled and hugged.

"You are my daughter, too, Margie. I want you stay here. Emilie says she must come care for her father. But you are nurse of his . . . heart." Catherine touched her chest. "I pray all is good with you and baby."

"And you are my mother, too, and this is my home. Thank you for everything, your kindness and love. I will miss you. But it is good for me to be with my parents."

Catherine turned away and wiped her eyes with her apron.

"I'll visit with Casper until my father comes."

"Yes, yes." She shooed Marjorie toward his room.

Marjorie took a deep breath and prepared a smile before she walked into Casper's room. She wanted him to see her strong. He always shored up her spirits—a cornerstone of strength, though his body lay weak.

Casper turned to her. "I know you go to make place for Emilie here." He reached toward her with his good arm. She held his hand and gave him a kiss.

"You always my dear nurse, Margie. You and baby, now together. Soon you come back when Lester finish training. Then we are family again."

"Yes." Marjorie fought her tears. She didn't want to lose control in front of him.

"Everything be okay."

210 | LOUISE RILL/

"Yes." Her voice crackled. "You are my hero. You will make a special grandpa to our baby." She leaned over and put her head on his chest so he couldn't see the tears wash over her eyes. "Please keep doing your exercises for me." She sat up.

"My job for my dear nurse." He smiled, his eyes twinkling at her.

Marjorie fixed his pillows, got water for him, and sat with him while she waited for her father.

Catherine appeared in the doorway. "Margie, I see car stop at house. Maybe father."

The time to leave had arrived faster than she wished. Peering out the window, she saw her father's grey Buick. He always bought grey Buicks because he said they showed less grime from the coal and steel factories in Johnstown. She was glad Betty had offered to keep her car at the apartment and drive it every few days. Gas may be rationed soon, so she would not drive it far.

Her father strode up the walk wearing his long wool overcoat and felt hat, and he carried his black medical bag containing pills, ointments, bandages, and bottles labeled *Homer. L. Hill, MD*. He came alone. She thought he would. Her mother was uncomfortable with Les's parents.

Marjorie opened the door for him and waved. He grinned and gave her his usual stiff hug of someone uneasy showing affection.

"You're looking fine, Marjorie."

"Thanks, Dad. Bet you're tired."

"Not bad. I like driving. The roads are clear now, but with snow due tonight, I'd like to drive back after just a little break in order to avoid it."

Catherine took Homer's hat and coat as if she were handling royal garments while Marjorie ushered her father into the living room.

Catherine said, "I make tea. Then I give you dinner before trip back. Long ride."

"That's kind of you. Thank you. I wanted to see Casper, if that is all right—just a little check. I could listen to his heart and take his blood pressure, test his reflexes."

"Yes, yes, thank you," Catherine nodded with vigor.

Marjorie accompanied her father to Casper's room, then left the two men alone while she helped Catherine prepare the meal. She set Casper's place for her father. After a few minutes, her father joined them in the kitchen.

"His heart is strong. I told him to keep exercising. He has some strength in his weak hand, which is good," her father said.

Catherine clapped and beamed at Marjorie. "Margie help him a lot."

After their early dinner, Catherine handed Marjorie a parcel wrapped in butcher's paper. "Here is *pierogi* and love knots. Take to mother." She whispered, "Eat some cookies in car. I give you many. And here is hot tea in thermos."

Marjorie smiled, grateful for Catherine's gifts of love. "Oh, thank you so much. We will enjoy them and think of you." Marjorie gave Catherine a lingering embrace.

"Wait, take pillow too." Catherine rushed to the bedroom and returned with a small pillow. "Sleep in car."

As her father loaded the car, Marjorie stood beside it and raised her hands, touching her heart to signal love to Catherine, who stood at the door, her rosary in her hand. Catherine pulled her apron up to her eyes, then waved her rosary.

"Thanks for coming for me, Dad. The car is so much more comfortable than the train. I think you were right about the train being taxing for me." They drove away. She could not look back. She put her head on the pillow and shut her eyes. It seemed only a moment when her father's voice stirred her awake.

"I'm stopping for gas, Marjorie." He chuckled. "You had a good hour-long nap."

Once on the road again, he mentioned her friends, Lorraine

and Ned, were looking forward to seeing her. Then he spoke of the war. Great Britain, still being bombed so badly, had run out of money to pay for much-needed American supplies. Roosevelt wanted to help the British with food and loans for supplies, military equipment, and war planes while still claiming US neutrality.

"I'm afraid that with Hitler controlling so much of Europe, the US may be forced to help them with troops," her father said.

"I've heard many in our country are against the US entering the war," Marjorie said.

"Yes, especially so soon after the great losses we suffered in the last war. I'm glad Lester is doing so well in his training and has engineering skills that may keep him here."

"I pray that every day."

They were quiet for a while. The hum of the car engine was soothing, and her thoughts were now of Les. Marjorie said a silent prayer for him. She mused about how happy he would be once he knew she was going to her parents. Then her mind shifted to her mother, and how best to cope with her controlling nature that burned red in Marjorie's memory.

Should she talk to her father about this now? He had helped her in the past by inviting Les's parents to the wedding. He might have some advice. Who knew when they would be alone again?

She clenched her teeth and began. "Dad, I have to tell you something I'm worried about." She paused, searching his face.

He glanced at her, his expression unchanging. "Tell me then. Your worries are important."

"Well, I'm afraid Mother will treat me like a frail ornament, monitoring my every move as if I were incapable. When she disagrees with what I want to do, with what I feel is important, I have this struggle. I want to yell at her, but at the same time, I feel myself crumble and I end up feeling angry and lost." She hesitated. "Can you understand, Dad?"

Her father cleared his throat. He spoke in almost a whisper.

"I'm sorry. I wish you didn't have this burden." He was si
for a while. "There is a story—one I should have told you lᴏng
ago, Marjorie. It's about a young girl of nine who was put in
charge of her younger sister. They were playing with dolls when
a friend of the older sister asked if she wanted to play with barrel
hoops. Distracted, the older girl didn't see her little sister wander
into the road before a horse and carriage came barreling along.
Unfortunately, the child was trampled and died. Guilt plagued
the older sister. As this girl became a woman, she vowed that if she
ever had a child, she would always protect her, no matter what."

Marjorie stared at her father. "That is so sad, so awful." She
hesitated. "But I'm not sure why you're telling me this?" Then
Marjorie's mouth fell open. "You mean . . . the girl was Mother?"

His voice was hoarse. "Yes."

"I'm telling you this to help you understand why your mother
is so protective, wanting what she believes is best for you, trying to
control things so you won't be hurt—so you'll be safe. She doesn't
always go about it the best way, I know. She just wants you to
make decisions that will give you an easier life. It's love for you
that's behind everything she does."

Marjorie's mind reeled. All these years, and she knew nothing
of this! She could hardly believe such a tragic thing had happened
to her mother. This horrible incident was behind her mother's
behavior? Her mother felt a desperate need to keep her child safe.
Yet her mother carried this so far that it prevented Marjorie from
developing necessary layers of self-confidence. Her thoughts raced.
Her mother must have had no idea how much it had damaged
Marjorie's spirit to be so controlled. Not supporting her decision
to marry Les, ordering her to quit a job she loved, and so many
instances over a lifetime had taken their toll. Shocked and bewil-
dered, Marjorie ventured a question.

"Dad, do you think *I* can do something different to make
things any better?"

"You have to decide each time, Marjorie, what is best for you to say or to not say. I am just so glad you are doing well in spite of everything—Les going off to war, Casper's stroke, having to move again. You haven't had any bad times that have gotten you down since you've been married." He glanced at her and gave her a reassuring pat. Her eyes were riveted to his face, grateful for his love.

In a low voice, he murmured, "I hope your health continues for you, always."

"Thanks, Dad, me too."

In this whirlwind of revelation, she spun her plan. She would focus on her baby and try to ignore any of her mother's caustic comments. Her wings were stronger now.

This time, though, she would not be a marionette, helplessly dancing to her mother's demands or sinking low from worry. Now she was armed with a new perspective. Her father's disclosure of her mother's failure to protect her little sister many years ago would allow her to make adjustments to her mother's behavior. She would express her ideas and feelings when she believed it was important to take a stand. But she would also remind herself of the deep need her mother had to protect her only daughter after having failed to protect her little sister.

Marjorie would also prepare for the silent treatments, the rejection that came when she contradicted her mother. She would not allow herself to be unnerved by it, and she would refuse to feel guilt for causing it. She'd roll through it. Life should be simpler now with no wedding to plan, no choice of a son-in-law, or guests to interfere with. However her mother might behave, she was primed to rise above it.

As they pulled onto the street near her house, a lump of apprehension formed in Marjorie's stomach. She really was back home.

Her mother met them at the side door near the kitchen. "I thought you'd never get here. It's almost ten o'clock," her mother said with a wide smile and a glow in her eyes. "Is that all you brought? Just two suitcases?"

Marjorie smiled and pointed to her tummy. "I don't have much that fits me."

"Well then, we'll have to go shopping." Her mother smiled.

When Marjorie hugged her mother, the fragrance of her lavender sachet evoked the familiar scent of home. The customary hairnet held her mother's auburn curls, carefully arranged to disguise the thin hair on top. Her mother had been chagrined that scarlet fever had left her temporarily bald in her twenties, with only a sparse regrowth of what had once been thick, red hair. Freckled arms and face revealed the redhead that illness had stolen. A freshly ironed and starched cotton dress sloped artificially at her waist as it followed the contour of her corset that flattened all that lay underneath.

Her mother took Marjorie's coat and hat, then called over her shoulder as she hung them in the closet beside the breakfast room, "Dad didn't want to miss office hours tomorrow or he would have stayed overnight. That was too much driving for one day."

"I offered to drive for a while, but Dad didn't want me to. We stopped for dinner on the turnpike."

Her father hung his coat on the newel post of the back stairs. "Well, the roads were good, and we got here just before the snow," he said.

She had never heard her father complain, but she never knew why. Perhaps nothing compared to the hard life he'd experienced growing up with ten siblings, all helping on their farm. Marjorie handed her mother the package from Catherine. "Here are some *pierogi* that Les's mother wanted you to have. We kept them in the trunk so they'd stay cool."

"What are *pierogi*?" Sara wrinkled her brow, holding the package away from her as if it were an object of revulsion. She put the package in the refrigerator.

"They're half circles made of dough filled with mashed potato, onion, and farmer's cheese. You sauté them with onions. They're delicious. I can fix them for us tomorrow."

"That's quite different!" Marjorie heard a note of disdain in her voice before it brightened up again.

"Well, you look good . . . but pale, Marjorie. I'm glad you decided to come home, where you can rest up for the little one. I know you and your dad are both exhausted. Let's have a little pie, then off to bed."

After a large slice of her mother's freshly baked apple pie and a glass of milk, Marjorie said her good nights. In the hall, she gave her father a second hug. "Thanks, Dad. I appreciate your driving so far to get me, and, well, everything."

Marjorie climbed the stairs carrying the cosmetic bag she'd used on her honeymoon. It held her toiletries, her rosary, and her wedding album. The homecoming had begun. It had already been an hour, but all was well so far. She sensed comfort in the familiarity of the spacious rooms, the burgundy carpet on the stairs, the oak banister curling around the landing, the tall ceilings. And tonight, she would have a bed of her own.

*

The night's snowfall turned out to be minimal and had melted by noon. Her mother suggested they take advantage of the sunshine that afternoon and go to town to get a few maternity outfits at Johnstown's sole department store.

Marjorie had written to Les that morning and could mail her letter in town. She finished, "I know you'll be happy I've come to Johnstown, though I will miss your parents, especially your father. He counted on me to tell him about the radio reports on the war. I enjoyed giving him the highlights and keeping him company." She knew Les would be pleased to get her letter. He'd been urging her to move back with her parents for weeks.

After lunch, Marjorie and her mother walked three blocks to the corner store to catch the trolley which would take them to town. It ran every hour. Although the seats were uncomfortable wooden ones, Marjorie loved riding the streetcar with its jerks and jangles. As soon as they arrived at the store, her mother shooed her to the maternity department. Marjorie was excited to have some new clothes, a luxury she had not been able to afford. Instead of new clothes, she had been wearing the tops Catherine had made for her on weekends. She tried on several outfits. A blue top with a navy skirt was her favorite. Her mother found several others for her to try on. "I really like these two, Mother."

"The blue one is quite snug," her mother said, dismissing it with a wave of her hand.

"I like it best. I think I'll still have room to grow!" Marjorie pulled the front of the top to show her the expanse of fabric.

"Well, suit yourself," she said in a tone of forced indifference. "And the skirt on the plaid one is too short. It almost comes up to your knees."

"That's the new style," Marjorie said. "And the plaid looks sophisticated."

Marjorie left with the blue outfit and a flowered one her mother liked. They had both compromised, she told herself.

"I'd like to stop at the counter where they sell yarn so I can knit the baby some booties and sweaters. Is that all right?" Marjorie asked.

"I bought some things for the baby already, dear. Why don't you look at them before you bother knitting?"

Marjorie swallowed hard. "That's nice, Mother, thank you, but I want the baby to have some special things I make," she said softly, trying to be patient with her mother.

"Hurry then. Your father will be picking us up in a few minutes."

Marjorie knew her father would pull in front of the store after his Saturday office hours and could not park there long. She quickly selected several skeins of fine yarn and a few skeins of thicker yarn. She planned to make warm hats and scarves for the soldiers as well as making things for the baby. After all, she would have the time.

After they got home, Marjorie reminded her mother about the *pierogi*.

"Are you sure you want to bother with them tonight? I don't think your father will like them. He's not much for trying new food. Also, I planned to serve the pork roast I cooked this morning, with mashed potatoes."

Marjorie weighed her response. "I think the *pierogi* would be a good substitute for mashed potatoes. They're easy to sauté. I'm anxious for you to try them, and I'm not sure how long they'll be good."

"You can use this apron, then," her mother said. In one jerk of her arm, she thrust the apron at her.

After Marjorie sautéed the *pierogi* in her mother's cast iron skillet, she placed them on a platter and carried them to the table. She missed Les, realizing that the last time she'd had dinner at this table was when the four of them had eaten here together before the wedding. *"Well it's a different four now!"* She caressed her tummy and passed the *pierogi* to her father, who took two. She took three and her mother took one.

Her parents chatted about filling the pantry with items like sugar, coffee, and canned goods, staples that were likely to be rationed soon if the US entered the war. Her father said factories would switch from automobile manufacturing to making munitions. He thought perhaps he should get a new car soon, before that happened.

"Did you like the Polish dish?" Marjorie asked. Her father's plate was empty, but her mother had taken only one bite from hers.

"Yes, tasty," her father said, smiling.

"Not bad," her mother said. "You ate for two, I see."

Marjorie snickered to herself. Perhaps it was her mother who didn't like to try new foods. So far, her time at home had been smoother than she'd expected. She'd stood up to her mother about her choice of outfits, but she had also compromised. Her mother had agreed to have the *pierogi* for dinner. This time at home was going to be okay. Marjorie felt stronger now than she ever had in this house.

CHAPTER 21

THE WEEK AFTER she arrived home, Marjorie decided to meet with her childhood friend, Lorraine, which she knew would boost her spirits. Marjorie's father used his lunchtime to pick her up from home and drop her off at Lorraine's around noon, and he would pick her up after his office hours.

Lorraine met her at the door, gave Marjorie a big squeeze, and ushered her into the living room. From the end table, Lorraine scooped up a package wrapped in pink and blue paper. "This is for you, Marjorie. Have a seat and go ahead and open it." Lorraine grinned, adjusted her glasses, and fluffed her curly dark hair.

Looking at the baby gift, she felt a rush of warmth move up her neck. She oohed over a little yellow baby dish with a cork on the side where hot water could be put in to keep the baby's food warm. Little kittens and pups chased each other around the rim. "This is so precious, thank you. Baby's first china," Marjorie said.

"When your mother told us you were expecting and coming back, I wanted you to have something useful. I'm so glad you could come home for a visit. Now, I can tell you in person. Guess what?" Lorraine put her hand up to her mouth, her eyes twinkling above. She paused for a moment, and before Marjorie could say anything, she blurted out, "I'm pregnant too!"

"Oh my goodness, congratulations! What fun! We'll have so

much to share. It's like we're sisters, each having babies." Marjorie jumped up and hugged her friend.

"I remember when you wanted a sister so badly you kept pestering your dad to bring an orphaned child home from the hospital. And he told you there was only a crippled little boy."

"Yes, and I said, 'Please bring him home.' I wanted a sister or brother to talk to and play with. I didn't care if they had a missing arm or leg!"

"They didn't know how badly you wished there was another child in the family. Marjorie, remember how your mother surprised me with a baby doll when I didn't have a doll like yours, and she bought one that was almost a twin to yours? How we would dress and undress them for hours, feeding and then changing them with diapers we made from hankies?" Lorraine gestured how they used to rock and cuddle their dolls.

"Oh, yes, and how much fun we had sewing clothes for our babies out of scraps of material?"

"And then when your mother saw our raggedy attempts, she sewed some lovely outfits for them."

Marjorie balked when she remembered that her lovingly stitched little outfits were replaced by her mother's finer craftsmanship. Marjorie shifted her thoughts and asked about Ned and the draft. Lorraine told her Ned was lucky since he worked in the steel mill where workers were exempt, at least for the present. Marjorie felt a momentary pang of jealousy, but scolded herself. She was glad Ned was safe for now.

"That's wonderful," Marjorie said. "Now, how about Dory? The three of us girls used to have a great time together. I'm sorry I couldn't make it back for her wedding. Has Bill been affected?"

"Yes, unfortunately. The draft really changed things for Dory. After Bill was drafted, she moved out of the house they were renting near here. They couldn't afford for her to stay."

"Like I had to do," Marjorie said, thinking of her beautiful little apartment.

Lorraine's eyebrows raised, then her brows knit together. "Your mother said you preferred to move in with Les's folks rather than live alone."

Marjorie flinched at this misleading information. How could her mother twist the truth that Marjorie couldn't afford to stay in their apartment? "Well . . . ." She started to correct Lorraine's misunderstanding of the facts, but realized it wasn't worth a debate. She stammered, "Well, financially, it was the best choice." Marjorie shrunk in her chair. She knew that Lorraine, although a good friend, would never doubt her mother's word. After all, her mother had always been good to Lorraine in many ways, and she had helped Lorraine and Ned find their house up the street from her father's office. Her mother had even negotiated the price with the previous owner.

"Oh," Lorraine said, cocking her head at Marjorie's response. She started to speak, then stopped. "So shall I call Dory and suggest getting together sometime? She doesn't know you're in town yet."

"Sure, that would be fun. The three of us haven't been together since my wedding. Where is she living?"

"She wanted to stay here in Johnstown, where she has friends, so she's moved into a little boarding house. A woman had two empty bedrooms she decided to rent out."

"Really? Poor gal, but I'm glad she found a place so she could stay in town."

For the rest of the afternoon, the two childhood friends caught up on their lives and shared ideas about preparing for delivery and infant care. They made promises to meet again soon and to knit for the soldiers.

As she walked stiffly to her father's car, Marjorie was unnerved. She knew that her father's story about her mother's behavior did not explain all of her conduct. Her mother would distort the truth to boost or salvage her own pride. The need to save face, to maintain a laudable position or a praiseworthy stance, seemed to be as strong as her need to protect her daughter. They were entwined somehow. Perhaps her mother's fear of not appearing admirable stemmed from the same underbelly of guilt that ran deep and wide beneath her. Marjorie sighed. However it was, she would overlook anything, as long as it didn't wound her.

*

Once home, Marjorie greeted her mother, who stood over the frying pan turning pieces of chicken. The aroma of the frying chicken fueled memories of this favorite dish. She was starving. Marjorie sat down at the kitchen table and shared the details of her visit with Lorraine. She told her mother of Lorraine's pregnancy, which her mother admitted she already knew. Lorraine had sworn her mother to secrecy, so apparently, the two had become confidants.

"Do I have any mail?"

"No, nothing from Lester."

Marjorie swallowed her disappointment, then said she was going upstairs to change. After hanging up her new navy outfit, she pulled on a housedress and uncovered her tissue-wrapped rosary. She wanted to pray for Les regularly. Marjorie made the sign of the cross from her brow to her chest and began reciting the Lord's Prayer aloud. Suddenly, she noticed her mother standing at the bedroom door.

"What is that?" Her mother's voice was pitched two octaves higher than usual.

"I'm saying a prayer for Les."

"I mean those beads. What are you doing with them?"

"Mother, I'm saying the Lord's Prayer that we always say in church."

"Let me see that!" Her mother plucked the rosary from her hand.

"This is a rosary. Did Lester give you this? He's not Catholic anymore, since he married you—he's a Protestant—or so he claimed. I saw you making the sign of the cross, the way *they* do."

Marjorie was shaken by her mother's rebuke, even though she knew that her mother's distaste of Catholics was second only to her objection to immigrants. These were prejudices she'd carried forward from her own mother. Marjorie quickly weighed the damage her answer might incur. If she let her mother think it was Les's rosary, it wouldn't be honest. He was no longer Catholic. But she hated to identify Catherine as the source, which would make her mother-in-law even more unlikeable in her mother's eyes.

"Well?" her mother said, impatience resonating in her voice.

"When I was upset over Les's departure for the navy, Catherine gave me this rosary—she thought it might help me over that rough time. I was glad to have the prayers to recite. The routine calmed me."

Her mother dangled the beads and handed the rosary back. "Presbyterians don't need necklaces in their talks with the Lord," she said, disdain resonating in her voice.

Marjorie looked into her mother's eyes. "I like the structure of the prayers. While I'm praying, I can't worry at the same time."

"You were baptized a Presbyterian, Marjorie. I hope you will remember that." Her face contorted into a misshaped mask. "I won't have a daughter of mine taking on a foreign name *and* another religion." She spat out the words.

Marjorie had touched a nerve. She gathered her strength, feeling her heartbeat race. "We all believe in God, Mother. There are many ways to pray to this same God." She paused. "And I'm not changing my religion."

Her mother's face softened slightly. She turned and walked down the hall, then went back downstairs.

Marjorie continued her prayers. She would do what comforted her. There was nothing more to say in defense of the rosary.

But she wondered if she should prepare for an ice storm at dinner, or just a bit of sleet. She could hear her mother and father talking downstairs. Her father spoke louder than usual, but she couldn't hear their conversation. She missed Catherine and Casper. She would call them soon.

When Marjorie reached the kitchen, she told her mother how wonderful the chicken smelled, then proceeded to set the table, pour the water into glasses, carry the beans to the table, and serve the potatoes. She eyed her mother's movements, watching for any sign of irritation or distress. Her mother banged no dishes and showed no brittle movements. Her jaw was not tight. All was well so far. During the meal, her mother's tone seemed natural.

Her father discussed Mrs. Sprock's ovarian tumor and the mistake the anesthesiologist had made. Nothing told of her mother's malcontent. By dessert, Marjorie breathed relief as she served the cobbler. *Thank you, God, for my strength.*

*

The next day, Marjorie was excited to start knitting her first baby sweater. Her mother coached her on how tightly to pull the yarn, and she reminded her frequently to measure her stitch so the sweater would match the pattern. Marjorie concentrated on the knitting needles as they moved in and out of the loops of the light-yellow yarn, producing at each movement something new that hadn't been there before. With every stitch, anxiety flowed from her fingers into the needles and out each turn of the yarn.

Marjorie listened to the radio while she knitted, alternating between news of the war in Europe and music. The announcer said the house of representatives passed the lend-lease bill to provide supplies and war equipment to allies in exchange for leases on army and naval bases. She feared this action would bring the US a step closer to entering the war. Marjorie switched the station back to music.

After a few days of needles flying, she'd knitted and sewn together a sweater for her baby. She had a pang of pleasure every time she held it up, envisioning a little one wearing it. One afternoon, when she was alone, she stuffed two skeins of yarn into the sweater and cuddled it, imagining her baby inside.

Several days later, her mother took a seat next to Marjorie. After a few minutes of idle chatting, her mother said, "That lipstick is much too red for your coloring, Marjorie. You don't want to look like a street walker."

"Oh, no," Marjorie said, and smiled. She started knitting a bootie, but didn't take the lipstick off.

"You should really crochet the booties, they'll be more delicate," her mother said. "I'll get the thread and the hook."

Over several days, Marjorie crocheted three sets of booties.

One day the following week, her mother said, "You shouldn't go out walking. It's freezing. You'll catch a cold, then what? If you get sick, don't complain to me."

Marjorie went out, every inch of her skin covered with wool—scarf, hat, sweater, coat, gloves, and socks. She paced stiffly back and forth in the driveway like a child stuffed in a snowsuit. The day was dark with heavy, low clouds that spoke of snow. Kicking a chunk of ice, she watched it chip apart. She drank in the cold air, suddenly feeling alive.

The next two weeks passed with ever-increasing challenges. Marjorie began to knit scarves for soldiers. Each row of knitting relieved the tension building within her and brought satisfaction, her tiny contribution to the men who committed their lives to the welfare of others.

"Why don't you part your hair further up? It would hide your cowlick better."

"That's an idea." Marjorie continued knitting scarves for soldiers. She winced as a twinge of pain shot through her left temple.

"Eat some more chicken, dear, you're starving that baby."

"Thanks, but I'm really full." Marjorie continued to knit more scarves for soldiers.

"Your face looks dry. Are you using your cream every night?"

"Yes, I am," Marjorie said, forcing a smile. She changed to knitting hats for soldiers.

"Are you alone providing scarves and hats for all the soldiers?"

"Just half of them." Marjorie smiled. She changed to knitting a hat for the baby. A throbbing pain behind her left eye wouldn't stop.

"Crocheted hats are really finer for a little one."

"Probably so." Marjorie crocheted a hat for the baby.

"Don't you want to sew a little ribbon there?"

Marjorie sewed a ribbon on the baby's hat. A pounding headache on the entire left side of her head distracted her.

"You shouldn't drink coffee anymore. It affects your kidneys."

Marjorie switched to drinking tea in the morning.

"Prop your feet up so they don't swell."

Marjorie used a footstool.

By the end of the month, Marjorie had stopped knitting and crocheting. Her headaches bothered her too much to concentrate. She had to rest in her room in the afternoons. Perhaps all pregnant women felt like this late in their pregnancy? She knew calling Catherine and Casper would cheer her. She missed them.

Marjorie gave the operator the number and waited for her to connect the long-distance call. When Marjorie heard Catherine's voice, she felt a surge like an electric current awaken her sleeping spirit. She smiled.

"Margie, Pops and I just speak about you. How are you? How is baby? Staying warm?" Then Catherine called out to Casper. "Margie is calling. Emilie, bring Pops here."

"Baby is fine, getting bigger. Yes, staying warm. We have snow and ice, so I'm mostly staying inside. How are you and Casper?"

"Okay, doing good. Emilie help Dad move to chair with wheels she buy him. He eat dinner in chair."

"That's wonderful." Marjorie wished she could be there.

"I hear your voice sad. You okay at home with mother and father?"

"I miss you and Casper, but I'm fine." Marjorie swallowed hard to ease the lump in her throat. "I loved living with you, and I liked my work."

"Here, here is Dad. I give him phone."

There was a rustling and then she heard Casper.

"Margie, my heart is happy now. Tell me how you are? I see you smile when I go to sleep. Then awake, I hear you say, 'Good morning my hero.' You are with me all days."

Marjorie's eyes filled with tears. "And you are always in my thoughts. I'm so happy to hear your voice, and that you can get up in the wheelchair. I'm knitting things for the baby, and some hats and scarves for soldiers."

"You think of soldiers too, so good. Baby play with dolls or football in tummy?"

Marjorie laughed. "I think footballs!"

"Then will be girl! Girls the busy ones. No matter, we will love. Our baby will give new beginning for everyone. Make more love in world, you will see."

Marjorie brightened. She was touched by Casper's humor and wisdom. "Thank you, my hero. It won't be long before I see you, with the baby in my arms."

"Yes, my angel."

Marjorie put the receiver on the cradle, energized by the deep connection she shared with them, buoyed by their love. She smiled broadly and reached into her bag for her knitting.

*

That week, Marjorie and Lorraine attended a meeting at the Red Cross to wrap bandages. They committed to helping every Tuesday and Thursday. Though she was still fatigued, Marjorie felt better taking some action for the war effort, no matter how small. As she handled the gauze with gloved hands, she couldn't help but think that the United States might soon come to the defense of the European countries. The newscaster said the Nazis had just bombed a town in Wales, almost to obliteration. The war raged on across the ocean. Marjorie prayed these bandages would not ever be wrapped around Les.

*

One day the next week, her mother called from her bedroom as Marjorie got up from a rest. "Marjorie, come and see what I fixed for the baby." Beside her mother's bed stood a white wicker bassinet trimmed in pale yellow ribbon. A stuffed bear lay inside on an embroidered pillow. "It used to be yours. I got it down from the attic and painted it with enamel so it's easy to clean."

"It's darling." Marjorie ran her fingers over the wide, satin ribbon. "What a wonderful surprise!"

"The baby can sleep here at night so you can get some sleep."

Marjorie steadied herself. Her baby would be sleeping beside *her*, not by her mother. What was her mother thinking?

"Then, when the little one wakes up, I'll change the diaper and take the baby downstairs until it's time for the scheduled feeding. That way, you can get your sleep."

"Mother, I—"

"You'll need your rest to be sure your milk comes in."

She would decide when to feed her baby, not her mother. Marjorie's stomach churned with the challenge of an impending clash.

Marjorie leaned against the dresser. "Mother, I don't believe in feeding a baby only when some rigid schedule says it's time."

"Newborns often cry for no apparent reason. They have gas, you know. You just have to let them exercise their lungs. It's good for them. You need to train the baby to eat every three or four hours."

"That is not what I want to do." Bile rose to her throat.

"If you feed the baby whenever it's uncomfortable, it will want to eat any old time, and you would get nothing else done."

This was a battle Marjorie could not lose. "I want to feed the baby when I think I should, regardless of a schedule." Marjorie stood resolute, determined that she would be the baby's mother and make these decisions.

"Then you'll be sorry and have a spoiled child." Her mother raised her head in a huff.

These words stung like venom. Marjorie's throat tightened. Her resolve began to splinter.

"I'll just have to figure things out," Marjorie said.

"Or take the advice of the experts. This is what the nurses all did in the hospital nursery." She swept her hand wide. "You can ask your father."

Marjorie didn't care *what* the experts said. Her mother's ideas of where the baby would sleep and when it would eat were unbearable. Marjorie would be in charge of her child's feedings whether others agreed or not.

"The bassinet is pretty," Marjorie choked out her words. She would protect her baby. She could not have her baby here.

*

After the conversation with her mother, Marjorie went down to the living room and paced on the green carpet. Her head still throbbed. She knew that beneath her mother's behavior was a deep need to protect her daughter. But now Marjorie would be the mother who must protect her child. She could not stay here and allow her mother to control her baby.

Marjorie slumped in her father's wingback chair, her hands grasping the wooden curves at the ends of the upholstered arms to steady her body. Her throat tightened at the crushing weight of having her mother's eyes and ears everywhere. The light within her was fading. Marjorie knew she had to get away before her anxiety turned into the blackness that had haunted her before she was married.

She couldn't go to Les's folks since Emilie was still there. Betty had no room. If only she could talk with Les. Could she feign an emergency and call him? But she knew Les would encourage her to disregard her mother's comments. Her fingers tugged at her hair. It was so easy to give this advice from a distance, but impossible to carry it out in the moment.

Maybe she could talk to a friend. She knew she could not put Lorraine in the middle. Perhaps she could confide in Dory. Dory might be able to empathize. After all, Dory was living in a boarding house while her husband was in the military. Then she thought of Betty. Her spirit leapt. She could call Betty and see if she knew of any such places in New Jersey where people rented rooms near Passaic or Elizabeth. Then she could be back near Catherine, Casper, and Betty. Fresh hope filled her lungs.

She hated to bother Betty with her problems yet again, especially since she would be at work now. But here it was a good time for her to call. Since her mother was still upstairs, she couldn't hear her talking if she phoned now. At almost eight months pregnant, she had no time to lose in order to travel safely. "Betty, I'm sending you kisses in advance," she thought.

She hurried to the coat closet for her purse to find Betty's phone number. When she came to the phone in the breakfast room, she heard that her mother was now in the kitchen nearby. Marjorie's heart hammered. She'd lost her opportunity.

"After I put the pork on to boil, I'm going up to iron. Would you check that there is enough water still in the pan in half an hour?" her mother asked.

Marjorie grinned. "Yes, I sure will." She looked at her watch. That would be at about three-fifteen. She waited until her mother walked up the back stairs. Then, a wave of guilt washed over her for sneaking this call behind her mother's back. But she had to know if she could find a place to stay before saying anything to her mother. She closed the swinging door to the kitchen so her voice would not travel upstairs. The operator connected her. It rang, and Betty said, "Hello," the answer to her prayer.

"Betty, I'm so sorry to call you at work. I won't keep you long. I'm fine. You will not believe this, but I need a favor once again! You are the only one who can help me. I'm afraid you won't agree, but I have to ask you. I beg you."

Marjorie told her briefly that for her health, she needed to come back to New Jersey. Les would be finishing his Officer Candidate School near the time the baby was due. She explained about her friend who lived in a rented room in a private house here.

"If I could find a similar situation, I'd be all set. I'd ask my dad to drive me. Do you know of anyone who rents rooms?" Impatience resonated in her voice.

"You want to have a baby in a rooming house?" Betty yelped. "How could that possibly be good for your baby?"

Betty's words stung. Marjorie stammered, "It's the . . . well . . . the only solution, Betty, believe me. I'm losing ground here. Mother is suffocating me with her constant advice. I'm being pecked to death."

"You have just over a month before the baby is born, Marge, surely—"

"Betty, please understand," Marjorie's lip trembled. "It's my health too. I can't care for a baby if I'm a wreck. It would be terrible for both of us—all of us."

"You sound pretty desperate. Oh, Marge, of course I want to

help you. I don't know of anything offhand, but I'll check around here at work. Are you positive about this, Marge?"

"I'm not crazy, really. A vagabond, perhaps, but a sane one. This means the world to me Betty. Believe me, I'm at my wits' end here."

"Okay. I'll call you as soon as I find out something. Uh . . . who's the President?"

"Jeez, Betty, Roosevelt!"

"What month is it?"

"Still March. Satisfied?" Marjorie grinned.

"Okay," Betty said, "just testing!"

"You are a dear. Bye-bye."

Marjorie heaved a sigh. She'd been shocked at Betty's first responses, but Betty was an ally who would try her best to help. Marjorie hurried to check on the pork. She poked it with a fork. It was tender, so she turned off the stove and called up to her mother that the meat was ready.

As she walked into the living room to listen to the radio report on the war, Marjorie decided to knit a hat for Betty. As she worked, she kept vigil for the ring of the phone. But no call came that evening.

Marjorie shuffled upstairs to her bedroom and pulled out her rosary. She began reciting Hail Marys and Our Fathers, but she also prayed God would give Betty guidance to find a place for her to stay.

*

In the morning, her headache was better. She hoped she would know today if Betty had found anything. After breakfast, Marjorie realized she should tell her mother about the phone call she was expecting. "My friend Betty said she was going to call today, Mother. She wants to tell me about something special, and she wanted to tell me in person."

"I'll call you if you're upstairs. Which friend?"

"Betty, who used to be my neighbor."

"That's nice you've kept in touch. Don't forget to prop your feet up when you sit. They look a little swollen."

Marjorie sat down in the living room and pulled out the hat she was working on for Betty so she could continue knitting while keeping an ear out for the phone. She kept checking her watch. The clock dragged its hands. She made good progress on the hat, but no call came all afternoon. Perhaps Betty wasn't able to find anything. Dismay lurked at the edge of her thoughts, taunting her. Then she remembered, Betty couldn't make a long-distance call from work. She reminded herself to be patient. After all, it had only been one day, though it seemed to have stretched to five.

If Betty found a place, Marjorie would talk with her father first. She hoped he would understand and would be willing to drive her. Going by train would not be good for her, or for the baby.

After dinner, when she was drying dishes, the phone rang. Marjorie jumped, but it was her mother who answered it.

"Yes, just a moment please." She handed the phone to Marjorie. "It's your friend, Betty." Her mother went back into the kitchen to finish the dinner dishes.

"Hello, Betty?"

"It's me. Well, Marge, I might have something for you. A friend at work, Sylvia, has a cousin who rents out several rooms in her house. Sylvia called the cousin on your behalf and recommended you since I had told her how polite and reliable you are. I decided I would take a look myself."

"Oh, how nice."

"The house is in a nice neighborhood in Patterson, about ten minutes or so from Les's parents in Passaic. She's willing to rent it to you for a month without an interview, and if all is well, you can continue to stay after that. The current resident will be leaving next week."

FROM FRAGILE FRAGMENTS | 235

"That's wonderful, Betty!" Marjorie whispered, "Perfect. How much does she charge?"

"Twenty-five dollars a month up front to hold the room."

Marjorie's thoughts raced. Though she hadn't saved much money because of quitting her job, she'd also had no expenses for the last month. She'd have enough to pay for two month's rent. Should she blindly commit to this? She was stretched out of shape from holding so much struggle inside.

"I'll call you by Wednesday to let you know how I'll send the deposit."

"Sure thing."

Marjorie spoke louder, choosing her words carefully in case her mother could hear. "Well that is wonderful. You're a terrific friend, Betty, a sister." Marjorie put down the phone, breathing an audible sigh. She had a place. Tomorrow she would talk with her father about all of this. She had to know if he would drive her back before making final arrangements. A sliver of light shone by the door that was opening.

CHAPTER 22

THAT NIGHT, MARJORIE dreamed she was standing outside a locked door, while behind it, voices argued about her. "She doesn't know what's best for her. She can't cope alone with a baby. She needs to be in a safe place."

She woke up perspiring and hugged her tummy. "I'm your mother and I'll do what's best for both of us. We're in this together."

At breakfast, her father mentioned he was going to make a home visit to check on a patient. This was her opportunity to talk with him alone. She asked if she could ride along to get out of the house. Her father welcomed her, and she ran to grab her coat and hat. She slid into the cold car, her nerves strung tight. The grey, low-slung clouds promised a snowstorm.

They rode in silence for a few miles. Trees, their branches naked, whirred by her window. Marjorie's eye twitched. How would he react to her appeal? She gathered her words and tried to sound stronger than she felt. "I wanted to talk with you Dad. It's hard for me to say this, but I have to let you know how I'm feeling." Her heart throbbed faster.

Her father glanced at her, navigating the winding, hilly road. "Go ahead," he said with a note of concern in his voice.

"I've had a difficult time with Mother's wanting to rule over me. I try to ignore her judgments and commands, keeping in mind what you'd said about her past and about her wanting to protect me." She hesitated, pulling at the fingers of her gloves. "But it's continued to build.

"I started getting my headaches again, and, well, I've been pretty disheartened—I'm having a hard time fighting it. I'm sinking. Then, when it came to how Mother planned to control feeding the baby, and where it would sleep,"—Marjorie swallowed hard. "I'd reached my limit. I just couldn't agree. Dad, I need to feed the baby the way I believe I should. And my baby needs to sleep in my room, not yours and Mother's." She stared at the road ahead for a moment, then looked back to her father. "I know once Mother has her mind made up about something, nothing will change it. There was no use in continuing to argue."

"Your mother told me about her idea of the baby sleeping in our room."

Marjorie blew out a flurry of air, wondering what her father's response had been. "I've tried to let things slide off, but I keep hearing her words—they suffocate me every time I take a breath." She shook her head. "I'm afraid it's not good for me, or the baby, to be here now."

Her father tensed. "Oh my, goodness, Marjorie, this is all so disappointing." He was silent a moment. "I want you to know that I intervened the other day and talked with your mother about the rosary. She came around, and understood that you were doing what helped you, and you were not becoming a Catholic." He paused and cleared his throat. "But I got nowhere in our discussion about the feeding schedule and taking control. I think her nursing experience has given her some authority on this." He was silent again for a few moments as his hand rubbed the steering wheel. "This is so sad for everyone." His voice cracked. "I was so looking forward to you having the baby here."

This was so much more difficult than she'd imagined it would be. Marjorie touched his arm. "I'm so sorry, Dad. Really, I am.

I would never want to hurt you, either of you." Tears welled in her eyes.

He shook his head. "This just seems such a shame, Marjorie. I don't know what to suggest to you."

She pulled out a handkerchief her mother had given her and wiped her eyes, then stared at the dashboard. "Well, I was hoping you might be able to drive me back to New Jersey. My friend Betty knows of a woman, actually a cousin of a friend, who is renting rooms in her house. Betty went over to meet the woman. The house isn't far from Les's parents."

"A room in a house?"

"Just until Les is finished with Officer Candidate School in six weeks, then he'll get his commission."

"What does Les think about all this?"

"He doesn't know yet." She fiddled with the window handle.

Her father's fingers tightened on the wheel. "Oh dear. Marjorie." He grimaced and shook his head. "Your mother will be . . . so . . . extremely upset. I can't imagine how she'll react to this." He clasped and unclasped his hands on the wheel. "I wish things were different for both of you." He pulled the car to a stop at the curb of a white clapboard bungalow, his patient's house. "The control she uses with you is somehow to make up for the control she let slip so long ago."

"I can understand that, Dad, but I've really tried my best."

Her father's voice softened. "You're not to blame. This is just how things are." He looked at her with eyes that reflected profound loss, then he reached in the back seat for his medical bag. "I'll leave the car running for the heat. We'll talk more when I come back."

Once her father was gone, uncertainty swept through Marjorie, pressing deeply inside where the darkness always chafed. She hadn't considered her father's thoughts or feelings in all of this. Such a mountain of hurt that had spread so far, born from an unguarded moment of a child so long ago. She would not carry the damage any further. Snow flurries swirled in a fury. The flakes blew down bigger and faster, melting on the warm windshield. Marjorie braced herself for what her father might say when he returned.

After a few minutes, her father was back in the car, his coat sprinkled white with snow. She waited for him to gather his thoughts, her nerves strung tight.

"Marjorie, I've seen too many parents ruin their children's lives because of expectations that they push on them. I want you to stay healthy and not fall into a depression again. You know, I'm torn about what is best to do." He turned and leaned his back against the car door to face her. "I believe it's best for your physical health for you to stay with us." He looked in her eyes as if to search for a glimpse of an opening for another path to peace. "If you go, your mother will be devastated. After all, her success in protecting you is what has kept her sane over the guilt about her sister."

He cleared his throat. "And if I take you, she'll be very angry with me." His voice fell. "Perhaps she'll never forgive me." He coughed. "But that's for me to deal with, not you. I must think a bit."

"Oh, Dad, I'm so sorry. I wish I could find another answer to this." Marjorie shrank in her seat. How could she do this to her father, and to her mother? Her heart throbbed. What would he say? Unnerved, she waited for his decision.

He turned on the windshield wipers that struggled to move, the snow piling up on the windshield. He put the car in reverse and turned it toward home. The only sounds were the rumble of the engine and the moan of the wipers. But the tension in the car was electric.

When they arrived home twenty minutes later, her father got out, opened the garage doors, got back into the car, and pulled it into the garage. He turned off the engine and faced her. "All things considered, this is what I think we should do. I will take you back to New Jersey on two conditions. You write to Les immediately, and you agree to see the obstetric doctor to be sure you can travel. Also, you must promise to call me if there is any problem with you or the baby. I want your doctor's name. If there is a problem, I will fly to New Jersey immediately. You are *my* only child."

At first, she wondered if his words were real, or if she'd only imagined them. She slid across the seat and hugged his shoulder. "Oh, thank you, Dad. I'm so sad about all of this. Please know I didn't want to cause any trouble. This is so difficult for everyone, and I'm very sorry. I love you."

"When you talk to your mother, be sure you tell her that too."

Marjorie exhaled, letting the pressure abate. Her father was a good doctor. He had relieved a pain that had seared so deep.

But there was still another hurt to heal.

*

After a restless night, Marjorie awoke at six o'clock to the darkness of early morning. She had tossed from one side to the other, unable to find a comfortable position. Thoughts of what to write Les to convince him to agree with her plan kept whirring in her mind. She needed his agreement so she could leave as soon as possible. As she turned on the lamp, she noticed condensation glistening on the windowpanes from the bitter cold outside. She'd forgotten to pull the drapes. She would compose her letter to Les early this morning so she could finish it with no interruptions, then put it in the mailbox before the postman came. She lifted the box of stationery from her dresser where she had placed it the night before, sat down in her chair, and balanced the box of paper on her lap.

After several starts, Marjorie finally finished her letter. She told Les of her mother's persistent monitoring, the constant attempts to control her, how Marjorie had tried to resist her mother's insistence on keeping the baby by her own bed at night and enforcing a rigid feeding schedule. She described the room Betty had found for her to rent in a house in Patterson. She told him that her father agreed to take her to New Jersey if he, Les, agreed, and if the doctor found both her and the baby to be well. She implored him to give his blessing so she could be free and independent—these being critical to her well-being. She pushed the letter into the envelope and tasted the sweetness of the glue as she licked it closed.

As she walked down the hall, she heard murmuring in her parents' bedroom. Slipping downstairs, she pulled open the heavy oak front door. Snow had drifted against it, creating a white wall at the bottom. She kicked the snow away, carefully stepped out in her slippered feet, and clinging to the doorframe with one hand, she placed the letter in the mailbox beside the door. There, it was done. She was one step closer to freedom. She wished she could shovel off the walk so the mailman could easily get up to the house. She brushed out the snow that had fallen in on the rug. Bending over with her expanding belly was becoming more difficult.

Once back upstairs, she called out, "Good morning," as she passed her parents' door. Their bedroom door opened.

"Marjorie, were you downstairs a few minutes ago? I thought I heard someone on the stairs." Her mother's eyebrows raised over her vexed stare.

For a moment, Marjorie was taken aback about how to answer, but she realized her mother might see the letter in the box anyway. "I just put a letter to Les in the mailbox. This morning will be busy, planning the shower for Lorraine, and I wanted to get it out first." Then she thought of the crumpled evidence of her plea to Les which lay in her room. She would have to shred them to pieces so no curious person could read her words.

"Are you feeling all right? You have been resting a lot in the afternoons."

"I don't have my normal energy, but I've been reading a wonderful book, *The Grapes of Wrath*. It's about the strength of people persevering in terrible conditions."

"That's good." Her mother stepped around the corner in her bedroom, walked over to her dresser, and pushed the end of her nail file into her bottle of lavender sachet, scooped some on the file, then dropped the fragrant powder inside the front of her dress. "I wanted you to know that your father made an appointment for you to have an exam with Dr. Longwell. He specializes in obstetrics. He has a good reputation in town. It's on Tuesday at nine."

"Good, thanks." Just three days away. She hoped the doctor would find both of them in good shape.

Time, though, was her enemy. On one hand, the clock dragged for a resolution to her predicament, but on the other hand, her pregnancy was advancing by the day, making travel riskier. She calculated that Les should get her letter by Wednesday. *Mister postman, there is no time to waste.*

*

Tuesday morning finally arrived, and her father drove her to the doctor's office for her checkup. Banks of dirt-spattered snow lined the roads. Her father took her arm, and they walked through rivers of slush to the office door.

As she entered the doctor's office, Marjorie crossed her fingers that the doctor's report would find both her and the baby fine. Once this was settled, the only hurdle would be Les's agreement. She would wait until after the exam to ask the doctor about traveling.

When the doctor had completed the examination, he told her that she was healthy, her blood pressure was good, she weighed 146 pounds, and the baby's heartbeat was strong. Marjorie wanted to hug him. All was well. She sputtered, "I'm planning to travel, and wanted to be sure that would be all right." She smiled at him.

"When are you going?" the doctor drummed his fingers on the table.

"In about a week."

"Hmmm. How far are you planning to go?"

She swallowed. "To New Jersey," she paused, "About a seven-hour drive."

"Oh, my." He clasped his hands. "In March and April there can be a lot of snow through these mountains, and it's risky, even with the new turnpike, especially for that distance. It's hazardous because of cars skidding on snowy and icy roads."

Marjorie felt a visceral tug. He wasn't going to agree. She looked up at him and asked in a hushed voice, "What would you advise, then?"

"I can't advise you one way or the other. I will say, if it were not an important trip, you might want to reconsider. Traveling that distance is hard on your body at this stage of pregnancy. Being confined in a car for lengths of time is bad for your circulation. If you go, frequent breaks would be good."

Marjorie was deflated, but she knew the doctor's response was realistic. She'd been ignoring the logical details of the weather. How foolish she was to focus just on her goal of leaving.

But, then, they could go by train. Trains go in all sorts of weather. You can get up and walk around a little, holding the backs of the seats. Perhaps her father had already thought of this.

Marjorie thanked him and walked out to meet her father in the waiting room, where he was reading the paper. Two patients sat waiting. He looked up as she entered the room.

She sat beside him. Opposing feelings of relief and anxiety battled in her mind. She leaned toward his ear and spoke quietly. "Dad, he said all is well. The baby has a strong heartbeat and is in a normal position. I've got good blood pressure and have only slight swelling of my ankles." She omitted her travel conversation with the doctor.

"Good," he said simply, giving her a quick pat on the knee. They left the office and walked back to the car. When they got in, he started to turn the key, then stopped. His eyes locked on hers.

"You know, we must have Les's agreement. There is no point upsetting your mother with all this until Les agrees you should go. After all, the baby is his too."

"I know, Dad." She squeezed her eyes shut and willed Les's approval. She had done everything else she could.

He started the engine and they rode back in silence. As Marjorie watched the snowy scene out the window, it seemed the landscape had lost its color. All the houses they passed were swathed in shades of grey, but as they slowed to turn, she saw a lone purple crocus peak through the snow, a promise that spring would come.

CHAPTER 23

EACH MORNING AT ten thirty, Marjorie opened the mailbox, full of hope that Les had received her letter quickly and agreed to her plan. Each day, there was nothing from Les. It had been several days. How much longer would it be? She wanted so badly to talk to him, but she knew only emergency calls were allowed. She would wait two more days, then fabricate an emergency to call him. Frigid evenings had begun to claim more of each day as she waited for Les to call.

She busied herself with making little favors for Lorraine's shower on Saturday, folding the diapers her mother bought and washed for her friend's baby. For herself, Marjorie began planning what baby things and clothes of hers would fit in her suitcase. How could she take a bulky stack of diapers on a train? Perhaps in a suitcase her father carried. Maybe she'd have to buy new diapers when she got to New Jersey.

On Friday, after Marjorie finished decorating cupcakes with blue and pink icing for Lorraine's shower, she went to the living room to listen to the BBC in order to keep up with the war in Europe. She worried the United States would soon be involved. Voices crackled on the radio. She heard Roosevelt announcing the plan to lend destroyers and anti-aircraft guns to meet Great Britain's desperate need for supplies in the war against the Nazis.

"Marjorie, come, Les is on the phone."

Marjorie jumped at her mother's words. She hadn't even heard the phone ring. He had finally called! Her heart leaped, then delight mingled with apprehension. She wanted so badly to talk to him, yet feared that he would not agree to her leaving. Her mother handed Marjorie the phone and walked into the living room.

She heard the radio go silent in the living room, her chance to speak privately gone. "Just a moment, honey," Marjorie said. To keep her mother from hearing her conversation, Marjorie moved the base of the phone to the floor in the hall as far as the cord would reach, then stretched the receiver to its limit around the doorway to the dining room. She got down on the floor, awkwardly lying on her side, propped on her elbow, giving the cord its longest reach.

After sharing the sweetness of hearing each other's voices, Les cleared his throat.

"I got your letter, honey. I'm sorry you are having a bad time with your mother. You didn't tell me about this in your other letters."

Marjorie spoke softly. "I didn't want to distract you with this. But then, I tried to explain in the last letter how difficult it had become. Not just unhappy, but miserable. Honey, my wishes count for almost nothing, my ideas are discounted. I need to leave, mostly because of her wanting to control the baby's care. I just can't bear that."

"Marge, I know you want me to agree that you should get away from your mother and travel to New Jersey. But I have to say, please don't make that dangerous ride at this point in your pregnancy and live in that house alone." His voice caught. "I couldn't stand it."

"The doctor says I'm healthy, and the baby is fine. Can you hear me?" She was talking softly.

"Yes, I hear you. I'm so glad all is well with you both. I can't be on the line very long, but I needed a chance to talk with you." He cleared his throat. "Please, Marge, I want you to be safe and protect our baby just a little longer. It's only seven more weeks before the baby is due."

"Honey, I—"

"My graduation and commission ceremony are in five weeks. I'm applying for the Brooklyn Navy Yard for my assignment. There is a good chance they will approve it since I'm still first in the class."

Her mouth went dry. "That's wonderful, but Les—"

"Then, I can call you almost every day. The baby will be born just a couple weeks after that and I will come to get you both as soon as you can travel. The weather will be better then. If you travel now, the weather could change in a moment, snow to sleet with slick, dangerous roads, both there and New Jersey."

Frustration wedged itself in Marjorie so deeply she couldn't think. "But I can take the—"

"Oh no. I have to hang up, I'm so sorry, Marge. I'll call back tomorrow."

She hurried, "Les, please understand, I have to go, for my peace of mind, my very health. I need you to agree—"

But the line was dead.

Out of the corner of her eye, she saw movement and looked up. Her mother was standing in the hall near her. Marjorie froze. She struggled to get up, nearly tripping on the phone cord. She tried to stop the trembling of her hand as she replaced the receiver and put the telephone on its stand.

Her mother stood still in the hall, staring at her. "Marjorie, where do you have to go? I heard you say you have to go, and something about peace of mind."

Marjorie's heart raced. She wasn't prepared to answer. She paused, then inhaled a long breath and chose her words carefully. "Mother . . . well . . . I feel it's best if I am close to Les in New

Jersey when our baby is born. I have always thought that. I just couldn't figure out how to make it happen before."

"But he hasn't completed his training yet. Doesn't he have another month or more, for heaven's sake?" Her hands flew to her hips.

Marjorie leaned against the doorframe for support. "Yes, five weeks until his graduation and commission. Since he's first in his class, Les has a very good chance of getting assigned to the Brooklyn Navy Yard, his first choice." Her knees grew wobbly.

"But he'll still be in Rhode Island another five weeks. And there's no guarantee he will get the Brooklyn Navy Yard. Nothing in the military happens quickly." She paused, shaking her head, her brow deeply knit. "So, you'd live with Les parents?"

She wished she could answer *yes*. Marjorie hesitated, choking out her words. "No. Les's sister, Emilie, is still living with them to help with Casper. Until Les knows for sure about his assignment, and gets married housing, a friend of Betty's has an extra room in her house where I can stay."

"For more than a month? Living at a stranger's house?" her mother's voice rose, her face contorted.

Marjorie shuddered, dreading her mother's response. "It's a room that she rents out."

"What?!" her mother barked, her eyes blazing. "A rooming house with a bunch of ne'er-do-wells?" Her mouth twisted with revulsion. "I can't believe this!" She shook her head. "And if Les doesn't get assigned to Brooklyn, you'd be stuck there with a baby, in a room, in some boarding house?" Her mother shook a finger at her. "What in the world are you thinking, Marjorie? This is so shortsighted," she screeched. "How would you even get there? The roads are too unpredictable with the snow and ice. This is so crazy. I can hardly believe you are considering such a thing." Her mother's eyes burned through her.

Marjorie drew from the courage she had stockpiled bit by bit. "Mother, can we sit down?"

"We'll go into the living room." Her mother marched into the living room ahead of her and sat down heavily in her usual arm-chair. She wiped her brow and fidgeted with her hairnet.

Marjorie collapsed in an easy chair, rubbing her chest where a sharp spasm of indigestion stabbed her.

"I could go by train."

"By yourself?"

She knew by her mother's question that her father had not shared a word of her plan with her mother. Marjorie would say nothing about him.

"I would be fine. Weather doesn't bother the trains. I could stand up and stretch."

"Your baby is due in seven weeks or so. What is the point of living in some stranger's room when Les will be in Rhode Island for another five weeks?" She enunciated each word distinctly, as if speaking to a child or a person hard of hearing.

Marjorie looked at her belly. "Because now is when I can still travel." She felt like the air had been sucked out of her body.

Her mother scowled. "You would prefer to live with strang-ers in a room you've never seen than here with us? This makes no sense. Why would you want to do this, risking a long train ride and the chance of having your baby in a rooming house?" Her voice was strained, her eyes bulging.

Marjorie couldn't answer. She hung her head. As her mother spoke, she realized her own rationale made little sense. Her mother had exposed the flaws in her story. Now what was there to do? Should she reveal the truth, her fear of her mother's dominance that had been thrust deep inside, shrouded in layers over the years?

Marjorie's thoughts surged wildly, then settled into the realiza-tion that she had been telling her mother these half-truths. What could she do? All her life, Marjorie's constant shadow had been this fear of her mother's rejection if she crossed her and didn't follow her mother's ideas.

Marjorie clutched the arms of her chair and reached down inside herself for the words. She plunged ahead. "You always tell me what I should do, Mother—which dress to buy, whether to crochet or knit the baby's booties, what food to eat. This is hard to say, but,"—Marjorie stopped, searching for the right words, ones that wouldn't sting. "I need to leave because you won't allow me to care for *my* baby the way I feel I should." She put her palms and fingers together as if in prayer and pressed on.

Her mother's mouth fell open.

"You made it clear that you would keep the baby at night, then take it downstairs until the scheduled feeding times. I told you I didn't agree with that, but you insisted. You didn't listen. I just can't stay and let you take care of *my* baby the way *you* wish." Tears welled in Marjorie's eyes. Her voice cracked. "I need to be the baby's mother and make those decisions *myself*."

Surprise and indignation scarred her mother's face. "My heavens, Marjorie! I try to help you, give you the advice of experts about feeding. It was all with your welfare in mind—to allow you extra sleep."

Marjorie summoned the last of her courage and continued. "Mother, I'm afraid it's more than just this. You've tried so hard all my life to make sure I never got dirty, had all the nice clothes, and so that I wouldn't get burned, you wouldn't allow me to cook. I've been having to teach myself how now." She cleared her throat. "You protected me so much that I had a difficult time learning what I needed to know to make a home. I had to learn it by myself." Her voice wavered, but Marjorie rode forward on a wave of adrenaline. She would tell her mother all that mattered.

"You even had me send my laundry home when I was at college. You wanted so badly to preserve me, keep me safe, keep a protective shell around me, that I never learned how to do anything for myself. I had no confidence I could be successful, to feel satisfied with my accomplishments. I've had so much—and so little."

Her mother tapped her foot with increasing agitation. "Marjorie, this is dreadful. I can't believe you are saying this. How ungrateful! Who put you up to this? You don't realize—"

"Please, Mother, let me finish. I know this is difficult for you to hear. It's even harder for me to say." She looked up at the ceiling as if to pull down encouragement from above. "I didn't have a chance to make mistakes to learn from, or to improve, to ever feel good that I had done better with my efforts." She took a deep breath, memories flooding like a dam bursting.

"You chose to control my every move so I wouldn't have a hard time, so I would have it easy, so I would be the perfect daughter you would be proud of, marry the country club boy who could provide for me well. But in the process, I didn't have the chance to become my own woman, a confident person." Tears fell down Marjorie's cheeks. "You know, Mother, I never wished to disappoint you. I always wanted to please you—afraid if I didn't, you wouldn't love me." Marjorie had forced the demons to be drawn into the light. Would they die or become enraged? Her stock of energy was now empty.

Her mother stared ahead as if looking at something far away. Her lips twisted like she was sucking alum. She said nothing but kept tapping her foot. Marjorie wiped her tears while her mother sat rigidly in her chair. Marjorie's whole life seemed to collapse into this moment. They sat in silence for what seemed an eternity.

Finally, her mother turned toward her. Pain contorted her face. She smoothed her dress over her knees and lifted her head high. "I raised you how it was best to protect you, my only daughter, to care for you in the way I knew—how my mother raised me." She stabbed her finger in the air. "Except you didn't have to press underwear with an iron you heated on a wood stove, clean horses' stalls, or wash the soot from the chimneys of all the oil lamps every day." She swept her arm. "You don't realize the sacrifices I've made so you could wear lovely clothes, go to a private college, and have the best of everything."

All this left Marjorie with the crushing frustration that her mother still didn't understand. She'd never asked for these sacrifices.

"But all that doesn't seem to matter to you. In fact, your baby will be lucky if you make half the sacrifices that I did." Her mother punctuated her words with a shake of her head. She got up and slowly left the room without looking back.

Guilt engulfed Marjorie. She had revealed so much, hoping to be understood, but in the process, she may have ruined any chance of a better relationship with her mother. She knew her mother was wounded. She had not barked angry retorts or walked off in a huff in the same way as she had so many times before. This time was different.

Too spent to move, Marjorie sank into the chair and held her head in her hands. She heard her mother's footsteps as she climbed the stairs and the sound of a door closing upstairs. A chorus of voices arose inside Marjorie. What would her mother do now? Would she flare up, or build another wall of silence between them?

Perhaps her mother was thinking she had failed her daughter as she had failed her little sister? The guilt of that time must have been suffocating. Those memories had surely burned a hole in her heart that she had filled with a promise to protect her little daughter, whatever the cost. Her mother had been fighting her own battle.

Had it all been for nothing? Exhaustion seeped out through Marjorie's pores. She pulled herself out of the chair and slowly climbed the stairs to lie down in her room. She had not wanted to hurt her mother, but the volcano had erupted, and she feared the lava would scorch everything in its path.

As she walked to her room, Marjorie realized that no matter what the future brought, she had finally crawled out of hiding, confronted her mother, and spoken her truth. She hadn't just shut her eyes and waited for the worst to pass, as she had done so many times before. Maybe this confrontation could lead to a change in their relationship. But nothing her mother had said indicated she would reverse her thinking. Change only happened from within, and it must be very difficult after so many years of habit. Sometimes it might not be possible. Was there a way to mend a heart?

Marjorie knew that at least *she* had turned a corner. In spite of everything, she saw herself with new eyes, feeling whole, no longer merely fragile fragments. She would stifle her feelings no more. In the future, she would deal honestly with each situation as it came. With this resolve, she lay down, her head sinking into the pillow.

CHAPTER 24

OPENING HER EYES, Marjorie realized that she had fallen asleep. Her watch said 5:40. It was evening. She'd slept almost two hours. Her parents were talking in low tones in their bedroom. How much had her mother told her father of what she'd blurted out? She realized that when her mother confronted her about leaving, she hadn't told her mother she loved her as she had promised her father she would. But the unexpected spewing of years of stifled feelings had hijacked Marjorie's senses. She knew her father always wanted to repair what could be mended, but perhaps no stitches could restore the fabric she had just torn apart.

She turned to her side, eased out of bed, and stepped to the bathroom, sensing her increasing girth. She gave her belly a caress and got a poke in response. "We will be fine, little one, don't worry," she said to her baby.

She washed her face with cold water and toddled back to her bedroom. From under the bed, she pulled out her small valise and tucked a pile of diapers in the bottom, then laid a few of the baby's things on top. She would pack more in the morning. When Les called tomorrow, she would insist that she had to leave. She would tell him she'd go by train next week, and she would ask Betty if she could pick her up at the station in Newark.

Marjorie sat down in her bedroom chair, and as she put her

shoes on, she saw how much her feet had swollen. She'd have to prop them up. Perhaps this was the one thing her mother was right about.

Footsteps in the hall caught her attention. She looked up to see her dad standing at her bedroom door, his face ashen.

"Marjorie, your mother doesn't feel well and wants to take a rest. She's not hungry but told me what to do in the kitchen for dinner. Will you come and help me?"

"Sure, Dad." Marjorie swept back her hair. "How is Mother?"

"We'll talk downstairs," he said, his voice weak.

She followed her father down the stairs, worrying about what had been said between her parents. She couldn't bear another hand-wringing episode, but she had to find out what happened with her mother. She and her dad prepared dinner. As Marjorie passed the platter of food to her father, she ventured, "How is Mother? What did she say?"

Her father put down his fork and straightened his napkin. "She was quite upset." He sighed. "She said . . . well . . . she had not been the best mother," he stammered. "I haven't seen her cry since her father died." He took off his glasses and wiped them with the neatly ironed handkerchief that her mother gave him each morning. "He favored her among the three sisters, you know. I believe her father saw how unforgiving her mother behaved after the accident and tried to make up for it." The wrinkles on her father's brow deepened, and he looked away. "These are just my thoughts about her father."

Marjorie was stunned that her mother had shed tears. She had never seen her mother cry. "Gosh Dad, I said much more than I meant to. All the pain and frustration of so many years poured out like a waterfall. I didn't want to hurt her."

"There is no good time for these things. I know it's been difficult for you, often trying to please your mother while putting yourself last. I see both sides." His voice was weary. "It's all so complicated." His eyes locked on Marjorie's. "Can we talk more tomorrow about your leaving? I think we're both tired." His eyes were glazed. He put his napkin on the table and pushed back his chair. "Now, just so you know, I will still help you how I can." He gave her hand a quick touch.

"Thanks, Dad." She wasn't sure what he meant by this comment. But she believed, like her mother's father, he was sensitive to his daughter's emotional needs. With the slight residue of energy she had left, she began clearing the table. Neither of them had eaten more than a few bites.

*

After a fitful night, Marjorie awoke thinking about Lorraine's shower, arranged for the next day. How could they get through their responsibilities as hostesses under these circumstances? As she pulled her dress over her ballooning belly, absorbed in these thoughts, she heard an odd, squeaking noise in the hallway.

A moment later, her mother entered her bedroom backward, pulling the bassinet she had redone. Baby clothes were stacked inside the bassinet. Her mother wore the same cotton print dress she'd had on the day before. It was very wrinkled, as if she'd slept in it. Marjorie had never seen her this unkempt before. Even her hairnet was askew.

Her mother stood just inside the bedroom and cleared her throat. "Marjorie, I wanted to show you some things I've saved from when you were a baby. I kept them in my cedar chest. I . . . thought you might want to use them." She moved the bassinet closer to the bed and lifted a few outfits, holding them out for Marjorie to see. "You were such a good baby, a happy little one. I was so lucky."

Marjorie wasn't certain about what she'd just heard. Her mother had never told her she was a good baby before. This warm overture left Marjorie speechless, but a voice in her head counseled caution. One by one, her mother showed her each baby outfit—flannel gowns with drawstrings at the bottom, pink sweaters, and crocheted booties—and laid them on Marjorie's bed. Her mother picked up a gown.

"The sleeves of this one tuck over the baby's fingers to keep it from scratching itself." She held up a pale-pink knit dress. "I knitted this for you when I was pregnant, hoping for a girl."

Overwhelmed, Marjorie ran her fingers over the outfits, feeling the softness of each one. She rubbed the pink dress against her cheek, inhaling the scent of cedar from the chest. Her mother had saved them all these years. A new place opened in Marjorie's heart. "Oh, this is so precious. I want to use them if I have a girl, or even if it's a boy." Marjorie felt herself glowing from within.

A slight smile ventured on her mother's face. She adjusted a ribbon on the bassinet and patted it. She looked again at Marjorie. "And this belongs here with you." Her mother's reddened eyes met hers. "I've had my baby. Now, it's your turn to care for your baby, as you think best." Her mother glanced down and looked away. "Where do you want me to put it?"

Marjorie hesitated, unsure of what to say. She was shocked by this seismic shift in her mother's attitude. "I'd . . . like it near the closet for now. Thank you, Mother."

Her mother wheeled the bassinet next to the closet and gave it another pat. She looked again at Marjorie and sniffled. Stray hairs, usually held captive by her hairnet, escaped down the side of her face. Her fingers brushed them aside. She smoothed her dress and shifted her weight from one foot to the other. "Will you stay to have the baby here, then?" she whispered. "We would like that—very much."

Marjorie stared at her mother, dazed. An overture had been made. A peace treaty offered. War was raging in Europe, but there was a truce here in her bedroom. Yesterday Marjorie had stormed the castle. Now, escaping and running seemed to be for prisoners.

She wouldn't allow her mind to hold her captive any longer. She had the power to leave when she wished, so her need to flee seemed no longer a necessity.

Her head spun. She faced so much uncertainty if she stayed, but life never held guarantees. Something had mended inside the bruised interior of her mother's heart. Could this last? Maybe not, but they were on new terrain, though it meant navigating the hills and valleys of the past and the present. Marjorie had found her strength in the moment. She believed she could again, grounded on a new foundation of confidence. She took some deep breaths.

She would follow this newfound path. Yes, she would stay, praying that the miracle of a child could merge their better selves. It was best for the baby, for Les, for her father, for her mother. And for once, staying here could be better for her, too.

Marjorie watched her mother gently fold each of the baby clothes and place them back in the basinet.

"Mother, I will stay and have the baby here. I think it's best for us all."

Her mother looked up, moved closer to Marjorie, and stood in front of her. She reached out and hugged her daughter. As they embraced for several moments, a tingling warmth coursed through Marjorie as if tightly held tensions had released and her nerves awakened to their newfound liberty.

"Good. We'll work things out." Drawing her handkerchief to her eyes, her mother quickly left the room.

Marjorie remembered Casper's message to her from his bed, "With baby, start again, fresh. Heal bad things. We know baby can do that."

Caressing her tummy, she whispered, "You're going to travel soon from this cozy cocoon to the brightness of a new world, little one. Our journey may have bumps now and then, but we will make this voyage together. Your dad and I will be there to support you always, with so much love. My gift to you is a family."

She would take one step at a time, savoring the moments that brought joy. This was an evolution, not a revolution. Marjorie grasped the edge of the headboard, eased down to the floor, reached under the bed, and pulled out her suitcase. Lifting the case onto the bed, she opened it. She picked up the baby outfits and the booties she had knitted, and she placed them with her own baby clothes in the bassinette. A mingling of generations and hope.

Reaching into the case again, she gathered the diapers that lay at the bottom and walked into the bathroom. She pushed the jar of cold cream aside and on the shelf beside the sink she placed the small stack of diapers. Looking into the mirror, the whole woman she saw there smiled back at her.

Made in the USA
Columbia, SC
05 October 2021